"SIT DOWN, WINGFIELD,"

called out Logan, "and eat with us."

"Thanks. Don't mind if I do," Kent Wingfield replied genially. On the other side of the long table sat four men—all of them members of the Hole in the Wall gang.

"Where you from?" sneered the man called Neberyull.

"I hail from the Tonto, mister. Men like you don't risk their hides there."

"Why, you—" Neberyull raised a bottle from the table. "When we're through with—"

"Cut it!" interrupted Kent, and as swift as a flash of light he drew his gun and shot. His bullet smashed the bottle in Neberyull's hand.

"Gentlemen, you'll please excuse my abruptness," Kent said as he laid the big blue gun beside his plate. "There's a sheriff on my trail, and I'm testy."

Books by Zane Grey

Published by POCKET BOOKS

ZANE GREY

STRANGER FROM THE TONTO

PUBLISHED BY POCKET BOOKS NEW YORK

**POCKET BOOKS, a Simon & Schuster division of
GULF & WESTERN CORPORATION**
1230 Avenue of the Americas, New York, N.Y. 10020

ISBN: 0-671-43946-4

First Pocket Books printing September, 1964

20   19   18   17   16   15   14   13   12   11   10

POCKET and colophon are trademarks of Simon & Schuster.

Printed in the U.S.A.

STRANGER
FROM
THE TONTO

1

ONE MORNING from a black slope of a desolate bluff the old prospector located, away to the southward, three red crags. He had grown tremendously excited and nothing could have held him back. These colorful hills seemed far away to the younger man, who ventured a suggestion that it might be wise, considering the time of year, to make for the cool altitudes instead of taking a risk of being caught in that stark and terrific contact with the hot rock.

They went on down into the labyrinth of black craters and red canyons, and across fields of cactus, ablaze with their varied and vivid blossoms. The *palo verde* shone gold in the sun, the *ocotilla* scarlet, and the dead *palo christi* like soft clouds of blue smoke in the glaring sand washes. The luxuriance of the desert growths deceived the eye, but at every end of a maze of verdure there loomed the appalling desolation and decay of the rock fastnesses of the earth.

From time to time the gold seekers caught a glimpse of the three crags that began to partake of the deceitfulness of desert distance. They grew no closer, apparently, but higher, larger, changing as if by magic into mountains. These glimpses spurred Bill Elway on, and Kent Wingfield, knowing they were lost, grew indifferent to the peril and gave himself fully to the adventure.

They had been marvelously fortunate about locating waterholes. Elway had keenness of sight and the judgment of experience. Added to this was the fact that one of his burros, Jenester, could scent water at incredible distances. But one night they had to make dry camp. The next day was hot. It took all of it to find water. And that day the crags disappeared as utterly as if the desert had opened to swallow them.

Cool sweet desert dawn, with a menacing red in the east, found the adventurers doubly lost, for now they did not even have a landmark to strive for. All points of the compass appeared about the same—barren mountains, dark cones, stark and naked shining ridges, pale blue ranges in the distance.

But Elway pushed on south, more bowed every day, and lame. The burros became troublesome to drive. Jenester wanted to turn back, and the others were dominated by her instinct. Elway, however, was ruthless. Kent watched him, no longer with blind faith, but with the perturbation of one who saw a man guided by some sixth sense, into which intelligence did not enter.

Nevertheless soon he changed their order of travel, in that they slept in the daytime and went on at night. The early dawn, soft and gray and exquisite, the glorious burst of sunrise, seemed to hold the younger man enthralled, as did the gorgeous sunsets, and the marvelous creeping twilight. As for the other hours, he slept in the shade of an ironwood tree, bathed in sweat and tortured by nightmares, or he stalked silently after the implacable prospector.

They talked but little. Once Elway asked how many days were left in June and Kent replied that he guessed about half.

"August is the hot month. We can still get out," said the prospector, rolling a pebble in his mouth. And by that he probably meant they could find gold and still escape from the fiery furnace of the desert. But he had ceased to pan sand in the washes or pick at the rocks.

The days multiplied. Spent in the shade they were not unendurable or utterly strength-prostrating. But the noon hours, during which the men invariably awoke, had a solemn menacing austerity. The nights were pleasant, so far as atmosphere was concerned. Try as Elway might he could not drive the burros in a straight line. Jenester edged away to the east which fact was not manifest until daylight.

Another dry camp, with the last of the water in their canteens used up, brought the wanderers to extremity. Elway had pitted his judgment against the instinct of Jenester, and catastrophe faced them.

Darkness brought relief from the sun, if not from over-whelming dread. The moon came up from behind black hills and the desert became a silvered chaos, silent as death, unreal and enchanting in its beauty.

This night Elway gave Jenester her head and with ears up she led to the east. The others followed eagerly. They went so fast that the men had to exert themselves to keep up. At midnight Kent was lending a hand to the older man. The sand dragged at their leaden feet. But they could not head the burros, which they were now following by the tinkling of Jenester's bell. The moon sank behind the dark horizon. White blinking pitiless stars shone piercingly. They paled into gray and when dawn broke the young man was half-supporting the old prospector.

All around, the desert looked precisely as it had for days. The eastern ranges were crowded with fire; those in the west gloomy in purple haze. The burros had traveled uphill. They had passed on out of hearing and had to be trailed. The older man appeared to be fast weakening. But sight of a jack rabbit and the sound of a mockingbird in melodious song saved him from collapse. Where these living creatures were it could not be far to water.

Elway sank less weightily upon Kent's strong arm. They climbed, trailing the tracks through the aisles between the cactus thickets, round the corners of cliffs, up a slow-rising ridge above the top of which three round peaks peeped, and rose, and loomed. Elway pointed with a shaking hand and cried out unintelligibly. His spirit was greater than his strength; it was Kent's sturdy arm that gained the summit for him.

"Look—old timer!" panted Kent hoarsely.

Three symmetrical mesas, singular in their sameness of size and contour, and magnifying all the mystery and

3

glory of reflected sunrise, dominated a wild and majestic reach of desert.

But the exceeding surprise of this sudden and totally unexpected discovery of the three peaks that had lured and betrayed the prospectors instantly gave way to an infinitely more beautiful sensation—the murmur of running water. A little below them ran a swift shallow stream, transparent as glass, yet taking on a tinge of the morning rose. The burros were drinking.

Elway staggered to the shade of the shelving rock and fell with a groan that was not all thanksgiving. Kent, with a thick whoop, raced down the gentle declivity.

The water was cold and sweet. It flowed out of granite or lava somewhere not far away. Kent filled his canteen and hurried back to his comrade, who lay with closed eyes and pallid moist face.

"Sit up, Bill. Here's water an' it's good," said Kent, kneeling. But he had to lift Bill's head and hold the canteen to his lips. After a long drink the old prospector smiled wanly.

"Reckon—we didn't—find it any—too soon," he said in a weak but clear voice. "Another day would have cooked us."

"Old timer, we're all right now, thanks to Jenester," replied Kent hoarsely. "Even if we are lost."

"We're not lost, son. We've found our three landmarks."

"Is that so? Well, it's sure great to know. But if my eyes aren't deceivin' me they're sure darned big," rejoined Kent, gazing up at the three peaks.

"Make camp here. We'll rest," said Elway.

"You take it easy, Bill. I'll unpack."

The old prospector nodded with the reluctant air of a man who had no alternative. Whereupon Kent went down and drove up the burros. Once unpacked they rolled and rolled, caking their sweaty backs with dirt.

By stretching a tarpaulin from the shelving rock where Elway reclined Kent made an admirable shelter. He unrolled his comrade's bed and helped him on it. Then he unpacked utensils and some food supplies, whistling at his work. The whole world bore a changed aspect. What a

4

miracle water could perform! He built up a stone fire-place, and then, ax on his shoulder, he sallied down in search of wood. This commodity might not be easy to find, though in an extremity dry cactus would burn. But soon to his gratification he found a dead ironwood tree, that most wonderful of all desert firewoods. It was well named, he decided, as he stopped chopping to wipe a wet face. Early as the hour was the sun shone hot. Kent looked up at the three peaks, conscious of an indefinable resentment and aloofness. What he had longed to behold somehow now left him cold. But seen from this side of the ridge they were exceedingly beautiful. The rose color of early dawn had faded. They were now bronze, strung with green dots and lines where desert growths straggled up the scarred slopes. The stream of water undoubtedly had its source under these mountains, and the distance was not many miles, though they appeared exceedingly rough.

Kent carried an armload of firewood back to camp. Elway was sleeping the sleep of exhaustion. The younger man gazed fondly and anxiously down at the worn wrinkled visage, unguarded now in slumber. The driving passion of the gold hunter was stilled now. Or had it strangely fled? Or had Bill ever possessed it? He had always been a mystery. Kent unrolled his own bed, on soft sand in the deep shade cast by the tarpaulin. Then removing his wet shirt he stretched himself on the blankets and with the closing of his eyes he too slept.

The golden sun mounted higher and changed to white. There was no cloud in the sky. Silence hung like a mantle over the desert scene, though the stream murmured sweetly, broken now and then by the musical tinkle of Jenester's bell. Bees hummed by. A black eagle sailed round and round, and a lean raw-necked vulture perched on a high cliff, watching the camp.

Late in the afternoon Kent awoke, to find his companion wide awake, lying with head propped high.

"Gee! I feel like I'd been beaten," exclaimed Kent, stretching and yawning. He was wet and hot. "Howdy, old rainbow chaser. Are you hungry?"

"Reckon I am," replied Elway.

"Gosh, I am, too. I'll rustle a meal pronto. Whew! Strikes me it's warm here," said Kent as he labored to get into his boots.

"Kent, looks like the hot weather is comin' early," rejoined Elway seriously.

"Comin'? Say, I think it's been with us for days."

"Wal, what I meant was *hot*."

"Bill, you're a queer one. What's the difference between hot an' *hot*?"

"Son, when it's *hot* you can't travel."

Kent stared at his old friend. What was he driving at? At the moment the idea of travel apparently refused to stay before Kent's consciousness. But a sober cast fell upon his countenance. Without more ado he got up and busied himself around the fireplace. Once he glanced at Elway as if wondering whether he was going to get up or not. Leisurely he cooked supper, sometimes standing erect with his stick in hand, during which moments he gazed unconsciously out across the desert. He was being influenced by forces of which he had no knowledge.

When the meal was ready he spread it on a canvas beside Elway's bed. The old man could not sit up straight, and he had to be waited upon, but there was nothing wrong with his appetite. This pleased Kent and reacted cheerfully upon him. While they were eating, the burro Jenester approached, her bell tinkling.

"I'll be darned. There's Jen. She's sure well trained," said Kent.

"I reckon. But if you'd lived with burros on the desert as long as I have you'd see more in it."

"Aw, she's only lookin' for some tin cans to lick," replied Kent.

Nevertheless the covert significance Elway attached to the act of the burro seemed not to be lost upon Kent. While doing the camp chores he no longer whistled. The sun grew dusky red and when it sank behind the mountain it was as if a furnace door had been closed. Presently with the shadows a cool breeze came across the desert. Twilight fell. Silence and loneliness seemed accentuated. The billets of ironwood in the fireplace glowed rosily; the stream flowed softly on; Jenester's bell tinkled faintly

6

from afar; and night seemed held back by a silver radiance from over the range.

The old prospector lay propped up, his bright eyes upon the peaks. Kent sat with his back to the rock, gazing out to see the moon come up over the weird formations of desert.

"Bill," said Kent, suddenly, as if a limit had been passed, "we spent weeks gettin' to your three peaks. Now what're we goin' to do that we are here?"

"Son, we used up our precious time," replied Elway sadly. "We got lost. We're lucky to be alive."

"Sure I'm thankful. But I'm hopin' you'll be up tomorrow, so we can look around."

If Elway nursed a like hope he did not voice it, which omission drew a long steady look from the younger man. In the darkness, however, he could not have gleaned much from his observation.

"Old timer, I hope, too, that you had somethin' in mind when you headed for these damn triplet hills."

If Kent expected his sole reproach to stir Elway he reckoned without his host, for the old prospector vouchsafed no word on that score. Kent's attempt to foster conversation, to break the oppressive silence, resulted in failure. Elway was brooding, aloof.

Meanwhile the moon arose, full this night, a huge silver orb in a pale green circle of sky. It added the last unreality to this wilderness of cacti and rock. By day it was possible for a human to keep his connection with life and rationality, but by night this seemed to be futile. Kent got up and walked out in the moonlight; he climbed a huge boulder and crouched there, his thought subservient to the listening, watching instincts that seemed to grow and encroach upon his consciousness. From this place he could not hear a sound, except the muffled beating of his heart. The silence was terrific. Nature worked imperceptibly here.

Kent went back to camp, treading softly by the old man, who lay asleep with the moonlight blanching his face. Soon the torture of the younger man likewise found oblivion in slumber.

But another day dawned and with it unrest.

7

After breakfast Elway called his young companion to his bedside.

"Set down an' let's talk," he said.

"Sure an' I'll be darn glad to," returned Kent, cheerfully, though his scrutiny of his friend's face noted a subtle change.

"Son, you've a lot on your mind," began Bill with a fleeting smile that was like a light on the dark worn face.

"Ahuh. I just found it out," replied Kent soberly.

"Worried about bein' lost?"

"Sure."

"An' thet worthless jade who'll jilt you?"

"Well, no, I can't say that. She seems sort of far off—But I reckon she'll stick to me, Bill."

"No, she never will, Kent. I know.... But—about bein' lost. We are an' we aren't."

"I don't savvy, old timer."

"Listen. I know where we are now, though I've never been anyways near here. An' I reckon now we're not far from what I was huntin'. There's gold here. An' old pard gave me a hunch. Water is scarce down here. An' he said water ran down that wash in the flood season. This stream peters out, of course, in the sand below here some place."

"Ahuh. An' what of all this?" queried Kent suspiciously.

"Wal, a fellow could mozy on down, stoppin' in likely places to shake a pan of gold, an' in a few days reach the Gulf with at least a couple thousand dollars worth.... Then he'd have, I reckon, about six days travel along the Gulf, bein' careful to go only by night an' at low tide, to the mouth of the Colorado. Then Yuma, where he could cash his gold dust.... An' then if he happened to live in Arizona he could get home pronto by stage."

"Sure would be wonderful, for that particular fellow," returned Kent, almost with sarcasm. "What you drivin' at, old timer?"

"Son, this desert is a queer place. I've been on the edge, an' talked a lot with prospectors who'd tried to learn it. But none of them ever did. They might have, but

8

for the Yaquis and Seris. I've known three who kept comin' in here, an' finally they never got back. They told me the Seris mined gold at low tide from the rocks along the Gulf shore. Dug out big hunks of gold eroded an' eat by salt water. They would give these to the Papagoes an' the Papagoes in turn would give them to the Yumas. An' the Yumas would do the tradin' an' buyin'. An' that's how such gold became known to white men. An' I could tell you stories about the Indians once takin' a doctor who'd cured a chief's sick eyes—about takin' him blind-fold three days an' then showin' him the ground every-where strewn with black manganese of gold!—That place too must be near here. For the doctor sighted three round hills of pink color, he said."

"Ahuh. Funny, old timer, now we're sittin' right under these amazin' hills that we don't give a damn much about the gold diggin's they're supposed to mark?"

"Not funny, son," reproved the grave old prospector. "But sure passin' strange. Gold makes men mad, usually. Though I could never see that I was, myself. . . . If we'd only had good luck!"

"To my notion we're most darned lucky," declared Kent vehemently.

"No. If that were so we'd got here weeks ago an' I wouldn't be on my back. We'd have had time to fill some sacks an' then get out before the hot weather came."

"Oh, I see, the *hot* weather."

"It takes a while to heat up this old desert. Then after a while the rock an' sand hold the heat over an' every day grows hotter, until it's a torrid blastin' hell, an' white men don't dare exert themselves."

"Ahuh. Then I'd say we haven't many days to waste," said Kent significantly.

"*You* haven't, son," replied the other gently.

"Me!"

"Yes, you Kent."

"I don't get your hunch, old timer. You strike me queer lately."

"Wal, even if I do, I've a clear mind now, an' you may be grateful for it some day. It may have been my dream

9

of gold that made me drag you into this hellhole, but I've got intelligence now to get you out."

"*Me!* What about yourself?" demanded Kent sharply.

"Too late, Kent. *I will never get out.*"

2

◘

"So THAT'S it, old timer!"

The younger man rose with clenched fist and bent eyes of blue fire down upon his reclining comrade.

"What's it, son?" queried Elway.

"You're knocked out an' need days to rest up. But you don't want me to risk waitin', so you'd send me on ahead."

"Kent, I meant to lie to you an' tell you that. But I can't do it, now I face you."

"What you mean?" flashed Kent suddenly, dropping back on his knees.

"Wal, son, I mean I couldn't follow you out."

"Why couldn't you?"

"Because the rest up I'm to do here will be forever," replied his friend.

"Bill, you're talkin' queer again," faltered Kent, plucking at his friend.

"No, son. I overreached my strength. My body was not up to my spirit. I cracked my heart. . . . An' now, Kent, pretty soon I'm goin' to die."

"Aw, my God! . . . Bill, you're only out of your mind," cried Kent, wringing his hands.

The old prospector shook his shaggy head. He scarcely needed to deny Kent's poignant assertion. "Listen," he went on. "You put water beside me here. Then pack Jenester an' one other burro. Pack light. But take both canteens. Start tonight an' keep in the stream bed. In the mornin's early pan some gold. But don't let the madness seize on you. It might. That yellow stuff has awful power over man. An' remember when you reach the Gulf to travel at low tide after dark."

"Bill, I couldn't leave you," rejoined Kent, shaking his head.

"But you must. It's your only chance. I'm a tough old bird an' I may live for days."

"I believe you will. An' for years yet. You're only tuckered out, an' sick, too. After a little you'll get better. Suppose I'd let you drive me to leave you, an' you didn't die!"

"Kent, a man who has lived on the desert knows the approach of death. . . . You must go before it is too late."

"I won't do it, old timer," returned Kent, his voice gaining.

"Son, you'll make my last days ones of grief an' regret. Sad things for the old an' dyin'."

"Bill, you wouldn't leave me," said Kent stubbornly.

"That would be different. You have everything to live for an' I have nothin'!"

"I don't care. I won't—I can't do it."

"There's your mother to think of."

"She'd be the last to want me to desert my friend."

"Perhaps I misjudged Nita. She really loved you. She might stick. An' you can't risk losin' her."

"Shut up, Bill! You know somethin' against her, an' you're lyin' to get me to leave."

"What's an old hulk like me? I'll be happy lyin' here when I know you're on your way. You're a wonderful fellow on a trail, Kent. I never seen your beat. Don't make a mistake you'll regret always. Leave me, son, an' go."

"No. It'd be inhuman."

"Kent, if you don't go *now* soon it'll be too late. I won't last long. Then you'll be stuck here. You couldn't stand the torrid months to come. You'll go mad from heat an' loneliness. But if you *did* survive them an' started out in the rainy season you'd be killed by the Seris."

"I'll stick," rasped out Kent, the big drops of sweat

11

standing on his pallid brow. He transfixed his friend with glowing eyes of reproach.

"Nita loves you, but she'll never wait that long," declared Elway, ruthless in his deceit.

Kent's gesture was one of supplication.

"Nita won't wait even as long as she promised," went on Elway, inexorably. "That Joe Raston will get round her. He'll persuade her you're lost. An' then he'll take her."

"Aw, Nita will wait," rejoined Kent, swallowing hard. Something about Bill convinced him Nita had already been taken.

"Not very long. She's weak an' vain. She needs you to bring out the good in her. An' son, there's a lot of bad in Nita, as I could prove to you. . . . Joe Raston or some other flash boy will work on thet, if you don't hurry home."

"You're lyin', old timer," replied Kent huskily.

"I saw Raston gettin' her kisses," said Elway. "That very day before we left."

"Honest, Bill?" whispered Kent.

"I give the word of a dyin' man."

Kent leaned against the rock and wrestled with his demon. Presently he turned again, haggard and wet of face.

"All right. I always was afraid. But we weren't really engaged till that Saturday night."

"She can't be true to you unless you're there to hold her. Go home now, Kent."

"No. I'll stand by you."

"Go, Kent. I'm beggin' you."

"No."

"For your mother's sake."

"No!"

"Then for Nita's. An' those kisses you'll never—never get—unless you go—now," shouted Elway in hoarse finality, as spent with passion he sank back on his pillow.

"No!" yelled Kent ringingly, and strode away down into the desert.

At length he came to a wide-spreading *palo verde* where the shade was dense and had a golden tinge. Half the yellow blossoms of this luxuriant tree lay on the ground, and it was that color rather than the shade which had halted Kent. The beauty was as appalling as its perils. He cast himself down here, sure indeed of a mocking loneliness. And in the agony of that hour, when he fought to be true to his passionate denial of Elway's entreaty, he acted like a man overwhelmed by solitude and catastrophe, yet laboring to victory under the eye of God. It was well indeed that the old prospector, who had brought him to this sad pass, could not likewise see him in his extremity. And what would it have meant to the wayward girl, whom he was losing in that bitter hour, to see him ascend the heights?

When it was over he rose, a man where he had been a boy, and retraced his steps to camp. The sun appeared to burn a hole through his hat. He found Elway asleep, or at least he lay with closed eyes, a tranquillity new to his face transforming it. Kent had the first instance of his reward, outside of his conscience.

That very day the hot weather Elway had predicted set in with a vengeance. Kent, awaking out of a torpid slumber, sweltered in his wet clothes. And Kent began his watchful vigil. That day dispelled any hope, if one had really existed, of his old friend's recovering. Elway drank water often, but he wanted no more food. Kent himself found hunger mitigating.

"Kent," said Elway, breaking his silence at sunset, "you're stuck here—till the rains come again."

"Looks like it, old timer," replied Kent cheerfully. "Perhaps that's just as well. Don't you worry."

"Quién sabe?" replied the prospector, as if he almost pierced the veil of the future.

At night they conversed more freely, as the effort cost less, but neither again mentioned gold or Nita Gail. The oppression of heat was on their minds. Elway had before given stock of his desert wisdom, but he repeated it. Kent should keep track of the burros, and keep them from straying, although it was unlikely that Jenester would leave, even if left to her own devices. He should eat sparingly, and protect his supplies from vermin and prowlers of the desert. He should keep out of the sun and

13

rest or sleep during the mid-hours of the day. Down toward the Gulf the waterholes would dry and travel for human beings would be impossible until the rains filled the holes again. Elway stressed that. Where he had been violently solicitous for Kent to go now—he advised against it. Lastly he cautioned Kent against the insidious encroachment of the desert upon a man's sanity. If he gave himself over to the unthinking sensorial perceptions of the savage he could survive. But to think and brood and grieve would be fatal. Let him watch and listen. Nothing in that wilderness was trivial. Nature was omnipresent. In a region where man could lose half his weight in a single day and die of thirst, and in a few more days dry up and wither and blow away on the desert winds, there was little sense in opposing the laws of the primal. What man needed to do was to go back in the scale of evolution and through a revival of primitive instincts live in the present one of the age-old experiences of mankind.

The days passed, wonderful in spite of their terror. And the nights were a relief from them. Kent did not leave the old prospector's side except when necessary. And as Bill imperceptibly faded away, Kent made these times more and more infrequent.

One afternoon upon awakening late Kent became at once aware of a change in the sky. Clouds were rare in this section during the hot dry season, yet the sky appeared obscured by pale green-yellow mushrooming clouds, through which the sun burned a fierce magenta hue.

Kent rubbed his eyes, and watched, as had become his habit. A hard hot wind, that had blown like a blast from a furnace earlier in the day, had gone down with the sinking sun. The yellow rolling canopy was dust, and the green tinge a reflection cast by desert foliage.

"What you make of that sky, old timer?" asked Kent, turning to his companion. But Elway, who was usually awake at this hour and gazing through the wide opening to the desert, did not make any response. Kent bent quickly, as had become his wont lately, to scrutinize the sleeping masklike face.

14

Getting up, Kent set about his few tasks. But the lure of the sky made him desist from camp work and set him out to drive up the burros. He found the lazy lop-eared Jenester close at hand, quickly directed to her by the tinkle of her bell, but the other three had strayed. Kent tracked them, as he had done often. There was really little danger, however, of them leaving the water and herbage in the vicinity of camp. Presently he located them and drove them back to where Jenester browsed her slow way toward the stream.

Meanwhile the singular atmospheric conditions had augmented. The sun, now duskily gold, set behind the hills. And the canopy of dust, or whatever it was, had begun to lift, so that it left a band of clear air along the desert floor, a transparent medium like that visible after a flash of lightning.

The phenomenon was so marvelous and new that Kent suffered a break in his idle sensorial attention. This stirred his consciousness to awe and conjecture as had no other desert aspect he had watched. Presently he thought to ask the old prospector what caused it and what it signified. To this end he hurried back to camp, realizing as he neared it, that there was an unaccountable boding oppression weighing upon him.

Elway leaned far forward from his bed, his spare frame strung like a whipcord, his long lean bare arm outstretched. He pointed to the west with quivering hand.

Kent wheeled in consternation and he called in alarm. "Hold on, old timer."

"Look!" rang out Elway exultantly.

"What do you see? . . . Bill!"

Kent flashed his gaze from the prospector's transfigured countenance out across the desert to see weird rocks and grotesque cacti exquisitely magnified in the trailing veil of luminous gold.

"Bill, it's only the afterglow of sunset," cried Kent, as if to try to convince himself.

"Boy, don't you see the great colored canyon? An' a red roarin' river shinin' through a hole in the wall?"

"No, I sure don't," returned Kent bluntly.

15

"Wal, I see them, an' it's a call fer me to tell my secret. . . . Come here."

Kent made haste to kneel beside his changed companion.

"Son, listen. I brought you on this journey to find gold, but thet wasn't my prime reason. I know Nita is faithless. You'll find out when you get back. My real motive was to try you out an' if you measured up to my hopes I meant to tell you of the most wonderful chance ever laid to an adventurous youth."

"Bill!—An' do I measure up?" queried Kent breathlessly. He was going to learn all about this mysterious man.

"You do! Your refusin' to leave me was the last an' final proof. An' now I'm goin' to put somethin' in yore way. . . . Kent, I'm not a real prospector. I only putter around lookin' fer gold. I had an easier way to riches than diggin' fer gold. I'm a robber—an outlaw. I belong to thet Hole in the Wall gang."

"My God! Bill, don't say that," cried the young man incredulously.

"It's true, Kent."

"Aw! I'm sorry, Bill—damn sorry. But it doesn't make any difference to me."

"I knew it wouldn't, Kent. . . . What do you know about the Hole in the Wall?"

"Not any more than anyone else down our way. An' that's little enough. I've heard of the outfit for years. They ride out of their canyon hidin' place, rob an' raid an' murder—then go back to hole up for a spell. That's all. They couldn't be trailed, so the story went. I'll bet by heaven I could track them."

"You could, Kent, an' you're goin' to."

"Me!—Say, old timer, the heat has unsettled your mind."

"No. I'm perfectly rational. I know now thet I'd have told you before if I hadn't hated to confess I'm a thief, an outlaw with red hands."

"But Bill!—You said I was goin' to track thet Hole in the Wall gang."

"I did, Kent."

"Sounds thrilling," laughed Wingfield. "Only I'm not goin' to do anythin' of the kind. . . . But *if* I did—what'd it be for?"

"To save the loveliest, sweetest, innocentest girl the sun ever shone on," declared Elway solemnly.

"Who?" blurted out Kent.

"Lucy Bonesteel."

"An' who in the devil is Lucy Bonesteel?" flashed Kent, his curiosity getting the better of incredulity.

"She's the daughter of Avil Bonesteel," went on the self-confessed outlaw. "She was a child—only five or six when Bonesteel went to hide in the canyon country. Thet was more'n ten years ago. I was one of his outfit. I owed Bonesteel my life. He was a friend, an' I was his right-hand man until Henry Slotte came to take my place. I was gettin' old. Slotte was younger—a daredevil, an' he caught the chief's fancy. He worked against me, put Bonesteel against me. I shot Slotte, left him for dead, an' fled. Thet was not so long ago—just before I came to Wagontongue. I heard a vague rumor that Slotte was still alive. But I did not dare risk goin' back. . . . There was twenty in the outfit when Bonesteel first went into thet hidin' hole down in the canyon. It came to be called the Hole in the Wall. There was three women with us, one of them the chief's wife. She was a woman of good family. She did not know he was chief of the wildest robber gang ever known in the West. When she found out she did not live long. Bonesteel worshiped the child. He never allowed her to be with the other women unless he was there. When we were out on long raids he left Lucy carefully guarded. I held thet trusted post fer several years. I taught Lucy all I knew—the same as her father had taught her before me. He was an educated man. She grew up in thet canyon. She never saw a child unless it was an Indian. The Piutes an' Navahos were Bonesteel's friends. They kept the secret of his hole in the canyon."

"Say, old timer!" exclaimed Wingfield, fascinated. "You're tellin' me somethin'. . . . Lucy Bonesteel!—How old was she when you saw her last?"

"Fifteen, at least. Thet is nearly two years ago. She's now seventeen."

"What was she like?"

"Boy, I couldn't find words to do Lucy justice. She had hair thet held the sunlight—eyes the color of the cornflowers I knew in my youth—lips as red an' sweet as ripe cherries. Her skin was tanned gold. She was strong-limbed, fleet as a doe, an' as beautiful an' wild."

"An' Bill—was she good?" asked Kent, ponderingly.

"Lucy did not know what evil was. She never knew Bonesteel was a hunted outlaw, nor thet his companions were bad. He was rigid in his rule. She must never know. He shot several men on Lucy's account. But fer thet matter none of our outfit ever wanted to tell her. What I always feared was the time when Bonesteel did not come back or thet he'd be killed in one of the fights among themselves. Then she would become prey fer the hardest men I ever trailed with. Up to the time I left all was well. But anythin' could happen. Thet outfit can't last. It's always haunted me—leavin' Lucy there. An' I've always been lookin' fer the boy to send after her."

"To send to his death, you mean!"

"Wal, it'd be a hundred to one, thet's shore. But, Kent, thet one chance is worth it. An' son, you are no ordinary young man."

"My God, old timer, I've no qualifications for that job!" burst out Kent in frank regret.

"Wal, you jest have," declared Elway, earnestly. "Before you got tame on Nita's account you was a pretty tall hombre, if all I learned is true. You had no beat on a hoss. You was a dead shot with a rifle, an' quicker'n hell with a gun. You've had gun fights, Kent, an' here you air tellin' me this job is too dangerous fer you."

"Bill, if Nita turns out what you say she is—I'll go," replied Kent, in cool deliberation. "It'd be tough for me to find Nita. . . . An' I'd welcome somethin' wild."

"Begin now to fortify yoreself, son."

"My mother liked you," went on Wingfield, thoughtfully, as if weighing things. "An' I believe you are honest. But it'd only be decent to give Nita the benefit of a doubt. That's all about her. . . . Now, Bill, how'd I ever find this Hole in the Wall?"

"I can tell you. Listen, an' remember these names.

18

Cross the Painted Desert. Don't start by hoss. It might cause notice. Take a couple of burros an' walk. Pack little bags of tobacco—little flasks of whisky—knives an' such to placate the Navahos. Go by Wild Cat an' Beckyshibeta. Go up the Segi an' cross the Utah uplands, down Noki to the San Juan River. The great blue mountain of the Navahos, Nothsis Ahn, will always be a landmark. You will meet Piutes. Buy a couple of hosses from them. They breed the finest hosses in thet country. Ford the San Juan at the mouth of Noki. Climb up on top of the rocks an' look fer Bonesteel's short cut over the bare stone down into the Hole. It can be found. A Piute could be prevailed upon to guide you. But if thet fails take the trail from the San Juan to the crossing of the Colorado. Only don't cross the Colorado. Go down river instead of across. It'll take nerve, son. Thet's a hell of a place. You can't see round the wall. But you can hear the roar of the rapids. Swim yore hoss close to the cliffs, around the corner, till you come to the Hole in the Wall."

"Then—what?" gasped Kent, aghast at this prospect.

"Boy, you must think, plan, be equal to the job," returned the old outlaw, with passion. "You *can*. It's a great job. . . . Take thet last step after dark or very early in the mornin'. The Hole is a big place. You can hide yoreself an' hoss. The gang may be away. Lucy runs wild over the rocks. You'd see her—meet her. She has never seen any fine upstandin' handsome lad like you. She'd fall in love with you, Kent. Jest like thet! An' you'll be near heaven, then, believe me. She would help you."

"Bill! You're crazy as a locoed colt. But you've got me stuck. Suppose the worst. Suppose Bonesteel caught me?"

"Pretend to be on the dodge yoreself—thet an Injun told you about the Hole—an' you wanted to hide. You could fool Bonesteel. He'd take anyone into his outfit. But shore as Gawd made little apples you'd have to fight some of his outfit. If Slotte *is* alive I'd want you to kill him."

"You bloodthirsty old devil," ejaculated Kent grimly. "But if I go an' you've given me an honest hunch, I'll bore Slotte for you. . . . What does he look like?"

"Slotte would be about thirty," returned Elway. "He

was short, powerfully built, swarthy of face. He had the hardest, coldest eyes I ever looked into. You'd know him from them."

"What color?"

"Wal, I'd say light steel-gray."

"An' how'd I know Bonesteel?"

"The chief was tall. He had an eagle's head. Hair once yellow, turnin' to tawny white. Eyes like lightnin'. He always wore a black sombrero."

"An' how many in that gang?"

"Ten when I left, includin' the chief."

Kent sat back running a nervous hand through his damp hair. He was intrigued. "Old timer, you've made me forget we're huntin' gold an' that this is the place you wanted to find."

"Gold!—Son, I forgot. There's gold in the Hole in the Wall. Bonesteel has buried stacks of gold. I don't know where. His outfit used to figger on it. An' some of them would have stole it. Slotte was one. Silk we called him 'cause he always wore a silk shirt. But I always felt that he wanted Lucy. He was waitin' till she grew up.... There's gold hidden in Bonesteel's canyon. He's savin' thet for Lucy. If you save her you'll get the gold."

"Bill, I reckon that'll be all for a while," rejoined Kent, thoroughly subdued by the overpowering conviction and sincerity of the outlaw.

"No need to say more, son. Only will you remember?"

"Yes, old pard."

"An' will you go after Lucy?" queried Elway in a hoarse whisper. He had taxed his strength too far.

"I promise," said Kent soberly, turning away.

He strode off among the rocks to think, to marvel upon what he had heard. The more he pondered over the story the more plausible it seemed to become. Life was like that in this sparsely populated West.

Kent stayed long away from camp. Upon his return, from quite a few rods distant, he saw in Elway's lax inert form a terrible suggestiveness. Kent had seen too many dead men to mistake one, even at a little distance. Therefore he was shocked but not surprised to find the old man dead.

He closed Bill's eyelids, to have them fly open again. Kent essayed a gentle force, with like result. Horrified, he shut the pale lids down hard. But they popped up.

"Aw!" he exclaimed, breathing hard.

Kent had never seen a dead man, much less a beloved friend, who even in death persisted in a ghastly counterfeit of life. Suddenly Kent saw strange shadows in the staring eyes. He bent lower. Did he imagine a reflection of the luminous golden effulgence in the sky, with its drifting magnifying veil? Or was there really an image there? He wiped the dimness from his own sight. He was like a man whom shock had gravely affected. There was something stamped in Bill's eyes. Perhaps the hope engraved upon his soul!

"Aw! It's only my mind," muttered Kent ponderingly.

But there shone that beautiful light in Elway's sightless eyes. And the sky had shaded over. The gold had vanished. The mysterious veil might never have transformed the desert. Kent covered the old prospector's face with a blanket.

That night Kent Wingfield kept reverent vigil beside the body of his departed friend. The desert seemed a sepulcher. If it sustained life then it let out no breath during the long slow hours. Kent Wingfield was no sensorial perceiving savage that night. The progress of the ages descended upon him. To him his thoughts were but the bewildered whirling of a mind rudely brought back to realities. But neither these nor silence nor desolation kept another day from dawning.

With the retreat of the somber shadows came a necessity for practical tasks. He ate a meager breakfast. Then he wrapped Bill in his blankets and tarpaulin, and bound them securely. Whereupon he stalked forth to find a grave.

It would never do to bury Bill in the sand. Of all the desert mediums sand was the most treacherous. It would blow away. So he hunted for a niche in the rocks. He found many, some too large and others too small. At last under a cliff he had overlooked he discovered a deep depression, clean and dry, as fine a last resting place as any man could desire. And it would be sweet to the old

21

prospector! It was sheltered from rain and flying sand, yet it looked out upon the desert. If properly filled and sealed it would last there as long as the rocks.

He carried Bill—now how light a burden!—and tenderly deposited him in the hole. Then Kent tried to remember a prayer, but he could not. Wherefore he made up one.

"To the rocks you loved, old timer! May God save your soul!"

It was going to take considerable work to fill that deep grave. Kent took another tarpaulin and folded it down over the body, and weighted each end with a stone. Then he shoveled in a layer of clean white sand. After that he began to carry stones and place them on the sand.

Small stones, such as he could lift, were remarkably scarce, considering it was a region of stone. It would be imperatively necessary to fill the grave, and wedge the last layer of stones, or the scavengers of the desert would dig poor Bill out and strew his old bones over the sands.

Kent went farther afield in search of rocks. Now he would gather a sack of small ones and then he would stagger back under burden of a heavy one. He performed Herculean labors. Despite the burning sun he kept faithfully to his task. He would not think of anything pertaining to the future until Bill was safely and permanently consigned to the desert that had claimed him.

The time came when his task was almost done. Only a few more heavy stones! But where to find them? He had sacked the surrounding desert of its loose fragments.

While allaying his thirst at the stream he espied the dull gleam of a rock out in a little pool, rather deep, where the burros liked to wade.

Kent waded out to secure it. His feet sank in the sand, and as the water was knee-deep he had to bend to get the stone. He lifted it easily enough, but soon found it heavy. All this toil in the hot sun had weakened him.

Bare sand edged on the stream there and Kent's stone, as he dropped it, gave forth a sodden thud. Some of the grains of sand adhering to the rock sparkled in the sunlight.

Frantically he crawled into the stream—grasped up

22

handfuls of wet sand. He spread them to the sun—gazed with piercing eyes.

Specks of gold! They were as many as the grains of sand.

Kent tore up the bank, his fists shut tight on his precious discovery, forgetting all but this wonderful strike.

"Bill! Bill!" he shouted, panting with rapture. "Look ahere!—A strike!"

He got no response to his wild outcry.

"Bill!"

Silence and loneliness emanated from the camp. They struck at Kent's heart with reality. An empty space marked where Bill's bed had lain in the shade.

3

□

ONCE ACROSS the Little Colorado, facing the colored steppes of this Painted Desert, Kent Wingfield passed into a country new to him. The years of his range-riding and hunting had embraced the cattle region south of the river, down to the black-timbered Tonto Basin. But for his mother Kent would have cast his lot with the Jorth faction in the Pleasant Valley War. All because when he was only sixteen he had seen Ellen Jorth once! That would have been a fatal choice for him. The Jorths, all except the girl, had been exterminated. Nevertheless Kent Wingfield had seen hard life enough before he was twenty. Red-headed Nita Gail had served Kent one good turn: she had coaxed him in off the wild range and from his questionable intimacy with the Hash Knife gang.

But this Navaho country was new to Kent. He liked it all the better for that. This desert brought out something in him that the timbered range had not. He had long been used to the menace of white men. His experience with Indians, however, had been almost limited to those who rode into Wagontongue. It had not been too many years since Kit Carson and his soldiers had rounded up the Navahos, which rude injustice had not been forgotten. Kent had heard old timers say that the enmity of the Navahos dated from Carson's campaign. There were Navahos and Piutes back in the canyons that had never known the indignity of being captured and herded into a reservation. Kent knew he must encounter Indians and felt equal to escaping those who might not be friendly.

Ten days out from the peaks he had met only a few shepherd boys and seen a few dark riders from the ridge-tops. He traveled around Moencopie, the Moki village, and gave Tuba, the Mormon settlement, a wide berth. From the salty, marshy lowland west of Tuba he climbed to a dry plateau, and knew his great concern from there on would be water. Therefore he kept a sharp lookout for bright green spots in the gray barrenness and for flocks of sheep. But he tramped twenty miles and more across that greasewood plateau before he came to a break in the level floor.

A deep wide wash yawned beneath him. Before Kent could stop them his two burros started down, no doubt scenting water that must run somewhere through the broad belt of dense green which wound through the gorge. Kent was about to follow when he sighted dust clouds. Then he espied a group of horsemen driving pack animals up the wash. Kent's sharp eyes quickly made them out to be white men. He hurried down after his burros, thinking the while that dark riders on dark horses were of keen interest to him.

"I'm gamblin' on my luck," he muttered.

The burros led Kent to water—a tiny shallow run with white-edged alkali borders, bitter but drinkable. He drove his burros in among the tall brush until he found an open spot where he unpacked. The day was far spent. A golden red limned the rock bluffs that peeped over the ramparts to the west.

Kent halted in the midst of his preparations for supper

and stood aghast at the discovery that he had caught himself whistling. It rendered him thoughtful. Ten days from Wagontongue—only ten days away from the red-haired little firebrand who he thought once might have broken his heart! Here was something to puzzle over. True the few days had seemed weeks. Loneliness and travel had augmented time and distance. There was no return of his jealous and bitter pangs. He could think of Nita Gail and her latest flame, Joe Raston, without that hot gush of blood.

"Doggone if that doesn't beat me!" soliloquized Kent gladly. "I've got over it. I always swore I would—if ever I found she was playin' fast an' loose with me. Gosh, I must be fickle. . . . But that awful drill with Bill Elway an' this job he set on me—they've changed me. But maybe old Bill was delirious an' it's all a dream. No matter! What have I got to lose?"

He bent again to his task of cleaning the rabbit he meant to cook for supper. He had shot it through the middle, spoiling much of the meat. Kent remembered the time when he could hit the top of a rabbit's head at fifty feet from the back of his horse. All the way across the desert he had practiced drawing and shooting his gun, soberly pleased that his old speed and accuracy could be brought back.

"Lucky I had all this practice before," muttered Kent, which admission made him conscious that he believed he could not travel long alone in this country without recourse to firearms. And he realized another fact: since his return to Wagontongue, with its bitter certainty for him, he had not the least concern about his safety. He had never been cautious, and now he found himself cold and hard, indifferent to danger. That was the second good turn he owed to Nita Gail. If the adventure he was bent upon turned into reality there did not seem a chance in a hundred of coming through alive.

Kent had about finished his supper when he heard hoofbeats some distance away. He could tell by the sound that they were being made on a hard trail and by three horses. The road was close, and any rider could have seen the light of his fire.

"Hey there," called a rough voice.

"Hey yourself," replied Kent, rising.

"Comin'. One man."

"All right. But come careful," warned Kent. He threw some dead brush upon his fire, and as a bright flame cracked up he drew back in the shadow of the high sage. Thud of hoof and crash of brush attested to the fact that the man approaching was hardly exercising caution. Presently he found the open lane and soon rode into the circle of light.

"Whar are you?" demanded the intruder impatiently. "I'm alone an' ain't lookin' fer trouble."

"So I see, stranger. Get down."

Kent saw a sturdy rider, roughly clad, booted, spurred and armed, and when he stepped down in the light he exposed the dark visage of a man of middle age, whose sullen eyes betrayed passion.

"Excuse me, friend," he said. "Step out an' talk to me. I'm in somethin' of a hurry."

"Reckon I can offer you a cup of coffee an' a biscuit. But I've about cleaned the platter," replied Kent.

"Thanks. I ain't hungry, but I'm shore goin' to be. So I'll take you up."

Whereupon Kent's visitor sat down, drank the cup of coffee in almost one gulp, and began munching the biscuit, his sloe-black eyes taking stock of his host.

"I know yore stripe," he said gruffly. "Kinda out of the cattle range, ain't you?"

"Yes, I am."

"Whar you bound?"

"Reckon I don't know. But you'd better be tellin' what you want, stranger, instead of askin' questions."

"Shore. Excuse me. I'm so damn sore thet I'm oncivil. I been cleaned out of my last dollar. Robbed, by Gawd! By my own outfit! I've split with them fer good. What I want is to sell one of these hosses."

"Were you with the outfit that rode by here just before sundown?" queried Kent.

"Yes. We made camp above. An' I had it out with Slotte right there, the — — — —!"

The leap of Kent's blood was so quick and strong that

his visitor might have seen his violent start had he been observant. Kent waited until he could speak casually.

"I'm not interested in your trouble, stranger."

"Hell no. Who's askin' you to be. But look at them two hosses."

At that Kent bent his gaze toward his visitor's animals. There were three, two saddled, and the other carrying a pack. Kent did not need to look twice to recognize two superb horses, one of which, coal-black and magnificently built, struck him as being as fine a thoroughbred as any he had ever seen. Horses had once been a passion with Kent. He suffered an awakening of that weakness.

"Wal, I see you love hosses, an' you know hosses. Thet's all I want to see. Pardner, the rider doesn't live who wouldn't buy the bay if he could, an' steal the black if he had a chance."

"You're right," agreed Kent reluctantly.

"Wal, which one will you pick an' what'll you give?"

"See here, fellow. How do I know you're not a horse thief?" demanded Kent seriously.

"Young man, I am a hoss thief, an' thet's the least I am. But I raised Spades from a colt. Shore I stole his mother. But thet job is outlawed these six years. How much? I've got to rustle."

"What's your rush?" asked Kent suspiciously.

"We're wastin' time. Can you buy thet hoss?"

"Yes, I'd give you a hundred dollars, if—"

"Done. I'd have taken less. I've got to have a little money pronto. I've got to leave the country. An' where I'm goin' the black would draw attention to me where the bay wouldn't. Gimme the money. He's the best hoss you ever forked an' wuth a thousand."

"Man, you're unreasonable. If you want to make a deal you'd better tell me somethin' to—"

"Here. I'm low-down enough to belong to the worst outfit in Utah. But I'm no liar. Thet hoss is mine. I raised him. You run no risk atall by buyin' him."

"But why are you so keen to leave the country?"

"Huh! I've damn good reason. The chief will kill me if he ever sees me again."

"The chief—what'd he kill you for?"

"He'd take it I'd double-crossed him by leavin' the outfit."

"Then what're you leavin' for?"

"I told you. This bunch I'm with is run by Slotte. Ever hear of him? Wal, you never rode southern Utah. He held out my share of. . . . He didn't pay what was owin' me. If I'd had the guts I'd drawed on him. But no man who knows Slotte would ever draw on him. So I cleared out. An' by doin' it I know I'm savin' my bacon."

"Here's your money," replied Kent tersely, producing some greenbacks.

The outlaw snatched at them, and without more ado leaped astride the bay.

"Be good to thet hoss, boy," he said. "He's used to softer hands than mine." Then the strange visitor drove his pack animal into the brush, and was soon out of sight and sound, leaving Kent standing at the head of the black, listening, wondering. Ten days from Wagontongue, on the edge of the canyon country, he had actually fallen in with some of the Hole in the Wall gang! Old Bill Elway had told the truth, at least as far as the existence of the outlaw band.

"What did he mean, Spades, that you're used to softer hands than his?" Kent said aloud to the horse. "Ah, the girl Lucy. But I still can't believe she exists."

"But Slotte!—Bill's enemy! He's real," whispered Kent to himself, in grim acceptance of an inexplicable step on this trail. "Campin' somewhere in this wash!—By all that's wonderful—I'm goin' to have a look at him!"

Kent turned his attention to the horse. "Spades, you belong to me now—at least for a while." The horse was spirited, but gentle. Kent soon won his confidence. He removed the saddle and bridle. The only thing tied on the saddle was a pair of soft rope hobbles, which Kent proceeded to put on the black. Then he turned him loose with the two burros.

The May night had fallen cold and a keen wind blew down off the rim. Nevertheless Kent divested himself of coat and boots, and taking his .44 Winchester he stole stealthily out to reconnoiter.

In a moment, it seemed to Kent, he had reverted to his

hunting instincts, always strong in him since early boy-
hood. While he rode with the Hash Knife outfit he had
often lived the hard raw experience of man-hunting.

Stepping down into the sandy wash, dry except in
potholes, he proceeded cautiously in the direction from
which his visitor had ridden. There was enough starlight
to enable him to see where he was going. Every few steps
he would halt to listen. It took him an hour at least to
travel half a mile. The wash widened and the brush
thinned. Kent at length came out into a comparatively
open flat of sage and grass. He heard horses not far off
and then he made out a pinpoint of light. The color was
red, which proved it to come from a campfire.

Kent swung to the right, and close under the bluff in
the shadow he glided on, careful not to make the slightest
sound. The light, which he saw at intervals through open-
ings, grew larger. Presently he made out dark forms of
men crossing in front of the blaze. He crept on. When
finally he drew close enough to hear voices he stopped to
consider. He saw that he could safely risk stealing almost
upon the camp. But in case he was detected he decided
what course he would pursue. Feeling his way with Indian
tread and bending low he gained a covert close upon the
campfire, and here he crouched on one knee, craning his
neck to find an aperture. Suddenly a peculiarly vibrant
voice sent a cold tingle over Kent.

"Goins, I'm not carin' a hook what you say."

"Wal, thet's plain as print," replied a gruff resentful
voice. "But I'm havin' my say. An' I say you wasn't on
the square with Ben."

"Who the hell said I was?"

"You did. Or you made out as much."

"That was about our cleanin' him out at poker. We
won his money honest. Ben always was a poor gambler. I
notice *you* kept what you won."

"Yes, an' it's burnin' my pocket right now. But I
wasn't meanin' the gamblin'. I meant you didn't give Ben
his share of—"

"Not so loud. There might be Indians hangin' around
here. . . . No, I didn't give Ben a dollar and that's why he
stole it all."

"What'll the chief say to it?"

"He won't know unless you or Kitsap tell him. How about you, Kit?"

A third man standing dark and tall, face to the fire, shook his head doubtfully. "It's too late now. I won't squeal. But I'm afraid thet sort of deal, if carried to extremes, will split the outfit."

This man Kitsap had a quiet cool voice and air that persuaded Kent to consider him more to be reckoned with than Goins.

"Kit, I counted on you," went on the harsh forceful voice.

"Wal, I'm not darn fool enough to queer myself with you," rejoined Goins, with less rancor. "But what eat me up was your treatin' Ben Bunge thet way. He's a good fellar. We all like him, except you. An' I figger if you give him a deal like thet you'll do the same to me an' Kit. Small wonder he robbed us."

"No. No!"

"All right. Why wouldn't you?"

"Well, it's not unreasonable for you to ask, that's sure. ... I had it in for Ben on account of Lucy."

"Lucy!"

"That's what I said," snapped the other.

"Fer Gawd's sake, Slotte!"

The tremor that ran through Kent's crouching frame ended in a tightening grip on his rifle. Slotte!—Kent peered at the wide-shouldered man who sat just out of the firelight. His bulk, like his voice, was formidable. But his features were in shadow. Slotte's reply to his comrade's exclamation of incredulous amaze and protest was a queer laugh, almost a cough. He did not speak.

"You hate Ben because of Lucy? Same as you hated Bill Elway!"

"They never helped my cause," said Slotte bitterly.

"Slotte, all of us, 'cept the chief, hev seen how hot you was after Lucy, ever since she was a kid. She never gave a damn fer you. An' that's why. Lucy is too innocent yet to understand what you feel, what you mean. But her instinct warns her agin you. She loved old Bill. An' I reckon she was fond of Ben."

30

"Bah! Lucy is fond of nothing but that black horse."

"Wal, Slotte, it's worked into a bad mix. Lucy has growed up. She's a woman an' doesn't know what ails her. I've a hunch she's goin' to wreck the Hole in the Wall outfit."

"That can't come too quick for me."

"Bonesteel won't give Lucy to you."

"I can make him."

"Hell, man! He'd rather see her dead than married to one of us."

"That's no compliment to me, Goins," rejoined Slotte harshly, his head thrown up and back. Kent had a fleeting look at his face, broad, big-eyed and dark with evil passions.

"Wal, I don't mean it as a slur," said Goins hastily. "You're young an' handsome. You hev a way with some women. But not Lucy. Why, Slotte, you're a thief same as Kit. Wuss, fer a woman, you're a gunman, with enemies of your ilk layin' to kill you."

"What of that? Lucy Bonesteel is the bastard daughter of a worse thief an' murderer an' gunman than me or any of us."

"Aw, Silk—not thet," expostulated Goins eloquently, spreading his hands. "Lucy ain't thet."

"Lucy wouldn't know what a bastard is."

"It's goin' to be my job to teach her a lot," returned Slotte with a ring of elation in his strange voice. It had its effect upon the listening Goins, who threw up his hands and appealed to the silent Kitsap, as if to get his corroboration of something heinous.

Kent Wingfield half-raised his rifle, his deadly intent to kill Slotte and the two outlaws with him. For an instant death hung in the balance. The fire sputtered; the cold wind rustled the brush and scattered the sparks. Kent almost yielded to the fierce desire to slay. Lucy Bonesteel had become a vivid reality. But it happened to flash into Kent's mind that he could track these members of Bonesteel's gang into the Hole in the Wall. Nothing else saved the lives of those unsuspecting robbers. Kent lowered the rifle, feeling that he could well wait. And as he stepped

31

back a twig snapped under his foot. In an instant then the terrible menace again hung over Slotte and his men.

"Did you hear that?" queried Slotte sharply. Slotte arose, showing himself to be so wide of shoulder as to look short.

"I didn't. But I'm deaf as a post," spoke up Kitsap.

"Somethin' cracked, like a piece of dead wood. It was over here," said Goins, pointing.

"No. behind you."

While they listened Kent turned and stole away in the gloom, careful not to make any more false steps. He looked back once. Apparently the robbers had lost their concern. Kent wiped the cold sweat from his brow, thinking darkly what a narrow shave they had had. He kept to the side of the trail, out of the dust. Once out of hearing he hurried down the wash. As he had neglected to locate a landmark on the rim he realized he would have difficulty finding his camp unless the fire still burned. He went far beyond it, he was positive, and had to turn back. His sense of direction, however, led him on until he recognized the waterhole where the burros had drunk. From here it was not far to the camp. He found his fire burned down to a red bed of embers. Quickly, he extinguished these. Then he got into his coat and boots, and unrolled his blankets.

At length Kent's excitement gave way to sober reflection. He went over every detail of his adventure. Its extraordinary nature ceased to confound him. It had happened. He had heard confirmation of old Bill's story, and he was no longer on a wild goose chase. But his curiosity intensified in proportion to the facts. The Hole in the Wall harbored a band of criminals divided against themselves, the most vicious of whom would sacrifice any or all of them to attain his own end—the possession of an innocent girl.

4

◘

AN OLD Navaho directed Kent off the trail to Becky-shibeta. It was a red waterhole, with a high bluff on one side and a sage flat on the other. There did not appear to be any outlet to it, but evidently it came from a spring, for the water was clean and cold.

Sunset came dull and dark through gathering sinister clouds that presaged storm.

"Rain?" he asked the Indian.

"Heap wind. Blow sand," replied the Navaho. He appeared to be rather a miserable specimen of the red man. His buckskin garments were ragged. The twisted cord that bound his black hair had once been white, but was now greasy and dirty. He had a seamed and lined visage, leathery in hue, gaunt and worn—a record of many desert years. His horse was a wiry little buckskin mustang that showed the white of its eyes. He used a blanket for a saddle and a leather thong for a bridle. He sat his mustang watching Kent with somber hungry eyes.

"Say, Navvy, get down an' help. Eat an' drink."

The native understood well enough and he complied without needing to be told what to do. Kent thought he might be a thief, or he might not, but Kent's intention was to adhere to Bill Elway's policy.

Kent attended to his black horse with careful hands. Two days in company with Spades had incurred his respect and admiration. The horse was a treasure. Kent tried to restrict a dawning love for the magnificent animal because he really did not entertain hopes of keeping him long.

"Weyno," said the Navaho, indicating Spades, and he made a singular gesture, slow and expressive, which told Kent as well as words that he knew the horse and that he came from far north and down in somewhere. And the word conveyed the idea of excellence.

The Indian carried dead sage to build a fire, and was otherwise helpful. Kent soon had a meal ready, cooking a little more for his guest. He was to learn that that food vanished miraculously. Kent laughed: "Heap hungry?"

"Injun old; no squaw," was the answer, in fairly understandable English.

When the meal and chores were ended a red dusk was mantling the desert. Kent got out some tobacco, and one of the little bottles of whisky. Sight of this fetched the Navaho's first grin. Kent put the bottle in the Indian's pouch.

"You keep. Smoke now."

And presently he was sitting before a warm fire beside the red man who smoked with evident relish.

"Live by Beckyshibeta?" asked Kent.

"Hogan," replied the Indian, with another of his impressive gestures. Kent concluded the hogan was not close.

"I run off. Sheriff," went on Kent. "Injun no tell?"

His companion shook his dark lean head. "Steal hoss?" he queried, pointing at the black.

Kent shook his head vehemently. "No. Bought him. You see four white men ride by?" And he pointed north.

The Navaho held up three fingers.

"There were four," went on Kent. "One run off. Come my fire. Sell hoss."

"Go me. Hide like fox." This reply was accompanied by a scrutinizing study of Kent's face. Evidently he had impressed the Indian favorably.

"No. Me go Utah. Ride far. Sheriff bad. . . . Navvy, you know three whites who went by?"

Kent scarcely credited the savage's cautious silent denial. He knew Slotte and his comrades.

"How far Segi?" went on Kent.

The Indian tapped his breast with one finger, then held it up, probably to signify one day's ride for him. Then he pointed to Kent and held up two fingers.

"Where white trader?"

"Logan. Squaw man. He no far Segi. Squaw man good. Stay him."

"Ahuh. How about Indians up that way. They good?"

"Heap good—heap bad."

"Piutes?"

"Pah-utes good. Trade hoss—firewater—gun."

"Navvy, tell me where Hole in Wall?"

"Uggh!" grunted the Navaho, and shook his head. "All hole in wall." His accompanying gesture acquainted Kent with a vast country full of holes. That was all Kent could elicit from the Navaho. Mention of Bonesteel's rendezvous had made him reticent. But Kent was satisfied. The Indian well knew of these raiding white men and was keeping their secret. Soon after that the Navaho without another word got on his mustang and rode off into the melancholy gloom. Kent sought his blankets and sleep.

The next day broke sunless and gray with a cold edge on the wind. Kent was soon mounted, heading his burros across the sage flat, taking a short cut to the trail. He gained it high on the ridge. A long black mesa swept majestically to the north, leading Kent's gaze to red domes and walls farther north. The east was not clear. A cold wind, laden with fine grains of dust blew from that direction. Kent picked up the trail of Slotte's six horses and followed it as he had for two days. Back off the trail, under the lee of the mesa, he espied mustangs and hogans, and more than one column of blue smoke rising. He had long passed the gateway to the Indian country. This high desert stretched north like an immense sage flat stepping up here and rolling there, gray and desolate, toward a dark line of cedars. The wind began to blow hard. Soon all landmarks were obscure in flying dust, and Kent settled down to a disagreeable day of travel. At times he was concerned about missing the trail, as clouds of dust swooped down to obscure even the burros. However, he soon lost this anxiety. Both the burros and the

35

black horse were not going to lose the trail. The wind lulled for periods, after which it blew harder. About noon sleet began to drive in the wind, to sting Kent's face. Covering his lower face with his scarf he bent his head to the cutting blast, as innumerable times he had done in his range-riding. This was nothing compared to the gale of winter.

But when the flying clouds of dust augmented to sheets of sand, heavy and swirling and suffocating, Kent had about all he wanted. The burros plodded on and the black bowed his head. Kent did not look up except when the trail lightened. The long afternoon wore by. Kent could see at rare intervals a dull magenta sun through the blowing sand. When at last he rode into a grove of cedars, which broke the wind, it was none too soon for him. He rode on until a particularly dense clump of cedars afforded good shelter when he halted to make dry camp.

The wind subsided by slow degrees. Kent was treated to a weird sunset—a great round red ball sinking down in haze. No walls were in sight. Even the mesa remained curtained in dust. Man and beast were weary that night.

But the following morning was beautiful, frosty and bright. Kent was off at sunrise. The trail led through a cedar forest and flat of sage growing perceptibly purple. Soon Kent rode down a declivity into a wide pass between the towering black mesa on his right and massed slopes and cliffs of bare red rock on the other. Ten miles north these two great walls appeared to meet in a bewildering barrier of upflung walls, cliffs, peaks and spires. That surely was the portal to the region of rocks.

Green squares showed at the base of the long red slope; and the red earthen roof of a cabin. As Kent rode on he made out a square of ground fenced in with scraggy uneven poles. This must be the house of the squaw man Logan. The hooftracks Kent was following sheered off the main trail toward the post. Kent reasoned that if Slotte and his men were at Logan's they would consider it suspicious if he passed by without calling. If they had gone on so much the better.

When a mile or two from the post he saw that the wooded ridge to his left ended in a sharp point some distance west of the post, and evidently was separate from the red slope. He soon made out the mouth of a canyon and green willows. Water came down there. He sheered off toward the point. Meanwhile he began to locate horses, bright colors, skins drying on the fence, Indians loping to and fro on wiry little mustangs. He made sure these Indians had seen him approaching. White men emerged from the door of the post to gaze his way, then re-enter. Kent admitted to more curiosity than they appeared to have. Reaching the point, he dismounted, watered the burros, tied them, threw their packs on the grassy plot he chose for camp. Spades went to drink of his own accord. Then he loosened his gun in its sheath, and taking up Spades' bridle he walked toward the post, his mind made up to meet any contingency.

But this stern resolve and the excited expectancy that accompanied it did not prevent his appreciation of the most interesting place he had yet seen in the Navaho country. The cabin was squat, but rambling with its several wings, all roofed with red adobe and growing weeds. It was built of stone, cedar and adobe, without a sawed piece of wood visible. The front had a huge door, but no windows. Red blankets gave the vivid colors Kent had caught from afar. They were hung over the porch railing. Shaggy mustangs, mostly grays and buckskins, stood before the post. Blanketed Indians watched him approach.

As Kent neared the front a tall man with a weather-beaten visage peered out over the heads of the Indians. Quickly he strode to the end of the porch to confront Kent.

"Are you Logan, the trader?" asked Kent.

"Howdy," replied the man gruffly. He had piercing slits of eyes that flashed over Kent and swept on to take in the black horse.

"Any objection to my campin' over there?" asked Kent.

"Wal, no *I* hevn't," he answered gruffly.

"Thanks. I'm not carin' a damn for anyone else," returned Kent curtly.

"Who air you?"

"Kent Wingfield. Tonto Basin rider. Lookin' for cover an' not overfriendly."

"Excuse me, Wingfield, if I 'peared oncivil," rejoined the trader hurriedly, as he glanced over his shoulder toward the post doorway. "But the fact is I've some visitors inside thet. . . . "

"I savvy. Logan, whatever I am it's sure not a horse thief."

"Boy, there's been hell over thet hoss clear from Lund to the Segi."

"How come?"

"He was Mormon bred an' the best hoss in Utah. Stole in the fust place—an' no man who owned him since could sleep in peace."

"Logan, I've been havin' tolerable good sleeps. . . . Can I buy some grain an' grub?"

"Shore. But you don't pay fer meals at my table. Suppose you rustle back to yore camp, leave yore hoss, then come in fer supper?"

"Ahuh. You'd like it better if your guests didn't see Spades?"

"I shore would, boy."

Kent leaped astride and rode leisurely back to camp. Once there he tethered Spades on a spot of grass around the point, and left him there free of saddle and bridle. This done he wended a more thoughtful way back to Logan's. The Indians stood as he had first seen them. Logan had gone in. Kent mounted the porch and stepped across the threshold.

He smelled wool, tobacco, rum, hides as he flashed a curious gaze around a big oblong room. It appeared crowded with bales, boxes, shelves of merchandise, innumerable objects suspended from the rafters. The back wall was broken by an immense fireplace of yellow stone, on the hearth of which a fat Indian squaw was adding fuel to the fire.

Kent had expected to face the Slotte triangle and perhaps more doubtful persons, but neither they nor Logan were visible. However, loud voices from the back told him where the men were. The Indian woman said: "Come eat."

She led Kent into a room that opened off to the right and which was screened from the post by a hanging fringed blanket. Kent faced a long table, and half a dozen men under the bright yellow flare of a huge lamp hanging from a center rafter.

"Set down, Wingfield, an' eat with us," called out Logan, waving a nervous hand.

"Thanks. Don't care if I do," replied Kent genially, as he stepped forward to straddle a bench.

"Howdy stranger. You step like you'd rid far," said the man who sat next to him.

"Sure have."

On the other side of the table sat four men, all of whom gave Kent a quick glance. None of them spoke. Kent gave them slow cool scrutiny. He recognized Kitsap and Goins. The third man, at the end, was younger, a brutish, heavily-jowled fellow, with heated face and ox eyes gleaming under a low brow and a mop of red hair. Then Kent's gaze traveled back to the fourth man, whom he knew before he looked, and against sight of whom he braced himself. For this was Slotte. The man's leonine head and large handsome face matched his remarkably wide shoulders. His eyes were so light as to appear abnormal, and they were windows of a tremendously violent and evil spirit.

At that moment an exceedingly pretty half-breed girl came in, carrying a wooden tray. Evidently she was the waitress and also Logan's daughter. She was about sixteen years old.

"Hyar you are, my little ole redskin sweetheart," sang out the man at the end of the table. He was verging upon being under the influence of rum. A black bottle stood in front of the men. The girl betrayed more fright than shyness.

"Lay off that talk, Neberyull," ordered Slotte. "Logan doesn't like it."

"Aw, you're jealous, Silk," jeered Neberyull. And when the girl paused beside him to set down a cup he obviously took some liberty with her under cover of the table. She moved so hurriedly that she almost upset the tray. Logan bent over his plate with face stained dark red. The girl

39

emptied her tray and glided away with soft moccasined tread.

"Logan, is that your daughter?" asked Kent. When the trader nodded Kent went on with deliberation. "You'll excuse me. I'm a stranger in these parts. Where I come from young women aren't insulted at table."

"Where'n hell is thet?" queried Neberyull belligerently.

"I hail from the Tonto, Mister Road Agent. Men like you don't risk their hides down there."

"Road agent!" shouted the other.

"Well, that's my hunch."

"Young fellar, you're triflin' with death."

"Sure. I've long been used to that. But not from meetin' such hombres as you."

"Pass the bottle, Silk," yelled the rowdy. "What'll I do to this flip range-rider?"

Kitsap reached for the bottle in front of Slotte and thumped it down before Neberyull.

"If you ask me I'd say rustle an' drink yoreself stiff before you get in trouble."

"Hell! I ain't askin' you."

Slotte flashed a speculative glance at Kent. If he read Kent correctly he did not appear overkeen to prevent a clash.

"Neb, the stranger from the Tonto called you right," he said dryly. "You disgust me, you annoy Logan. And it was plain Geysha didn't invite your vulgar attention."

"Geysha didn't, huh?" growled Neberyull, as he lifted the black bottle off the table. "An' neither did Lucy? . . . Silk, you won't let no one but you look at a woman."

"I told you not to mention that name in public," rasped Slotte.

"Aw hell—My tongue's loose. . . . All the same I'm gonna wag it at this smart-alec stranger from the Tonto. . . . Hey you!" And he raised the bottle from the table while he bent his ox eyes malignantly upon Kent. "When we're through grub I'm gonna call you out—you — —"

"Cut it!" interrupted Kent piercingly, and swift as a flash of light he drew his gun and shot. The heavy clap almost drowned the crash of breaking blass. Kent's bullet broke the top of the bottle which fell with a clatter upon

40

the table to empty its dark contents. The splintered glass had manifestly stung Neberyull's face, especially his mouth and chin, which began to bleed. The shock of the deafening boom of the gun appeared not improbably as stultifying as the pain.

Kent pounded the table with his smoking gun and he held that quartet as one man.

"You — — loud-mouthed rummy!" he rang out. "You can't talk to me that way. I'm Kent Wingfield. Does it mean anythin' to you? . . . Well, you'd heard if you hadn't lived like a skunk in a hole in the rocks."

Neberyull for the time being at least had been effectually stampeded. The pallor had just begun to recede from his face. With shaking hand he wiped off the blood and sweat.

"What'd I tell you, Neb?" asked Slotte curtly.

"Gentlemen, you'll please excuse my abruptness," said Kent, looking from Logan to Slotte as he laid the big blue gun beside his plate. "There's a sheriff on my trail an' I'm testy."

The tension eased. Logan called to his Indian woman. He coughed nervously, but the look he gave Kent held more than curiosity. The fat squaw, obviously Logan's wife, brought in a tray of steaming food. Geysha did not appear again. There was no more conversation at table. Kent gulped down his supper. He wanted to leave the dining room when the others left. He had gambled on a chance with these robbers; and his motive had been to establish in their minds something unforgettable and formidable while at the same time he hoped to make a friend of this squaw man. Opportunity had presented itself.

Slotte was the first to get up. But Neberyull beat him to the door. The others followed while Kent came last. They went into the big post, now brightly lit by lamp and fireplace. Kent stood back a little in the shadow where he could watch. Neberyull paced to and fro before the open door. He would have to be reckoned with. Kent sensed an affront of some kind. He did not intend to give Neberyull a chance to shoot him in the back.

"Thet was the last bottle of liquor I had in stock," said

41

Logan. "An' mebbe it's jest as well." He began to wait upon sloe-eyed Indian customers. Goins and Kitsap lighted pipes and found seats on bags.

"Neb, come an' hev a smoke an' forgit what riled you," called Kitsap. "You was to blame."

Slotte bent over the hearth to pick up a bit of burning stick, the red end of which he applied to a cigarette. Standing square in the firelight he made a remarkable picture. He was most powerfully built. His garb was dark. Kent saw the tips of two gun sheaths protruding from under his long coat, one on each side. In Kent's opinion that long coat precluded Slotte from the ranks of gun fighters such as created awe and respect in the Tonto. Slotte's prime business in life was not gunslinging.

"Have a smoke?" he asked Kent.

"No thanks. Swore off smokin' an' drinkin' lately."

"Well, with no thanks to you, we couldn't offer you a drink. . . . Kent Wingfield, eh, from the Tonto Basin? Bet you rode for that Hash Knife outfit."

"Won't take you up," laughed Kent.

"Ha! If you belong to that outfit I should think you'd be safer from a sheriff with them than riding into the canyon country alone."

"Sure. But I'm lookin' for a man harder'n that sheriff is for me."

"Ah, I see. *All same Texan!*"

"My father came from Texas. But I'm just plain cussed sidewinder Arizona."

"Well, don't take offense if I give you a hunch. Stay away from Utah."

"Thanks. You talk like you're some pumpkin—in Utah."

Slotte vibrated to that, but obviously controlled strong feelings. At this juncture Neberyull leaped into the light. Sober now, vindictive, possessed by some hard passion, he prepared Kent for what in all probability was speedily coming.

"Whar's the rider?" he called, peering into the shadow.

"Wingfield?—He's here. Can't you see, man?" replied Slotte.

"Slotte, he's got Spades," shouted Neberyull hoarsely.

"What?—Who?"

"Why this hyar rider who yells about bein' from the Tonto. Wal sir, he's got thet — — black hoss Spades."

"No!"

"Fact. Tobiki seen him ride down the pass—an' up to this post. Logan came out, seen the hoss, said somethin' to Wingfield, who rode back pronto to the cedars. . . . Slotte, thet Navaho knows Spades as well as you or me."

"*Logan!*—Come here," yelled Slotte, and in those trenchant words the nature of the man pealed out. The trader appeared in much perturbation.

"Did you hear Neberyull?" demanded Slotte.

"I'm not deaf."

"Is it true? Has this rider Wingfield got Spades?"

"Slotte, I wouldn't gamble on it," returned the trader hurriedly. "He rode a black thet look some like Spades. An' I told him—"

"Say," called out Kent coldly, striding out of the shadow. His cue to act had come when Slotte lined up beside the furious Neberyull. "What the hell you fellows ravin' about?"

His interposition reacted markedly upon the two men. Slotte's furious amaze subsided to a suppressed calculation; Neberyull began to pale and glint and crouch quiveringly with a passion that betrayed the deadliest intent.

"Wingfield, did you ride in here on a black horse?"

"Sure I did, Slotte. Blacker'n the ace of spades."

"Name Spades, by any chance?"

"Right again. Spades is his name."

"Where'd you get that horse?"

"Slotte, I don't like your tone an' I don't like your pardner's look."

"Like them or lump them, Wingfield," hissed Slotte. "You stole Spades—"

"You're a liar, Slotte. Be careful! Don't sling talk around like your pard there. . . . If it's any of your business I bought the black. Several nights ago. Back in a deep wash a day's ride from Moencopie. A man rode into my camp. He had the black, he rode a bay, an' also had a pack horse. He wore high boots an' a wide belt. His face was dark. He had on leather wristbands an'. . . . "

"Enough. That was Bunge. Well, what'd he say? What did he want?"

"He said a hell of a lot. But all he wanted was to sell Spades. I gave him one hundred dollars."

"Bunge took *that* for Spades?"

"Silk, the fellar's lyin'. Ben wouldn't hev sold Spades fer as much money again as he had on him," burst out Neberyull.

"He swore he was absolutely strapped an' had to sell Spades," went on Kent.

"Haw! Haw! Haw!" roared Neberyull in harsh mirth.

"By God, men! I see Bunge's dodge," exclaimed Slotte. "He figured I'd chase that black horse and let the money go. But we missed Spades. We rode right by this rider's camp. And Bunge gave us the slip down that rocky wash."

"Slotte, did the horse belong to you?" queried Kent.

"No. He belonged to a girl. Bunge stole him. What was as bad, he robbed us of ten thousand dollars. . . . Wingfield, our pard had a deep game. He stole my girl's horse. He lied to me about finding Spades way up the San Juan. I believed him. We had to take Spades along with us. But all the time he meant to rob us an' never go back to Utah."

"Ahuh. Bunge was a double-crosser, all right. When did you find out he'd robbed you?" returned Kent curiously.

"Not long after dark that night. He took Spades and the bay out to hobble them on grass. He must have had the pack horse ready. We never suspected until Kitsap missed his sack of greenbacks."

"Well, it's tough on you," replied Kent sarcastically. "But you're all thieves. Bunge went you one better. Take your medicine."

Slotte's evident laboring under a passion of surprise and fury suffered a break. He spat like a snake. His thick neck corded. And his luminous eyes glared like pale opal balls upon Neberyull.

"Silk, the — has squealed," said that worthy huskily.

Slotte turned to face Kent, his face working. "Wingfield, it's no fault of yours—this mess. If you tell us what Bunge said we'll take Spades and let you off."

"Take Spades? Let me off!" echoed Kent derisively. "You must be loco. The black is mine. I bought him. If he does belong to Lucy Bonesteel and I can find her I'll be decent enough to return Spades. But not to you, gentlemen."

"What do *you* know about—Lucy Bonesteel?" asked Slotte in a whisper of bated breath that was scarcely audible. A tremendous astonishment emanated from him.

Kent had the better of that situation and he knew it. Slotte was dominated by a mighty passion that would put him at the mercy of any man. Neberyull was just a ruffianly lout who could not be dangerous to Kent face to face. Kent sensed that in their whirling minds he was already doomed. As dead as if they had already shot him! Kent eyed them, hiding his knowledge and interest, swiftly certain that he could inflame Slotte by rage and Neberyull by fear to such extent that they would be easy to frustrate.

"Bunge sure talked," Kent began slowly, turning his right side slightly away from them. "But it wouldn't have been particularly interestin' to me if I hadn't rode plumb into you all. What's a few robbers to a Tonto Basin rider? Say, men, we have raiders an' rustlers down there who don't run an' don't hide. . . . Bunge told me you had beat him out of his share of money. Admitted he was a thief, but not a liar. Told me all about you, Slotte. How you had fallen in with Bonesteel's outfit some years ago, an' did dirt to the best robber who ever forked a horse. Elway—Bill Elway was the man. How you double-crossed Elway 'cause the girl Lucy liked him. Told me all about Bonesteel an' his Hole in the Wall—an' thet he was goin' to tell the same round every campfire he happened on. Swore you meant to split Bonesteel's outfit—an' even murder Bonesteel himself—just to get the girl. . . . Bunge wasn't a very good pard of yours, Slotte. He sure got satisfaction out of tellin' me how Lucy liked all her father's outfit except you . . . how she loathed the sight of—"

"Aghh!" screamed Slotte, his face black. He lunged for

45

his gun. As it leaped up Kent shot and Slotte went down with a crash, the gun spinning across the stone floor. Neberyull was drawing when Kent's second shot beat him down as if a battering-ram had struck him in the breast. Kent leaped behind a pile of sacks. The others were running. Slotte appeared to be threshing on the floor. Kent ran for the door, colliding with Logan.

"I'll wait outside by the fence," he whispered. Then he scattered the frightened Indians and bounded through the door, out into the darkness. He ran a few rods, then drew up panting. Cold sweat began to break out over him. His passion leaped now. His gun felt hot. With shaking hand he slipped two fresh cartridges into the empty chambers. His impulse was to go back. But he conquered it. He gasped a little, swallowed hard, fought back the weakness of repugnance. He had meant that for Slotte. The meeting had come soon, but that was well.

Kent peered around, and as his eyes became accustomed to the darkness he distinguished the pale line of fence. He approached it to lean there and wait, watching the post. He heard Logan driving the Indians out. They shuffled off to mount their mustangs and ride away in the gloom, the unshod hoofs pattering on the hard trail. A loud hum of angry voices inside the post and the stamping of boots gradually lessened and finally ceased. The night air felt bitter cold to Kent's hot face; coyotes were wailing out in the pass; the light disappeared in the post. Kent was about to give up seeing Logan when he heard guarded steps, coming from the other direction. Presently he made out a tall dark form, stealing along the fence. It was a man carrying a bag in each hand.

"Here, Logan," whispered Kent.

The trader came up. "I slipped—out—the back way," he panted. "Here's your grain—an' a sack of canned grub."

"Sorry to mess up your post, Logan," rejoined Kent, taking the sacks. "Let's move out a ways."

"Wal, youngster—you needn't apologize," said the trader grimly. "I was afraid to open my mouth at table. But, by Gawd, you made a friend of Cy Logan! My lass, Geysha, is a half-breed, yes, but she's good. An' thet

46

outfit hound her as if she was a slut. . . . Wingfield, you shot Neberyull through the heart. But Slotte escaped by a miracle. Yore bullet hit his gun an' glanced to plow along his ear. He was stunned. But he came to—the maddest man I ever seen."

"I'll have to do it all over again," muttered Kent, in chagrin.

"Who air you, son?" queried the trader earnestly.

"Logan, I'm a Tonto rider all right, but the rest was just blab."

"Then you're not on the dodge?"

"Sure not. But I reckon I'll have to dodge bullets from now on."

"You shore will. My advice is for you to rustle out of hyar. What's yore game, son? There's somethin' kind of queer about you."

"Doggone if I don't think so myself," retorted Kent. "Logan, did you know Bill Elway?"

"Yes. He was the whitest man in thet outfit."

"I met Bill once. . . . Logan, where's the Segi?"

"Jest a few miles north. It opens out of thet red wall. Fer Gawd's sake, boy, don't go up thet canyon."

"An' why not?"

"It's a turrible deceivin' canyon. Got a hundred offshoots. Bad Injuns up there an' some renegade whites."

"I'm curious about this Hole in the Wall."

"Wingfield, it's days down in the rocks. A hell-hole! I don't know where, but some place beyond the San Juan."

"Ahuh. . . . Logan, I hope I haven't made Slotte your enemy."

"Wal, he jest used me. I'll be afraid now. I'll swear I didn't hear what you said Bunge told you. But no man who heerd you could ever be safe from him."

"Look out for him, then. An' keep that pretty Geysha in. Good night. I'll be ridin' in on you some day."

5

AFTER SHOOTING frays of the past Kent Wingfield had had recourse to the bottle whenever the sensations of remorse or terror or sickness that inevitably attacked a young man for having snuffed out a human life had to be deadened or drowned in drink.

He set down the sacks Logan had given him and bent over his pack. All of a sudden a thought struck him and he stood up straight, as if he had heard a voice. The fitful starlight made objects dim. A faint wind moaned in the cedars. He heard Spades cropping the grass nearby, but could not see him in the darkness. There was no other sound. He was as much alone as on any other of the numberless nights he had made camp. Yet there seemed to be something. Kent shuddered a little. Night was always different.

"I got to think," he muttered, knocking his head. "Sure I never did think. Well, it's high time." And he sat down upon the pack he had intended to open to get the liquor. His thoughts came vivid and sharp, and he repeated them audibly. "No more red-eye for me! My mind has to be clear. My eye keen. My hand swift an' steady. Reckon I don't savvy, but sure a grand job has been wished on me. I like it. I reckoned I was runnin' away from myself. All right. I just threw my gun on a couple of skunks. Nothin' to be sick over! All in the day's work! I'll have a lot of that to do. . . . So far so good. But what's drivin' me? Old

Bill's trust in me? His love for a little girl hidden over here in the canyon? To get even with the man who drove him away from her? . . . Yes, all that. But that isn't all. The idea of savin' Lucy Bonesteel! It's in my mind. It's no dream. . . . She may not be what Bill claimed. She might be lost already. She might not want to leave her father. . . . What's the difference—I'd fall in love with her anyway. . . . What sense is there in lovin' a girl—havin' faith in her? . . . I'm loco to dream she might. . . . All the same, so help me God, I'm goin' on!"

Kent stood up as fixed and unalterable as the towering black wall to the north, beyond which called this irresistible adventure. If indeed he were not out of his head there came a whisper on the cold wind. Lucy Bonesteel could not know that her old guard and teacher Elway had set in motion a tremendous force in her behalf. But Kent realized it as he stood there in the lonely darkness. There was no telling what one man might accomplish. It was as if doubt and fear had never tortured him.

Dawn caught him climbing the pass with Logan's post miles behind, and to the fore the ever-growing, frowning stone-walled gateway to the north. Sunrise found Kent at the top of the pass with the magnificent portal of the Segi beneath him. A green-floored canyon, bisected by a deep wash, wound back between the high red walls. A winding trail crossed the sage flats. The red flush of sunrise deepened the red of the walls and crowned the pinnacles and peaks that spired the ramparts. A mysterious silent menace warned Kent not to enter that gate to the rocky fastnesses of the wilderness. It went unheeded.

A backward glance down the long slope of the pass claimed Kent's attention from the cardinal duty of the hour—which was to watch for Slotte and his men. The beauty of the valley, however, struck Kent so forcibly that he reveled in it. Soft misty gray sage, spotted with green cedars, rolled down to the purple flat in the distance. The sun had not yet burned away the shadow and mystery of the lowland. High up the rim of the mesa gleamed gold and the vast bare slope opposite lay in shadow.

Logan's post showed up like a black square in the gray. Kent's searching gaze then sought the trails. On the lower one he sighted a string of horses. Dismounting he led Spades and the burros back into the cedars and tied them. Then he came out, rifle in hand, to watch.

The line of horses disappeared and were out of sight for a while. Then it came into view again. At length Kent made out three riders and three pack horses. They had not come across toward the mesa slope far enough to find his tracks. The lower trail kept to the wash and did not ascend the pass. Kent lost sight of the trail below him in the network of rough ground, but he had no doubt that it wound in and out to enter the Segi. When he ascertained that the three riders were not Indians he had a moment of satisfaction. This was Slotte and his two men. They were coming at a trot, which augured a desire or need of hurry. A mile to the left and below Kent's position they passed out of sight. Kent sat down to wait for them to reappear. In half an hour he saw them in the red wash, headed into the Segi. Their horses floundered in quicksand. They turned a corner of the deep wash, and eventually reappeared far beyond, climbing up the steep slope. The men were on foot dragging the horses up. It was a hard pull. One horse slid down, recovered and went at the ascent again. The pack horses labored. At last they were up and the three men followed. They left dark tracks of disturbed sand behind them. Mounting then the riders drove their pack animals up the trail, across the sage flat, into the cedars and on out of sight up the Segi.

Uncertainty ceased for Kent. He lighted a cigarette and sat back comfortably to let time pass. Slotte had entered the Segi. He was in a hurry to cover ground, to reach the robber rendezvous. They would leave telltale tracks behind.

"Slotte, you can't shake me on a trail," soliloquized Kent grimly. "Even if you tried, which you're sure not doin'. So far as the way to your old Hole in the Wall is concerned I'm as good as there."

The robbers were traveling four or five miles an hour. Kent concluded it would be wise to let them get several hours ahead of him, to allow for accidents, early camps, or anything that might permit him to catch up with them.

In due time Kent was on the move again, his rifle

across his saddle. He had to work to and fro to find a way down off the slope into the canyon. When he reached the deep wash he found the wall a hundred feet straight down, and he had to ride along it to where the branch came in from the west. This was deep and steep also. But eventually he found a place where Spades piled down hock deep in sand, and the burros slid down on their haunches. In the half-baked floor of the wash he found the horse tracks he was seeking. They led into the main wash, where a thin sheet of water ran over quicksand. The tracks of Slotte's horses disappeared here. Spades went in readily, driving the reluctant burros. Kent saw that as long as he kept moving there was no danger of miring down. But how easily he could have been ambushed from above! That was one of the perilous chances he had to take.

The burros waded around a sharp bend and out upon a bench, from which the fresh tracks of the robbers' horses led up almost perpendicularly. The burros balked. Kent dismounted and half-led, half-dragged them up. To his surprise and pleasure Spades came plunging up of his own accord. He snorted his disdain and there was fire in his eye. Every hour Kent succumbed more and more to appreciation of the black. He seemed to be back again in the Tonto, his life dependent upon his horse.

The Segi was wider than it had looked from above, and the walls were higher. Kent headed up the trail into a marvelous region. But at every turn in the trail before he exposed the burros or Spades to possible riders or watchers beyond he halted to peer around and study the land ahead with a passion of keenness. It appeared to be the loneliest canyon imaginable. Deer and rabbits, coyotes and mustangs were not in evidence at all. Old deserted hogans stood among the cedars, their black vacant doors open to the east. The trail played out in stretches, and would have been hard to follow but for Slotte's fresh tracks. The robbers held to a brisk trot. It was easy, almost level going.

Every feature of this remarkable gorge magnified until Kent felt bewildered. He could not get lost because he had fresh tracks to follow, yet nevertheless he felt lost.

He had never dreamed of a place like the Segi. It was strange, sad, beautiful, a desolated rent in the crust of the earth, with sage growing luxuriantly, with patches of scrub oak and cedars growing on the flats, and a fringe of spruce at the base of the cliffs. Intersecting canyons on both sides opened into the main gorge, and each yawned deep and red-walled. In some places sections of wall had splintered into fragments, strewing numberless rocks of all sizes and shapes down the slope. In other places the walls were sheer, looming red and unscalable to the notched rims a thousand feet above.

At length Kent came upon an outlook that held him spellbound. The canyon widened to a great oval into which branch canyons opened like the spokes of a wheel joining with the hub. Here Kent got off his horse and long sought for signs of life. All he heard was a shrill piping whistle which he concluded came from a cliff animal or a bird. He spent more time studying this valley of decay and ruin than he did in crossing it.

Afternoon had far advanced when he rode out of this oval up the main artery which led out of it. And he was to find that the Segi narrowed considerably. The wash diminished in its formidable steep walls, the stream to a thin thread of clear water, and the peaks and crags were no longer lofty. Kent figured that he had been climbing for ten miles toward the head of the canyon. The sun sank early behind the western rampart, after which Kent began to look for a secluded campsite. He had to travel on for a goodly distance before he found a patch of oaks, well off the trail. He penetrated this scrubby growth to an open spot next to the cliff, where he was fortunate enough to find a tiny spring of cold water.

"Wonder where the bad Injuns are," he said, as he unsaddled Spades. He did not relax vigilance, but this was a most desirable and well-hidden spot. Having unpacked, Kent sallied out with his rifle to hunt for meat, a quest he believed would be quite a forlorn hope. But some distance up a brushy side canyon he found rabbits and succeeded in killing a couple.

Upon his return his quick eye caught sight of an animal in the trail. At first he thought it a coyote, because it slunk away looking back. He passed and the animal glided along through the cedars. It might have been a wolf. As he reached camp, however, and had a better look at the animal which appeared to want to keep him in sight he decided it was an Indian dog. He had seen dogs, half-shepherd and half-coyote that resembled this one. And he forgot about it until as he was eating his supper he espied the dog sneaking along on the inside of the belt of oaks. It was a lean, hungry, long-haired dog, a dirty white in color, as wild in aspect as any wolf.

"Hey, doggie, I won't hurt you," called Kent.

The animal appeared to take fright and went away. But soon it came back and hung around. Kent threw it the parts of the rabbits he had not cooked and soon had evidence that his guess was correct. The dog was starved. Kent called and whistled, but the dog would not come closer.

"Say, boy, you could do worse than hang around me. Can't you see I like dogs?"

Dusk fell, and night. Kent lay in his secluded camp, wide awake and thoughtful. He began to sense an intimacy in these canyon walls, far removed from the vast emptiness and homelessness of the desert. They gave him a feeling of protection. He could not get rid of the haunting idea that something great and terrible was going to happen to him under them.

Morning disclosed the fact that Spades and the burros had remained in the inclosure, though they had been free to leave. Next he discovered the white dog hanging around.

"You son-of-a-gun. Come here," called Kent. "Well, wait till you smell meat."

While Kent was frying the second rabbit the dog came closer, and finally out of the brush. But for his gaunt frame and stained hair he might have been a handsome dog. Kent threw him meat and biscuits. Later when he took to the trail again he was surprised to see that the dog followed.

Kent had not traveled far before he sighted a mustang and rider turn a corner ahead. Presently the Indian espied Kent and slowed down. They met in the trail and halted.

"How," said Kent. The Indian was a young brave, buckskinned and beaded. He did not have a weapon that Kent could see. He was eagle-eyed, brown-skinned and prepossessing. His answer to Kent's greeting was a grunt. He did not appear curious or hostile or friendly. Kent held up three fingers and motioned up the trail.

"Palefaces? How far?"

"Kitseel," replied the savage.

"Ahuh. Have one on me," said Kent with a laugh, offering a cigarette. Kitseel was a place somewhere beyond. Probably this Indian took him for a member of Slotte's party.

Navahos live Segi?" asked Kent.

The Indian understood that, for his sign probably meant his people were farther up the canyon. He was not in the least unfriendly. But he kicked his shaggy mustang and whipped his plaited bridle. Kent turned in his saddle. A few rods down the trail stood the white dog.

"Hey. Navaho dog?"

"Piute," called the brave with something of scorn, and rode on.

Kent watched the savage lope out of sight. "Gosh! I thought the Tonto riders could fork a horse. But these Navahos must have been born on horseback. . . . Come on, Piute."

The dog trailed along, keeping about the same distance from Kent.

This morning the sun was hidden by clouds. A dull redness showed over the rim. The clouds thickened and bore down, obscuring the crags. Then rain began to fall. After a while it turned to snow which melted almost as soon as it alighted on sage or sand. The rocks glistened wet. Kent kept on, unmindful of his growing discomfort. And the white dog kept on his trail.

A troop of mustangs, wilder than deer, bolted from a cliff shelter and ran out a few hundred yards to halt and whistle. Kent slowed to a walk. He passed a hogan from which a thin wisp of blue smoke showed in the white snowflakes. Dogs barked. But no Indian shoved aside the blanket at the door to peer out. After that Kent passed more hogans, across the wash, barely discernible through the snow. He grew grateful for the storm, despite his sloppy cold feet and numb hands. In his rush to get away he had forgotten slicker and gloves, indispensable things for the desert rider. Finally Kent got off to plod along, leading Spades, and driving the burros ahead. As the day neared its end the snow gave place to sleet and a bitter north wind whirled down the canyon. Kent knew he had enough. The first clump of cedars claimed him and a good hot fire changed the dreary world. The grass here was long and wet, which Spades went at with a relish, his black back all shiny and his long mane sprinkled with raindrops. Then the sleet ceased to fall, as the wind grew colder. The canyon was engulfed in dull clouds which hung half way to the level. Dusk was not far away. Warm and dry again Kent turned to his tasks.

There before him, scarcely a rod away, stood the white dog, muddy and bedraggled.

"I'll be doggoned!" ejaculated Kent. "Piute, are you throwin' in with me?"

Even at such distance Kent saw that the dog had remarkable fine and piercing eyes. They were not brown or dark like those of most dogs, but a strange shade of gray or yellow, flecked with spots. But that was only the physical characteristic. Kent imagined he saw something wild, fierce, searching in these desert eyes. And as more than once before in his life, in the case of animals, he sensed something out of the ordinary in the meeting. This Piute dog has passed hogan after hogan. He was homeless. He was studying the white man. Kent pretended to pay no more attention to the dog. And before he had supper cooked he had the satisfaction of seeing the dog edge closer and closer until he felt the warmth of the fire. Kent fed him generously, without speaking. The dog had not known a white man's voice.

That night turned out to be exceedingly cold. Kent kept his fire burning, despite which he did not sleep much. His last nap carried him past daybreak. When he awoke he found the white dog curled at his feet. That was the pleasantest surprise of all.

"Piute, you're makin' no mistake," he said. "I'm no good with women, but I sure stand high with dogs an' horses. An' I'm tellin' you if a poor lost wild dog of the Piutes can cotton to Kent Wingfield he's a real hombre."

The clouds lifted, the sun came out, the cold disappeared. Kent's first incident of that morning's trail was to meet a shepherd boy with his flock of sheep. He was a ragged barefoot lad with black hair straggling around his brown face. He had big, eager, unaffrighted eyes. His shepherd dog attacked Piute and in short order got a severe drubbing. But at Kent's stern call the white dog left off. The sheep ran bleating down the canyon. Kent gave the lad a knife. That poor Indian boy surely had never had a gift before in all his life.

"Where Kitseel?" asked Kent.

The answer was untranslatable, but eyes and hands supplied Kent with the intelligence that Kitseel was not far away. He rode on, reflecting that Spades had seen or sensed those sheep before he had. Thereafter he meant to keep a close watch on the horse, and the dog, too. This was his third day up the Segi and though he had looked carefully he had not yet come upon signs of where Slotte had camped.

Turning a cliff corner Kent came upon a colossal cavern on the left side across the face of which and high up stretched a magnificent cliff dwelling. Kent had seen a few ruins near Wagontongue, enough to recognize in this a marvelous monument to the ancient aborigines. He did not waste time to halt, but he looked with eyes intent and fascinated, to imprint on his memory that weird bridge of little stone houses crossing the cavern, the vacant eyelike windows, the smoke-stained walls and the vast looming roof of yellow rock.

Beyond this point the canyon narrowed until it was a mere winding lane with low walls, and with a trail that had a very perceptible ascent. Huge rocks blocked the way. Little streams of water cut across the trail. The sage grew luxuriant and exceedingly fragrant. Still Slotte's tracks led on. At length the canyon walls notched and Kent had to climb up a crack between them. He had suspected before that Spades had been along this trail, but when the horse went boldly at bad steps he knew it. He walked almost on the heels of the burros, driving them ahead.

Kent came out on top to be confronted with so stupendous and awe-inspiring a view that if Slotte had ambushed him there he would have been easy prey.

For a moment Kent was stunned. He had gazed across farflung desert distances, but this was extraordinarily different. He had climbed out on the Utah uplands. Purple rolling sage, dotted with green cedars and outcroppings of red rock, stretched down for leagues to what appeared a red-streaked haze. Kent could not hold his gaze there because of something looming black and grand to his left. It was a half-round mountain towering into the blue, banded by sage at its base, by cedars beyond, by green pine to the domelike summit. As striking as was the front of this mountain, the north face dwarfed any other aspect of it. For that side sheered down abruptly, a riven and blasted spectacle of colored crags and cliffs, its lower half vanishing in a red chaos.

It was too dim, too hazy, too aloof under that north front for Kent to make out anything except the abyss which seemed to be the end of the world.

Kent had to face north himself and gaze down these beautiful upland steps to where they fell off into a seared and seamed gulf that reached to infinity. If it had an end somewhere across that awful space it was lost in the haze of obscurity. But that gulf was the crust of the earth, denuded of soil and green, an endless rock-ribbed region more rough and terrible than the ocean with its hurricanes.

As Kent's desert eyes began to discern and trace and magnify, he gathered that this stretch, two hundred miles and more, must be the canyon country of Utah. The lines and cleavages were numberless canyons. The three ragged black irregular demarcations cutting across at all angles with these were the great canyons of which he had heard —the Colorado, the Escalante, the San Juan. Surely this was the grandest scene that man's eyes had ever dwelt upon. The immensity of it limited the faculties of beauty. But an appalling beauty vied with the majesty, the sublimity of that illimitable area of rain-washed, wind-sculptured, sun-blasted rock. This was Utah. This was the grand hole in the earth, and down in there somewhere, hidden, all but inaccessible, was the Hole in the Wall.

Shrill concatenated whoops, unquestionably Indian, rudely disrupted Kent. Spades jumped as if he knew the nature of that yell. The sound of light hoofs succeeded it. Turning in his saddle Kent saw three Indians riding down upon him. They came from a clump of cedars not far distant.

"Humph! Sounded kind of wild—that yell," exclaimed Kent aloud.

They were not Navahos, so therefore they must be Piutes. He had been told that the Utah Indians wore black high-peaked conical sombreros, and one of these at least had on that kind of head gear. They rode on apace, matchless horsemen, on lean racy mustangs the like of which Kent had not seen before on the desert. They dashed up to him, and pulled their mounts hard. Spades did not like this encounter any more than Kent. The leader began to jabber. He was squat of build, had a wide dark face with large features and black wild eyes that Kent at once distrusted. The other two·were younger, leaner and less impressive, but they were every bit as wild and aggressive as their leader.

"Piute? What you want?" demanded Kent, not any too conciliatorily. He did not like being whooped at and then harangued by a trio of savages. The leader had an old muzzle-loading musket over his saddle, and his companions were armed with bows and arrows.

"Yah! Yah! —Yip-sa-teda-el-eki," shouted the high-sombreroed savage, or words that sounded like that to Kent.

"No savvy," returned Kent impatiently. "Me belong Bonesteel clan."

"Nuh! Nuh!" vehemently replied this Piute, shaking his big head until his straight black hair danced around his ears. He followed that with a volley of native language. But his expression and his gestures, together with his fierce eyes hardly needed any interpretation in words. The Piute took Kent for an intruder. Moreover, when he pointed a dark lean hand at Spades and turned to his companions, as if to get their vindication of whatever it was that he was claiming, then Kent passed from annoyance to a sharp consideration of trouble, if not peril.

"Say, what the hell you yellin' about?" he called, and he began to calculate chances. He pulled Spades back a step and turned his head somewhat away. Just so long as this Piute did not move that old musket barrel toward him, and his two allies did not separate their bows from the handful of arrows they held, just that long would Kent talk and try to be patient. But he did not like this. He had fallen in with bad Piutes. They recognized Spades. They knew he did not belong to Kent, and that Kent was not a member of Bonesteel's outfit. So much Kent gathered.

Apparently the Piute had no fear of Kent. In fact he could not see the gun low down on Kent's leg. And the rifle was in its saddle sheath. Suddenly Kent filled his lungs full and let out a yell that stopped the Piutes' torrent of Indian language.

"Me Pak-a-guti," the leader rolled out, striking his breast.

"Say, redskin, I don't give a damn who you are," declared Kent. "If you want whisky or tobac I'll give you some. But——"

"Injun want hoss."

"Ahuh. You want swap hoss?"

"Nuh swap. Me take."

"Oh, is that all? ... Piute, this hoss is mine. I swap money with Bunge."

"Nuh swap. Paleface steal."

"You lie, you ornery Piute. Don't you call me a horse-thief."

The savage urged his mustang a few steps closer to Kent, which action turned the muzzle of the musket farther away. Then he snatched at Kent's bridle. Spades jerked up his head.

"Lay off, Injun," warned Kent, cursing under his breath. He would have to shoot the fool Piute. And his hand went to his gun. Perhaps the Indian saw the stealthy move, for he reined his mustang back, and all his squat body appeared to stiffen. Kent read murder in the black gaze.

"Look out, Piute," yelled Kent in cold fury. He saw the Indian let go the rawhide halter. He saw his left hand shift from the stock of the old musket to the stubby hammer. The lean thumb was drawing the hammer back.

"Take it, you crazy redskin," hissed Kent, flashing his gun.

The shot battered the Piute half off his mustang. The musket boomed and went flying in the air. A horrid strangling cry issued from the Piute as the mustang wheeled away.

Spades stood like a rock. He had been shot from before. Both the other Indians had evidently drawn their bows simultaneously with their leader's menacing action. Both bows twanged before Kent had time to duck. One arrow stuck quivering in the saddle and the other, striking Kent's shoulder with a fiery wrench, spoiled his aim so that he missed. His third shot, however, knocked the Piute clean off his mustang. The other Indian was already speeding away, and as Kent sought to align his gun on the bobbing form the Indian slid around under the neck of the mustang leaving no mark to shoot at. Kent let that Indian go. The first Piute was still hanging on to his mustang, spent and swaying, evidently hard hit. Kent sat a moment longer, swearing at the burn in his shoulder, then urged Spades away after the burros. Reloading his gun he sheathed it and then lay hold of the arrow in his shoulder. It was loose and readily came out without causing him further pain. The flint arrowhead was red. Kent felt the wound. His thick leather coat had saved him from a bad hurt. Slipping his hand inside the coat he found a rent in his shirt and a wet stinging groove in his shoulder. His fingers came forth bloody. Kent stuffed his scarf inside over the wound, grimly reflecting that the more that happened to him the more luck he had. The dog was trotting at the heels of the burros.

"Piute, if that's a sample of your redskins I don't wonder you left them," said Kent.

During the next half hour Kent looked back more than forward. He drove the burros at a fast trot. He had made out some bright dots on the sage that he believed were mustangs and he thought he saw thin smoke rising from a cedar grove. Soon that part of the sage upland fell out of sight behind him, and when he sought ahead to see the vast hollow of rocks that too had dropped under the gray-green upland.

Kent now had enemies in front and enemies behind. He expected pursuit more than ambush. Slotte had no idea Kent was trailing him. There were many places where he could have made his tracks difficult to follow, but these tracks he left were like leaves of an open book.

The minutes passed by. The burros kept their brisk trot downhill, the ground began to show the heave and break which indicated the near presence of a change in the plateau. Then passing through a belt of stunted cedars he came to a void in the earth. The burros went down out of sight over a rim. In another moment Spades halted where the trail started down.

First Kent saw a slanting wall of jumbled red rock—a vast slope of talus the color of fire. This was the opposite slope to a mile-wide canyon, deep and empty and glaring. Used as Kent had been to desert scenes he had never gazed upon such a barren and desolated rent.

"This is Noki—the red canyon old Bill told me about," said Kent, excited and elated. For this canyon emptied into the San Juan—and once across the river and unburdened by the slow burros, Kent had no fear of any pursuit by Indians. Spades could outdistance any mustangs over any kind of going.

EAGERLY KENT dismounted to walk down and save his horse. The travel ahead would be all but impossible. Rifle in hand he stepped out on the extreme edge of the rim and gazed down. Noki was a canyon like a notch cut out of solid rock, in all shades of red. There were no walls, no cliffs. Both slopes from the rim to the ghastly white wash in the depths consisted of a frightful slanted mass of rocks small at the top and growing larger until they consisted of huge masses as large as houses. Everywhere they lay, the hugest ones far out on the canyon floor, mute evidences of the ruin and devastation of the rock crust of the earth, glistening, burning red under the sun.

The only spot of green in all that arid rent shone intensely bright and strange far down the canyon—a small oval of cottonwood and grass, an oasis in that desert of stone.

A few zigzags down the Noki trail, dust and earth gave way in some places to a sliding treacherous slant of weathered stones, in others to stretches and steps of bare rock. Kent had to keep going or be stepped on by the snorting horse. And both of them pressed too hard on the heels of the burros. Kent was relieved to reach the bottom with his horse and burros without mishap.

The trail led around and among huge boulders. Kent headed off the burros to straighten their packs. It was hot down here. He was wringing wet with sweat, and Spades dripped as if he had just emerged from water. Kent searched the trail he had just descended and the rim two thousand feet above. But nothing moved. The slope was dead. Mounting Spades he rode down the canyon, concentrating on the wilderness of rock ahead.

Long before Kent expected to, he came upon the oasis. Set in that glaring furnace of red rocks the vivid green of cottonwood, the white sand, the blooming desert flowers appeared to make a little paradise. Lizards, the only living creatures, scurried across the sand. Kent found the remains of a campfire, which upon close scrutiny he decided had been left the preceding morning. So he was less than thirty hours and more behind Slotte. Too close! This oasis would have been a fine campsite if there had been any water above ground and the certainty of no Piutes behind him. But it was as dry as a bone. By the end of the day both he and his animals would be badly in need of water.

Kent rode on, and the character of the canyon

changed. It deepened and widened. Denuded slopes of clay, gray and blue and yellow, vied with the red rocks in lending color to the stark and naked canyon. The tips of walls to the fore rose higher and higher. Kent had a feeling that he was descending into the rocky bowels of the earth. But while he went deeper all the time the great slopes spread until he could no longer see the rims. In front rose a barrier—the frowning walls that he had seen from far back on the uplands. He was now beneath the seamed and lined floor of the vast basin. That wall ahead looked unsurmountable and impenetrable. The trail led deeper and soon Kent lost sight of the formidable wall. He appeared lost in a winding gorge.

When hours later, toward the end of the afternoon, he emerged into the open he found that he had passed through the mouth of Noki into San Juan Canyon. He heard a sullen roar of water, but could not see the river. The formidable wall that had daunted him had apparently shrunk to a low bluff. But that probably was only the first step. A wide bench covered with scant sage and greasewood led out to an irregular break across which rose the red bluff. This break would be where the river ran. That sullen roar disturbed Kent. It seemed to have a hollow menace. Noki had had some beauty to help one to endure its desolateness and heat. But San Juan was drab and forbidding with a terrible loneliness. No living creature crossed Kent's sight.

On the flat sides of great boulders he saw crude Indian paintings of distorted animals and images of grotesque design. Then under a shelving rock, against a yellow background, Kent's roving eye caught the imprint of bloody hands. How suggestive of the awfulness of this region! Kent felt that they were meant to intimidate him. The trail turned to the right, under a slope of scattered rocks, from around which the river sound increased.

Turning a corner Kent came abruptly upon a wide sandy bar, a fringe of willows, and a swift sliding river of muddy red water a hundred yards wide. A break in the wall opposite showed steps and ledges where the trail went upward.

The river appeared to be in flood and impassable.

63

Nevertheless a little study of the canyon above this point and below assured Kent that the ford was here. On both sides the canyon boxed. Besides there were Slotte's tracks straight toward the river. He had not halted here, even for a rest. Kent's alarm receded, so far as crossing here was concerned. To make doubly sure he let Spades have his head. The black went down to the water, waded in, slaked his thirst, and then headed across. Kent had to turn him back.

He tied Spades and fed him the last of the grain. The burros he unpacked for the last time. He hated to see them go, for they had belonged to Bill Elway and had been faithful beasts of burden. But he could not take them further. They would wander away into the wilderness and be free.

Kent hurried through a cold meal, at once busy and preoccupied. He ate all he could hold. Thus his pack would be lighter. He could not keep from listening to this river of the rocks. If the San Juan slid along so sullen and dark and sinister what would the Colorado be like?

The approach of sunset found him sorting his pack. Most of its contents would have to be hidden. He espied a niche up in the rocks that could be utilized for a cache. Kent donned his extra shirt, jeans and socks, and rolled the old ones to hide with the bulk of his tinned goods. The wound in his shoulder had caked over with clotted blood. Kent bound it up and let that suffice. It was painful, yet did not inconvenience him. While choosing what he should take along—ammunition, supplies for a few days, the extra gun he had brought along—he happened to remember the dog Piute.

"Doggone! . . . Where'd I see Piute last?"

He remembered last seeing him come down the rocky trail in Noki Canyon. Perhaps the dog had gotten tired and had left him. But Kent thought better of that. Somehow he had faith in Piute. There was going to be something between him and that Indian dog.

Carefully Kent weighed the new pack which Spades was to carry. He limited it to about fifty pounds. Then he hid all that was left and wedged stones in the niche. He was satisfied with that job. Coyotes could not reach the cache and Indians were not likely to find it there.

Suddenly Kent was more than astounded to see Piute coming up the slope, carrying a dead rabbit in his bloody jaws. His distended stomach was further proof that he had eaten prodigiously. He laid the rabbit down and gazed intelligently up at Kent. He was wet, dirty and bedraggled. And he panted heavily. Then he lay down and began to lick his foot.

"See here, Piute," said Kent solemnly. "This will never do. Suppose I'd get fond of you? . . . By gosh, I am already."

Whereupon Kent skinned the rabbit, cleaned it, salted it generously and wrapping it in a cloth he deposited it in the back of his leather coat. Then, tying the compact pack behind the saddle, he mounted Spades.

Kent rode the black down to the edge of the river at the place where Slotte's tracks led into the water. Spades had been across there, perhaps often. He did not need to be spurred or even spoken to. He waded in boldly. Kent looked back. This was the crucial test for Piute.

"Come on, Piute," he called.

The dog whined, ran to and fro along the sand bar, looked back at the wide gloomy mouth of Noki, and then turned to enter the water.

Kent expected quicksand. But the iron hoofs of the black cracked on stones. The water was shallow. The heavy rolling current with its queer waves had deceived Kent. Spades headed for the break in the wall opposite. It was somewhat downstream. When he reached the middle the water grew deeper reaching his flanks. Piute swam by quartering downstream. Spades plunged on. The current foamed reddish around him, making him slip, but he did not lose his footing. Kent lifted his boots high. There came a moment of hard striving on the part of the horse, then shallower water intervened, and with disdainful snorts he waded on and out. Piute was on the bank waiting for them. Dusk was now at hand.

Kent selected a campsite off the trail under a cliff and hidden from the shore opposite by rocks the size of a house. He chanced building a small fire and over it broiled the rabbit. Then he put it out. He staked out Spades so the horse would not wander into sight from across the river.

His tasks done he could no longer be inattentive to the strangeness of this place, to the encroaching of irrepressible thoughts, to the feeling engendered by the fact that he could not be many miles from the Hole in the Wall.

For a bed he lay his saddle blankets on the sand, after scooping out a hollow for his hips, and placing his saddle for a pillow. This left him his blanket for a coverlet, something he would not need very soon that night. A warm air stirred down the canyons. Spades stamped his annoyance at being haltered. Kent went down to the willows and cut an armful of long bushes and branches, which he carried back and threw in front of the horse. Then Kent went to bed, and lay there with the black walls leaning against the sky, the stars blinking white, and the changing roar of the river in his ears.

If his luck held the next night would find him awake under the stars in the stronghold of the Utah robbers. The thought awed him with its peril, its thrill, its romance. His consciousness would not admit of failure, and his wild imaginings got him as far as meeting Lucy Bonesteel. Beyond that tremendous event his consciousness did not work. Somewhere beyond that bold black rim, deep in a hole in the walls at a level with the river so much unknown, so mysteriously famed, lived a young and innocent girl, as lovely as the sleeping beauty Kent's sister used to babble about, awaiting her rescuer and love and life and happiness. Night after night he had dreamed in this wise, unable to stop it, despite the doubt engendered by the blackness and the solitude.

Besides this he had to contend with his throbbing wound and the aftermath of the shooting fray with the Indians. If there were no specters in the canyon there surely were some flitting through Kent's consciousness. Still he knew he was thinking right—that on that line he would succeed. All night through his slumbers the river rolled and roared. Several times he had awakened to turn over, trying to find a soft spot in his hard bed, and each time Piute heard him and stirred. The Indian dog was uncanny. Kent wondered, Did Piute have the instinct to know his needs? At last Kent realized and accepted the fact that no savages or robbers or beasts could surprise him while that dog lay at his feet.

The night passed. Gray shadow curtained the walls. The sullen roar went on. Kent got up with a leap. This was the day that he would discover Lucy Bonesteel's retreat if he did not actually get into it. He made short work of saddling up and took to the trail, leading Spades. The first two short slants were easy. The next was a narrow shelf, and succeeding that were steps no horse should have been put to. The black horse knew the danger as well as Kent. But so long as Kent led on he followed with careful sure steps. Intent on the trying ascent Kent did not take note of anything save the bad places and how to surmount them. For that reason he reached the top of the bluff before he had any idea he was near it. Spades heaved. And Kent found himself laboring for breath and sweating freely. Bare rounded slopes rose gradually before him. And across the red rock showed the wicked trail. Kent did not look back. Everything in the world for him lay ahead.

Stepping into the saddle he let the black go and gave him free rein. Piute trotted close behind. Never in his life had Kent been so curious, so obsessed, so intensely keen. This was a plain trail over the rocks to the Colorado, and though it was little traveled other riders besides robbers had used it for many years. Trails told their story to Kent Wingfield.

A long weaving climb up and over curves and mounds and slopes of bare rock brought Kent up on what appeared to be a level of this matchless and incredible sea of rock. But for the many deep crevices and pits and deep apparently bottomless cracks it would have resembled a sea of rounded irregular swells. Not a single vestige of green did Kent espy until he had gotten far from the San Juan, and then bits of green began to lend contrast to the barren red.

Surmounting another and still higher rounded ridge Kent halted to gaze about him in awe. There was no direction in which he could see far over the smooth rock.

But all around stood up the grand landmarks that identified this canyon country. Dim black mountains rose to the north; to the east ran a magnificent red escarpment, fringed with black, an almost endless barrier which broke off in a purple haze of distance; to the south the red and yellow sloped front of the uplands walled in the canyoned area; and to the west loomed the great mountain of the Navahos, with its colossal face of colored crags and cliffs.

"Wonderful!" cried Kent, breathing hard. "No place like it on earth, I'll bet. . . . Will Lucy Bonesteel want to leave it?"

But the stern exigency of his enterprise precluded all else. He let Spades go on. With hawk eyes he scanned the scalloped horizon, then bent them for a moment upon the trail. And at last he came to the conclusion that if Bonesteel had a branch trail off this main one he traversed it with unshod horses or padded hoofs. The latter was likely to be the case. Kent remembered Elway's assertion that there was a way over the rocks into the Hole in the Wall. Kent thought he had better trust his horse. Spades was going home; that seemed a certainty to the rider.

At length Kent reached a point in which all aspects of this extraordinary rock region seemed augmented to unbelievable proportions. The levels disappeared; the long hogbacks lengthened and rose and descended between canyons that sheered down into black shadows; the holes and pits resembled craters, only they were smoothly whorled; and green ledges and benches enlivened the world of red sandstone, and most striking of all were the oval depressions, deep down, where sage and cedars grew out of white sand.

Then the tortuous trail led down once again. Kent got off to walk. There were slants where he almost slipped himself, and narrow strips around red mounds, and at last a long descent of a massive slope down to the head of a canyon.

It became so narrow that Kent, once more mounted, could touch the walls on both sides, and they sloped up, V-shaped as far as he could see. Kent figured that he had covered miles. But old Elway might have meant the distance to the Colorado as short as the way a crow flies.

The sun penetrated this narrow chasm only at turns where an intersecting canyon opened. The trail always led down. Finally a clear stream flowed out from somewhere under a wall, and beyond that point brush and sage and flowers and grass grew profusely. It was hot, shady and fragrant, and the stream made a hollow murmur under the walls.

Kent rode on as if he were a magnet drawn by a loadstone. He preserved his extreme vigilance, still he could not but attend to the overmastering changing, mounting growth of every feature pertaining to this canyon, except its width. For it widened very little if at all.

Sunshine failed him. Either the lofty walls shut off the sun or else the afternoon was far spent, perhaps both. Gloom began to pervade the caverns. At times he thought the hollow shallow bubble of the stream was permeated by a deeper sound. Then he thought he imagined it. But as he rounded one of the jutting abutments of rock suddenly his ears caught a note of something else. There was a fall below or another stream joined this one or a cataract poured off the wall. He rode on, straining his ears. And the time came when a dull heavy rumble obliterated the murmur of the brook. The river! The Rio Colorado!

The gloom lightened. Kent appeared to be approaching the open, or at least space less restricted than that between these narrow canyon walls. He knew of course that presently he would look into the Grand Canyon of the Colorado. Yet he could hardly wait. What strange low thunder! It lulled, then pealed anew.

Sunlight again on the wall—a golden shaft far above his head! The shadow dispersed. Kent turned another bend to see close at hand a walled gateway through which shone a red sliding terrible river.

"End of the trail," muttered Kent. "But my God!— What did Bill stack me up against?"

He gazed, he listened, and what he saw and heard told him how little he had been prepared for the actuality. Kent had no thought of turning back. But the prospect was frightful. And the thing which saved him from sheer panic was the evident fact that Spades did not share his terror. The Colorado was no more to Spades than the San Juan.

Kent pulled himself together. Sunset was on the water. He had tracked Slotte down to the river. The fresh hoofmarks were there in the mud where the river had receded recently. They went into the water and they did not come out. He gazed across to see the outlet of a canyon on that side and the deep rut of a trail in the yellow bank. It was not so far across there but that he could detect fresh tracks made by half a dozen horses. Slotte had crossed. That was the ford on into Utah. Kent pondered in much concern. Had old Bill given him wrong directions? Or did this place look so different from the picture Kent had in his mind? No! He remembered perfectly. He was to swim his horse down the river and round a jutting corner. But for some reason Slotte and his companions had gone on. Kent did not know whether to be concerned or relieved. If this was the place, the outlaw would certainly return.

The trouble was that the actual river, with its swirling current, its treacherous look, its hidden thunder, and the long distance down the wall to the bold barrier jutting out simply raised Kent's hair stiff on his head and clove his tongue to the roof of his mouth.

Spades clamped his bit and pounded with impatient hoofs.

"Say horse!—What ails you?" ejaculated Kent, and he slackened the reins. Spades headed down river and stepped in the water up to his fetlocks. He was about to plunge when Kent hauled him back. Again the horse knew where he was going.

"Wait, Spades," called Kent huskily, triumph driving out fear. "I savvy. Wait till tonight! . . ."

Kent urged the impatient Spades back a few rods from the river behind a break in the wall. There he dismounted to quiet the horse. Spades seemed to understand that they would go presently and ceased his restlessness. He was learning to trust Kent.

The sun sank and the brightness faded from the river.

70

Kent saw the shade climb up the walls slowly raising the gold belt. It lingered on the towering rim, then vanished. And the canyon changed magically.

Kent did not realize when his decision was made. His intelligence, which he had called so persistently upon, told him that this whole adventure was foolhardy, and that this trusting himself to horse and river was sheer madness. Wherefore he repudiated his reason and answered to nerve and passion. If he ever got into the Hole in the Wall alive it would be time then to think.

Piute was as keen as the horse. The dog rested at Kent's feet watching him with wonderful eyes. Kent ventured a first time to lay a caressing hand upon the lean wolflike head.

Twilight always fell swiftly in the canyons. Here there was scarcely an appreciable moment between twilight and dusk. Kent strapped his gunbelt high around his waist. He would carry his rifle in his hand. These two things he would keep dry if possible. He looked at the saddle cinches. Spades, understanding these actions, regained his impatience. Then Kent got on and rode out and down to the river.

In the gathering darkness this strange river of the rocks magnified the characteristics that by day were frightful. There did not appear to be any rapid near yet the river muttered its low thunder, now low now high, a deep undercurrent chafe of siltladen water against its rocky confines.

"Go, Spades," called Kent, cold and grim, dropping the knot of his bridle over the pommel. "Come, Piute."

The horse took off as before, only this time, after the second step, he plunged and went in. The water surged almost over his head, and high up around Kent's waist. But it receded to his hips as Spades began to swim. Kent saw at once that the horse was at home in the water as well as upon land. His tremendous muscular activity appeared to be more violent than when at a gallop. Kent turned to see Piute almost even with them swimming easily. So far so good! The icy damp on Kent's breast lessened. Wherever the horse was headed for he would make it.

71

They passed the point of canyon wall into a current which swept Spades on. The wall sheered in a curve, so that there was comparatively dead water close to shore. No doubt on the return upriver from the rendezvous the robbers kept their horses close in out of the current.

That dark corner of wall had appeared far off and almost unattainable to Kent Wingfield. But he saw very soon that the current, aiding the horse, would bring them abreast of it in a few minutes of actual time. Kent held his rifle up, which was about all he could do, although he held himself in readiness to slide off and let Spades drag him in case the horse got in difficulties. But Spades breasted the river powerfully. Kent, in those moments of strain, seeing how his life depended upon the black, conceived such a love for him as he had never had for any other animal. Piute too came in for his share of strong feeling. His lean pointed head kept even with Kent, not an arm's length away.

From around the bold black corner of wall pealed that low thunder. All was veiled in shadow there. The wall loomed terrifically. Kent's suspense seemed to stretch the labored beats of his heart to long intervals. He heard the current chafing at the corner, saw the swirling surface of the river rise a little against the rock. Then Spades swept around it and headed into eddying water.

In the gloaming Kent saw a break in the black cliff. Sky and stars! His eyes pierced the gloomy obscurity. All he could make sure of was that the wall ended some score or more rods below where Spades swam. A pale strip of sandy shore gave Kent's clamped heart release. He saw the foliage of cottonwood trees against the sky. On and on the brave horse swam, at length to check his smooth rhythmic motion by a violent halt. He had struck bottom. A plunge, a heave and then he was wading out to a sandy beach now plain to Kent's gaze.

7

□

A TRAIL as wide as a road led up the beach, cut through a
low bank to a level, into a grove of cottonwoods. Caution
came to hold Kent's eagerness in abeyance. He bent low
in the saddle. The hooftracks he had been following for
days showed plainly in the starlight. Others, fresher
tracks, led back down into the river. A sudden terrible
fear welled up inside Kent. Slotte had been here and gone
on. That explained the tracks Kent had seen across the
river. No one else had come this way, or across the ford
ahead of him. Had there been a fight? Had Slotte killed
Bonesteel and ridden away with Lucy? Or was Kent's
imagination running riot?

Kent rode up the bank into grass and sheared off into
deep shadow. Far on through the trees flicked a campfire.
Someone was still here. Instantly he was Kent Wingfield
of the Tonto again, multiplied by a hundredfold in all
that had ever made him keen, resourceful, implacable.

He did not need to call the dog to him. Piute hung
silently beside him. The horse drooped. All that rough
travel over hot desert and slippery trails, and that last
desperate expenditure of strength were past. Spades was
home again.

Kent thought swiftly. It would not do for him to leave
the horse there while he stole into the grove toward the
light. He must make a wide detour to get far around on
the other side of that camp. To this end he peered to the

left, as that was the only direction safe for him to ride. He did not want to leave his boot tracks in the sand near the trail. So he mounted again and rode to the left, out into the open. A wall of rock loomed prodigiously above him, but he could not tell whether or not it was close. The ground was covered with turf which gave forth only soft thuds. Kent rode on, amazed not to come upon the wall. When at length he did approach it he had another surprise in the discovery that there was no slope, no weathered rock leading up to the cliff. A line of dark scrub oak ran along in a long curve away from the river.

The Hole in the Wall was a big place. From time to time Kent turned to keep his relation to the grove of cottonwoods. He rode fully a mile along this wall before there was any change in the level. Then it began to slope up and sage gave place to turf. Kent kept to the edge of the slope.

All about him the black walls towered, their peaked and spired rims against the stars. The roar of the river lightened in the sound of a shallow waterfall not far away. A rushing brook blocked Kent's advance, so he held to its course up toward what appeared a high broken notch in the wall.

It led into a zone of oak and spruce, and scattered sections of cliff that had fallen from above. Kent could not see far, but he guessed that back up this brook he would find a wild enough country to suit even him. Grass grew almost to his knees. He heard animals in the brush. When he thought he had placed enough cover between where he was and the open flat he got off Spades, freed him of saddle, pack and bridle, and tied him out on a long halter. He was wet up to his waist, but had kept his ammunition and weapons dry.

Then he strode for the open flat. Once on the edge he looked up at the walls behind to pick out a landmark by which he could return. Two sharp spires stood up like sentinels. Piute trotted at his heels, a silent dog, a hunting dog, with his own intelligent idea of all this strange maneuvering. Kent followed the brook back to the point where he had first come upon it. He waded in, finding the water swift and cold, and knee-deep. From here he struck straight for the dark patch of cottonwoods. Presently he stepped into a grassy road.

It led along alfalfa fields, vineyards and gardens, all smelling of rich soil and fresh water. He heard calves bawling. Through the obscurity of greater distances he made out the dim shapes of horses grazing. Bonesteel's Hole in the Wall was not only a retreat for robbers but a ranch that insured them the best of living.

Kent came to the cottonwoods and that ended amaze and conjecture. They were big trees, far apart and full-foliaged. Summer lasted almost all the year round down in the canyons. He stole from tree to tree, halting to peer ahead. Piute stopped when he stopped, and at these intervals he was a listening, scenting, watching dog. The gloom was thick under the cottonwoods. There was no brush to avoid. The thick turf under his feet would leave no tracks.

Suddenly a light pierced the gloom. It appeared too high off the ground and too yellow to come from a campfire. Noiselessly and stealthily Kent made his way toward it. Once a black shape barred it for a second. That electrified Kent. A man or possibly a woman, had crossed that light. Presently a space opened in the grove of trees and a long low structure showed in the shadow. It was a log cabin. The light flared from an open window.

Like an Indian Kent stole up close. A wide porch on that side would have to be crossed before he could peep in at the window. He slipped along toward the corner of the cabin, turned it; and presently caught a glint of light from a crack in the mud chink between the walls.

Breathlessly Kent applied his eye to that crevice. He saw a big room made bright by a lamp on a table, a fair-haired girl sitting in its light, a huge oven fireplace where fagots blazed, a man smoking beside it, and floor and walls covered with skins and blankets.

Kent took all this in at a glance, then he sank down in such an intense relief that he was weak.

The girl's low voice lifted Kent as if it had been the hand of a giant. Silently he peeped in again.

"Slotte promised to bring my horse back," she was

saying, petulantly. "I don't believe Bunge stole Spades. I don't believe he sold him to some range-rider."

"Wal, neither do I, Lucy. An' admittin' as much I'm not square with either Slotte or yore dad," replied the man.

Kent could not spare a second then to look at the girl's companion. But his dry drawling voice was one to prompt a favorable impression. Kent could only gape in wonder at Lucy Bonesteel.

She was young and wondrously lovely, as Elway had sworn. She had wavy hair like the gold of sunlight with dark tints in it, as Elway had so lovingly claimed. She had great dark eyes and the sweetest face Kent had ever seen in all his life. Old Bill had not lied. The moment was so staggeringly great for Kent Wingfield that he stood in strong rapture. Then as he grasped the truth he shook like a leaf.

"Jeff, you have said that before," went on the girl, after a troubled pause. "I don't understand you."

"Shore I shouldn't hev said that much," returned the man Jeff. "You see, lass, you're growin' up. You can't be kept a child an' fooled forever."

"Fooled!" exclaimed the girl, her wide eyes upon her companion.

Kent's gaze followed their glance. Jeff appeared to be a spare gray man of uncertain age, with his gaunt visage softening its hard record through kindly feelings he could not help.

"Thet's what I said, Lucy. An' it ain't easy for me to be left hyar alone with you so much."

"Jeff, you've been most as good to me as my dear old friend Bill," she said softly. "I'm happy here—except when they come back. And lately I haven't been happy, Jeff. Slotte took Spades with him. Why did he do that?"

"Wal, I reckon he needed a fast hoss. They all want Spades. Only Slotte was the only man who dared take him."

"Why do they want fast horses?"

Jeff vouchsafed no reply to that. Lucy Bonesteel did not yet know she belonged to a band of robbers, raiders, rustlers who often had dire need of the swiftest horses.

"Jeff, I didn't tell you," resumed Lucy. "It's harder to tell things than it used to be. Maybe I am growing up. . . . But last night Slotte came in here and called me from my room. I had heard him swearing at Goins out on the porch. He was furious because Dad had left the message for them to come on across the river at once. . . . Well, Slotte looked black and fierce. But seeing me he changed. He seized me—held me tight—put his mouth to mine— and bit my neck. Then he tore at my skirt. At that I became so frightened I broke away from him, ran into my room and barred my door. He begged me to come out. But I was disgusted. I didn't. Then he stamped out."

"Yeah. So Silk did all thet, did he?" queried Jeff, a note of iron in his voice. "Was thet the fust time, Lucy?"

"Yes, that way. He always kissed me. I liked him before. He always fetched me pretty things from outside. But this was different, Jeff. I didn't like it. You know I did not come out for breakfast until he had left. Why did he treat me that way last night?"

"Slotte is in love with you, lass."

"He has told me that twice this year. Says he intends to marry me. I told Dad. And Dad was furious. He swore. 'I guess *not*,' he said. 'I'll have to kill this silk-shirted renegade!'—That frightened me. I don't want to see Dad in any more fights. . . . But, Jeff, even if Slotte does love me and wants to marry me, why did he kiss me that sickening way and try to tear my dress off?"

"Lucy, do you remember your mother?" asked Jeff gravely.

"Yes, a little. She was pretty, except when she cried."

"You was too much of a kid to remember anythin' she ever told you?"

"I must have been."

"Wal, didn't your father or old Bill ever tell you *anythin'*?"

"Jeff, they taught me to read and write. All I know."

"Listen, child. Bonesteel has shot men on yore account. An' he'd never let the women he had hyar from time to time be with you when he was away. Old Bill saw to thet. He was yore guard hyar from the time you was twelve to fifteen years old. . . . The reason of thet is

77

because yore Dad wanted to keep you innocent until he could take you away."

"Innocent? Of what? He never told me he was going to take me away. I don't want to leave home."

"Wal, I mean innocent of the hunger of man fer woman."

"Hunger? So that is what was the matter with Slotte," rejoined Lucy with a perplexed laugh. "He did act as if he wanted to eat me."

Jeff writhed in despair and knocked the ashes out of his pipe with a resentful finality.

"You're a child in knowledge," he said bitterly. "An' a buddin' woman in body. You've been hid hyar all your life, lass. All yore life! An' you're the purtiest thing the sun ever shone on. You ought to hev the same chance fer happiness thet other girls hev."

"I am happy, Jeff. I will be, I mean, if I get Spades back."

"But, child, listen to me," retorted the man, as if driven. "Don't you want to get out of this lonely hole in the rocks?"

"I don't think I do. Sometimes I wonder. . . . That newspaper I found and which Dad snatched from me. It made me curious. But even if I ever did want to go I wouldn't leave Dad."

"Suppose he'd get shot?" queried Jeff bluntly.

"Oh!" cried the girl, her eyes dilating. "I've thought of that. It terrifies me."

"Wal, it might happen. He's had more than one narrow shave."

"Dad promised me he would not go in any more gambling halls or drink any more or go near bad men," protested Lucy in a faith that was pitiful.

"Shore, shore. I was only supposin'," hastily went on the outlaw. "We ain't gettin' no whar. . . . Lass, promise me you won't never tell Bonesteel about my talkin' this way to you."

"I'll try, Jeff. He used to ask me what you talked about. But not any more. If he should ever ask me again I'd have to tell."

"He'd kill me, Lucy. Wouldn't you lie to save my life?"

"Yes, I'd lie for you," she replied, stoutly pondering. "But not for Slotte. . . . I'll not want to see Slotte any more. Dad will find out. He'll ask me."

"Wal, there's always the chance Slotte won't come back to the Hole," said Jeff, darkly.

"That would please me. But he always will come. I feel it."

"Mebbe not. . . . Go to bed, lass. I'm sorry I fetched thet troubled look to yore eyes. I'm gettin' to be an old fool. Don't pay—"

"Fool! No, you're not, Jeff dear," she interrupted earnestly. "But you said 'fooled forever'—What did you mean, Jeff? Don't double-cross me."

"Aw, I didn't mean nothin'," returned the outlaw lamely.

"Yes, you did. You were serious. You said 'they can't fool you forever.' By that you meant Dad and Slotte—Kitsap, Goins, Forman—all my Dad's riders."

"Forget it, Lucy."

"I always forget unpleasant things," she rejoined wistfully. "But maybe some day I won't be able to."

"Wal, goodnight lass," rejoined the outlaw, with a pathos that matched hers, and he got up to go toward the door. He wore high boots. A gun sheath swung from under his coat. As he opened a door on the porch side of the cabin Lucy ran to him.

"Goodnight, Jeff. Don't feel sad about me."

She closed the door behind him and leaned against it deep in thought. Kent heard the heavy slow footfalls of the outlaw pass down the porch. The girl then left the door to come slowly back toward the light, to stand with it showing full upon her.

"There is something wrong here," she mused aloud. "With Jeff—with Slotte—with my father. . . . But I mustn't try to find out what."

She was a little above medium height, lithe and strong. Her dress appeared to be of finer quality and cut than what would have been expected of a girl living in the depths of the canyon country. She appeared beautiful with a strange charm apart from physical perfection—her lovely waving hair, her broad low brow unlined and serene, her starry brooding eyes, her oval face of golden tan, and the red lips with their sweet curve.

She blew out the lamp. The room darkened except for the blazing sticks and ruddy coals on the hearth. She stood for a moment before these, gazing down, her profile faintly lighted, clear and clean-cut. Then she stepped away into the shadow. A door closed and a bar dropped into place.

Kent drew back from the wall stiff and dizzy. If she had stayed another moment he would have been mad enough to call her. Wrenching himself away Kent glided out under the cottonwoods with Piute beside him. He had never been in a trance, but this state he now palpitated under he thought might be one. His instinct, his habit of caution, returning doubly strong, guided him despite the fact that he had been struck to the very depths of his soul.

Under this cottonwood and that one he halted to listen, to peer into the gloom, to choose his way out to the open. And all the while his heart beat thick in his ears, his blood raced tinglingly through his veins, and his thoughts whirled with the tumult of his emotions.

Lucy Bonesteel, waif of the canyons, daughter of the chief of the Hole in the Wall gang—he had found her. And all that Elway had told him and prophesied leaped true in his mind. He came to the road that led out through the fields. He saw the green-fire eyes of deer grazing in the gardens. He stole on like an Indian, as stealthily as before, only on his return he had that which made him a vastly changed man—a glorious certainty to replace doubt, an exaltation that drove fear like mist before the sun, a passion of love that made all he had felt before pale and insignificant ghosts.

And the ghost of Nita Gail passed by in his memory. Poor Nita, with her greed for gold, her yearning for gaudy things, her luring eyes, her false heart—what indeed but a pale ghost of a woman compared to Lucy Bonesteel! With that pitying vision she passed out of Kent's thought forever.

He hurried now, beyond the fields, out into the sage, across the swift brook—the cold of which he scarcely felt, on to the spruces and the patches of oak, the great standing rocks, and at last his camp under the two tall sentinel spires. Behind the shelving rock Kent built a fire, hung his overalls and socks and boots to dry, and rolled in his blanket with his feet to the blaze.

The night seemed enchanted. The hidden waterfall murmured and beat and sang, and lulled to let in the low deep thunder of the terrible river of the canyons. Coyotes mourned. The melancholy canyon owls hooted their to whoo-te whoo-te whoo-oo-oo, and under the burning white stars the monuments and spires, the peaks and crags and the vast dark unbroken walls pierced the sky. The Sonoran desert had never called to Kent as did this lonely lost amphitheater of the rocks.

Bonesteel's hole in the canyon closed Kent in with warm protective barriers. He felt these sensations while his mind revolved around Lucy. Sight of her, the indubitable proof of her living lovely self, the sound of her voice, the dawning in her of a consciousness of boding trouble, the evidence to his own eyes of her revolt against the advances of the first man to disturb her innocence— these kept Kent awake for long hours, until at last his weary body succumbed and dragged him into slumber.

Mockingbirds awakened Kent. Broad daylight had come. He lay still, listening, letting his bewildered gaze rove around.

High up shiny mists of silver and pearl canopied an upflung broken wilderness of rock. The colossal wall presented a spectacle of sublime ruin, infinitely more beautiful for the endless forms of wind and water-worn stone. What Kent's gaze beheld in one direction without moving his head to right or left beggared his power to grasp. It was unreal, another world. Purple sage and golden flowers began at his feet, patches of gray cedar and green, black-pointed spruce trees peeping about masses of red rock, aisles and lanes leading into this maze of splintered mountain wall, and higher, out of a notch a lacy white waterfall, sliding down like smoke, murmurous in hum and drowsy melody, and dark chasms choked with green growths, and on higher still above the jumbled savage slope a heave and bulge of red mounds and billowed ridges, and yet towering higher the sunrise-flushed shafts and spires and monuments, their tips lost in the pearl mists of the morning.

That was one aspect of Kent Wingfield's environment, as he lay prostrate upon the grass. He was wide awake. Night had fled. The break of the morning was such as dwarfed in glory all the desert dawns he had seen. This was the back barrier of Bonesteel's Hole in the Wall.

Kent got up and dressed, marveling at his presence there. Clear daylight brought a returning of logic and caution, but did not dispel his excitement. His first move was to spread and hide the remains of his fire. Then calling the dog, with rifle in hand and his pack on his shoulder, he started back along the brook to find a secluded nook where there would be little possibility of his being discovered. He would return for his horse and saddle.

The brook wound back through the maze, bordered by banks of wild rose, yellow columbine and strange white lilies with purple centers. Deer and rabbits watched him pass; foxes stole into the red crevices; mockingbirds and jays flitted from cedar to spruce; and long-maned mustangs, far wilder than the deer, fled at his approach. The grass was a rich luxuriant carpet. Hard thorny growths of the desert, like cacti, manzanita, buck-brush appeared conspicuous by their absence.

He penetrated far into this maze without climbing. Always the massed slope of rocks, trees, cliffs, seemed a little farther. But the open spots grew smaller and less in number. On all sides stood up sections of red cliff that had fallen from above, to become half-hidden by spruce or overgrown by vine. His hurry made it impossible to make more than a superficial study of his surroundings. He wanted a safe hiding place, but there were so many of these that he could not choose. At length he followed a tiny tributary of the brook far in among shafts of stone and clumps of spruce to its source, a crystal spring at the base of a high lichened cliff. There was a little glade that would be sunny part of the day, a huge spreading cedar, a wall of rock on one side and a wall of spruce on the other, with a carpet of flowers and grass. Along the wall he espied a break the grassy ledges of which stepped up out of sight.

This was the camp of Kent's dreams, the most perfect sylvan hidden nook imaginable, steeped in solitude brooded over by the grand wall and murmuring waterfalls, fragrant and dry and sweet, lonely as the spot where the first man evolved upon the earth.

"If I can persuade Lucy Bonesteel to meet me here—I am lost. I would never leave," whispered Kent, as he dropped his burden, and gazed about with dreamy prophetic eyes.

Then he noted the absence of Piute. The dog had gone hunting. No doubt he would return to last night's camp. Kent took up his rifle and began to retrace his steps, no easy task over that soft rich grass. He had come much farther than he had thought.

Meanwhile the sun dispelled the mists, shining somewhere behind him over the walls and towers, but had not yet gotten down into the glades and aisles. The rock rim stood up golden red against the azure blue. Again Kent had to concede in amazement the bigness of just this section of the Hole in the Wall. If it had other ramifications like this he had penetrated, it was surely the most astounding place in all the West.

As Kent followed the brook and was approaching the more open spots, one of which would be the camp he had left, the whinny of a horse startled him. That might be Spades heralding his return. Nevertheless it disturbed Kent. Then when he heard the angry snarl of a dog he became thoroughly alarmed and broke into a run.

Suddenly he rounded the spruce bordered shaft of rock, which marked the glade where he had camp, to halt with sharp cry and stand rooted in his tracks.

8

PIUTE STOOD like a wild wolf, the hair on his neck up in a stiff mane. He was snapping at a shepherd dog which Lucy Bonesteel could scarcely hold back.

"Here, Piute," yelled Kent harshly, leaping out of his stupefaction.

"Oh!" cried the girl. "Stop him. I thought he was a wolf."

Kent got between the dogs, and cuffed Piute, and shoved him back. The Indian dog gave ground but slowly, his growl deep and his strange eyes burning with green fire. This was a difficult situation for Kent, as he did not want to hurt or alienate.

In a moment he turned to the girl, who stood erect now, profoundly surprised and interested. Behind her a buckskin mustang stood bridle down grazing on the grass. It was Lucy, yet in the bright sunlight, with her bare head a blaze of gold, and her great dark eyes, which he saw were blue instead of black, wide with wonder, she appeared so infinitely more than he had idealized last night, so alive and vital, so dazzlingly beautiful that he burst out incoherently: "Lucy Bonesteel?"

"Yes. Who are you?" replied Lucy, not in the least alarmed. She was not afraid of men. Frank surprise appeared to be the dominant note in her impression of the moment. She flashed her blue gaze from his face to his feet and back again. Kent did not need to be told that he was a new type to her.

"I'm—Kent Wingfield," he returned thickly, and struggled with his agitation.

"Kent Wingfield?—I never heard of you. Are you one of Dad's riders?"

"No."

"Are you someone driven to hide here?"

"No."

"Are you lost?"

"Lost! —I reckon I am—a thousand times lost," replied Kent with a laugh of relief. He was finding his voice. Her curiosity, her flattering unconscious appreciation of his lithe rider's build, his lean pale handsome face as he stood bareheaded before her, began to work a magic in his mind and heart.

"How strangely you talk—and look! I never saw anyone like you. . . . Did you come down over the rocks by the Piute Trail?"

"I came by the river on a horse."

"Did you just happen to find this place by accident? That happened once to a man. They shot him. . . . Oh, I hope you . . ."

"I was told how to get in here."

"Then you must be known to my father?"

"He never saw me—never heard of me."

"Then you couldn't be an enemy?"

"Thank God I couldn't, though his men, or even he would think so."

"Why?"

"Because of my reason for coming here."

"Will you tell me?"

"Lucy Bonesteel, can I trust you?"

"Trust me? That is a queer request. Here I find you hidden among the rocks back of my home—a stranger—somehow different from all the men I've seen, younger, softer-spoken indeed, but a trespasser—and you ask me if you can trust me."

"That's all true, Lucy. But if I prove I'm your friend will you promise not to betray me?"

"I wouldn't betray you. They'd shoot you on sight. But

you must leave. They are away now. Only Jeff is here. He takes care of me. He would shoot you, too, if you happened to meet him alone."

"So you wouldn't give me away?" he asked earnestly, his eyes intent on hers.

She was beginning to pass from interest and amaze to stronger feelings. "No, whether you are friend or not. I've seen men killed here. It's horrible. . . . But you must go."

"Lucy, I will go when you go with me," he replied softly.

The girl staggered back a little and sat down upon a rock, as if her legs had sagged under her, and her parted lips, her suddenly dilated eyes betokened an incredulity verging on alarm.

"Young man—are you crazy?" she gasped.

"I reckon I am, only not the way you think. I was crazy for tacklin' this job, but now I've seen you I'm glad." Kent had found himself. His emotion made him eloquent and his sympathy for this girl lent him all that was in contrast to boldness or evil. It worked upon her, despite the abruptness of their meeting and his preposterous statement.

"Crazy? —Job? —Glad?" she echoed, fascinated out of her momentary fear. "You seem kind. I—I like your eyes. . . . But—but . . . don't keep me in suspense. What do you mean?"

Kent took a carved bone-handled knife from his pocket and held it out before her. "Did you ever see that?"

"I'm sure I have," she replied, puzzled. "Somewhere! —But I've never been out of this place in my life."

"Lucy, you'll remember this," went on Kent, thrilling to the changing, wondering dark eyes. And he drew forth his old friend's watch and placed it in her hand.

"That's Elway's," she exclaimed instantly. "My old friend Bill!—Tell me of him. Oh, please tell me."

"All in good time, Lucy. You recognize the watch. Does that satisfy you I'm no imposter?"

"You might have killed Elway—or robbed him," she answered tragically.

"Sure I might have—only I didn't."

"Bill would not have given that watch to anyone in the

86

world," she said solemnly. "Have you ever opened the case?"

"No. It's a stem-winder. Funny I never thought of that. Let me see." He took the heavy worn silver watch and with difficulty opened the case. Inside lay a curl of golden hair. With a start Kent glanced from it to her head.

"Yours!" he asserted.

"Yes. I put it there. Bill had to go away. He said he would come back. But I knew he never would. None of them ever come back—when they leave that way. I never knew why, except Dad lost faith in him."

"That was Slotte's vile tongue. He hated Bill. He undermined Bill with your father."

"Slotte! —Do you know of him, too?"

"Well, I reckon I do. Lucy, when did you see that hombre last?"

"Night before last."

"Had he been shot recently?"

"I don't know. Jeff thought so. Slotte had a bandage around his head over his ear. He kept his hat on. He was as sore as when he loses at cards."

"Lucy, I shot him. But my bullet hit his gun and glanced. I did not know that then. Logan, the squaw man trader, told me afterward."

"Oh heavens! —You said you were not an enemy."

"Would I have been an enemy of yours if I had killed Slotte?" Kent queried, forcefully.

"Kent Wingfield! —You know more than you tell me."

"Yes, I do. I'm burning up with excitement. Lucy, I'm so—so happy I'm loco. Never mind that. . . . Last night, I peeped through a chink between the logs of your cabin. I heard you tell Jeff how Slotte had kissed you—mauled you and . . ."

A vivid scarlet wave of shame suffused Lucy's face. It was new and distressing to her—that blush. Kent with his youth, his force, his scorn had given to her vague troubled doubts a dismaying reality.

"I—I couldn't help—" she faltered. Then she flared up, "I hated him for that."

"Sure you hated him—and I'll kill him for it," returned Kent passionately. "But I'm upsettin' you. Please bear with me, Lucy ... to the end about Slotte. He was Bill's enemy. He ruined Bill with your Dad. On my way here I had the luck to run into Slotte twice. The second time was at Logan's post. Neberyull, the little drunken skunk, was forcin' his attentions on Geysha, Logan's half-breed daughter. That gave me a cue to start a fight. But it didn't happen then. Later, in the big storeroom Neberyull came ravin' in, red-eyed because an Indian had told him about my horse. That started a hot argument. Neberyull was deadly as a rattlesnake, half-drunk in the bargain, an' was backed up by Slotte. They didn't know me. They meant to kill me. I beat them both to a gun. Slotte escaped by the skin of his teeth. He will know me when he sees me next."

"You will—fight—him?"

"I'll kill him, Lucy. For Bill's sake as I tried before, but now a thousand times more for yours."

"Oh, please—please—you must go before you meet Slotte," wailed the girl, as if overcome by unfamiliar calamity. "Dad swears by Slotte. You would have to fight Dad too."

"No, I could avoid that. I wouldn't draw on him, Lucy."

"Oh, you bloody man! —You seemed different at first. I—I ... you must leave here, Kent Wingfield. we don't expect Dad back till midsummer. But he might come."

"Lucy, I won't leave," declared Kent ringingly. "Now I've seen you I couldn't."

"You won't!—What has seeing me got to do with it? Oh, why did you come?"

She slipped off the rock and stood before him with swelling breast and eyes haunted by fear of the unknown.

"Look here," said Kent, throbbing with the knowledge that he had not yet imparted, thrilling with delight at the prospect of seeing her transported and undone. Seizing her hand he drew her, struggling to hold back, protesting, beyond the rock to where the black horse grazed.

"Spades!" she screamed in rapture, and flew toward him. Certain it was that the horse saw her and whinnying he trotted to meet her. If ever Kent had seen love between a horse and a human he saw it then. Lucy clasped

his neck and buried her face in his mane. That also was the only time Kent Wingfield had ever been jealous of a horse. But he reveled in her joy. He understood it. Spades' dark eyes were warm and bright. He tried to reach her with his nose and if his whinnies were not response to her Kent did not know what to call them. He turned away, his eyes a little blurred. This lonely girl had not much to love except a horse and perhaps other pets. Presently he heard her low voice, sweet and broken, and the thud of Spades' hoofs. Kent wheeled. Lucy had slipped the halter and was coming with the horse.

Kent trembled. Her face was perfectly white and her eyes had a magnificent glow.

"You brought him back to me!"

Before Kent could move she ran to clasp her arms around his neck. She hugged him with a strength he could not have credited to those slender round arms, and she kissed him blindly with passionate gratitude.

"There!" she cried, leaning back yet still clasping him. Her eyelids trembled up wet with tears. "Bless you! — Nothing else could have made me so happy.... I thank you with all my heart, Kent Wingfield!"

Perhaps his breathless mute response or the restraint that quivered over him or something about him then that he had no cognizance of, but something made her conscious of herself, of her joyous impulse, of an inexplicable committing of herself. For blushing almost as vividly as before she hastily released Kent and drew back. But in her confusion and uncertainty there was no hint of regret or shame.

"You might have told me first off pronto," she said reproachfully.

"Well, I was keepin'—that," replied Kent unsteadily, averting his face. He felt unattached in space, in a glamour of enthrallment, the details of which were azure sky, white clouds, red walls, and a green sage glade, all whirling round the vision of a golden girl.

"Kent, where did you find my horse?" she asked warmly. "How did you get him?"

"I bought him from Bunge."

"Ah!—Then they told the truth. Slotte took him away

from me while Dad was absent. And Bunge stole him from Slotte."

"Yes. And Bunge stole more—ten thousand dollars."

"What?" exclaimed Lucy, astonishment again possessing her.

Kent told her briefly of the circumstances of his getting possession of Spades, and all that followed up to the shooting fray at Logan's.

As he ended her lovely eyes clouded again and her expressive face lost its happy light.

"It worries me, Kent," she murmured.

"I'm sorry. If I hadn't gone for my gun Slotte would have gotten back your horse."

"I meant the ten thousand dollars. Dad's riders have large sums of money from time to time. When I have been curious Dad would put me off: 'Big cattle deals, lass. I have ranches and herds all over southern Utah.'"

Kent hated to tell her the truth and though he recognized the moment had struck he found it desperately hard to betray her beloved father.

"Only last night Jeff said: 'They can't fool you forever!'"

"Lucy, listen," interrupted Kent huskily. "Old Bill sent me on this mission. He worshiped you. Before he died he told me all about this Hole in the Wall—and about you. He made me promise to find you—and take you away."

"Oh, my poor old Bill! My dear friend! Dead! . . . I knew—Oh, I knew. It came to me lately. . . . Where and how did he die, Kent?"

"On the desert, down in Sonora. We were lost. At last we found gold. Bill gave out. He begged me to leave him there to die. He swore I could not travel when the hot summer came. But I couldn't leave him, Lucy, I couldn't. So I stayed an' Bill told me your story an' he died happy."

"You would not leave him? You stayed! You made his last days comfortable. You are brave, Kent Wingfield. I could love you for that if I didn't love you for bringing my horse back to me. . . . But why did Bill send you after me?"

"I told you. To take you away."

"He knew I'd never leave Dad."

"Yes, but he thought I might persuade you. He told me I must get you out of here. So desperate was he that he even told me to—to make love to you—an' if that failed, then to pack you out against your will."

"Mercy! —The wretched old villian! —Make love to me! —I'd like to see you try it, mister. . . . And if you took me by force I'd shoot you in your sleep."

"What a nice gentle disposition you have! Like father like daughter!"

"Kent, I am my father's daughter. But I have never hurt any living thing, much less shed blood. How could I kill you!—Forgive me. . . . But why, why, *why* in heaven's name did Bill send you on this terrible task?"

Kent looked around into the shadowed eyes and replied deliberately: "Your father is chief of the Hole in the Wall outfit—the hardest, bloodiest gang of outlaws and rustlers in the West."

"Oh, my God!" she whispered, her warm face blanching. "Don't say that. For pity's sake, take it back!"

"Tough as hell on you, girl, but it's true," replied Kent hoarsely. "That's why old Bill sent me. To get you out before it is too late."

She swayed blindly, and would have fallen had Kent not caught her. Then she sagged against him, with clutching hands.

"So that is—what was wrong," she moaned in anguish. "That is what Jeff meant. That explains all—the women, stacks of bills and rolls of gold—the gambling—the fights —the long absences from home—the returns home, sometimes ragged and bloody, sometimes without old riders, sometimes with new ones, always spent, elated, close-mouthed. . . . And the drunken spree to follow. . . . Oh, I see it all now. . . . God have mercy on me!"

"Lucy, don't take on so," implored Kent, holding her close. "It's awful, but not that bad. I will get you out safely. I will take care of—"

"I wouldn't leave my father—any more than would you leave old Bill. No matter what he is! What could I do away from here? I'd die of loneliness out among strange people. I love it here. It's the only home I ever had. How

91

could I learn to live in a town or a city, away from my thundering river and my red rocks? No! No!"

"But, child, that might not be so hard as you imagine. You are a girl, young, full of life. You would come to enjoy—to—"

"A rustler chief's daughter!"

"No one would ever find out."

"*I* would always know."

"Dear girl, I don't know what to say. Only, you're wrong—you are not to blame. No—no disgrace can ... I see, Lucy. It is not what people might hear an' say that you would care about. It's the truth. Bonesteel has brought you up in ignorance and innocence."

"Damn him!" cried Lucy, with a sudden birth of passion. "Why didn't he let me grow up like the women who have come here? Hussies, old Bill called them. Dad would never let me know a single one."

"Yes, it's plain now, Lucy," said Kent sadly.

"Now I'll be worse than any one of them," she blazed, straining in his arms.

"What you mean, girl?" he queried in stern alarm.

"I'll be worse.... I'll drink and gamble.... I'll consort with these robbers—rustlers.... I'll be a hussy! ... I'll let Slotte—"

"Shut up," interrupted Kent, harsh with grief for her. "That's wild talk. Lord, I'm sorry, Lucy, I had to be the one. ... *No!* I'm glad. Now see here, you—"

"I'll throw myself at Slotte," she raged.

"Like hell you will! Didn't I tell you I'm going to kill that hombre?"

"You hurt me. ... please don't grip me—shake me so hard. ... Oh, I don't know what I'm saying. ... I never —was—unhappy before."

"Lucy, say you will go away with me," he entreated. All the long days and nights of thought of her made their short acquaintance something unreal.

"No! —No!" she sobbed.

"Can't you think, child? This is the critical time in your life. You must think, despite your misery. Your innocence, your ignorance of what awaits you here make it my sacred duty to take you away. I promised Bill. He was dyin' then. He had a vision. Lucy, he saw that red slidin' terrible river. He saw *you*. He saw you as a white lamb in a pack of bloody-mouthed wolves."

"Oh, I know now, Kent. I can see now. Bill was right. He loved me, and he lost his place, and died for me before his time. . . . You are good and kind, too, Kent Wingfield. You're brave. You'd fight like a devil for me. And it tears my heart. . . . But—I won't leave this Hole in the Wall—and my dad."

"Sooner or later Bonesteel will be killed," replied Kent inexorably.

"Oh! —Better sooner than later."

"Slotte will take you—make a rag of you—tire of you an' abandon you for outlaws an' evil."

"I won't go," she rang out, goaded.

Kent drew a long deep breath. This was defeat for him, but he had half-expected it. Old Bill had not mentioned Lucy Bonesteel's character. But then it was two years and more since he had left the Hole in the Wall.

"All right, Lucy. Then I will stay."

She vibrated to that. *"What?"* And she wheeled from his hold to turn a tear-wet working face and widening eyes of dark havoc that began to light and blaze even as he looked.

"I shall not leave you."

"But you must go," she rejoined wildly. "You can't save me. I am a rustler's daughter. You would be mad to hide here. What was Bill Elway to you—what am I to you that you sacrifice your life? I will not let you."

"How can you prevent me?"

"Man! I'm not able to pack you out or drive you away. But I can beg you with all my heart and soul. I do. Oh, I do.—I think you're wonderful to promise Bill you'd save me—fight your way here with my horse. I'll never forget you—I'll always love you. . . ."

"Lucy, don't talk of love to me, as you loved old Bill, as you love Jeff now. As far as I am concerned that is only gratitude. I'll take it. I'd rather have only that than all from some other girl. Now I've seen you—know what trouble hangs over you—I mean to stay."

"You've done your best to persuade me. I refuse. I won't leave. I beg you to go."

"No, Lucy Bonesteel."

"What do I mean to you that you will stay here to hide among the rocks like a fox? To starve! To be found out some day! To be shot!"

"What do you think it could mean?" he counterqueried.

"I think you're different from all the men I've seen here. You're like I dreamed my father was—and ah! —is not."

"But I shall not starve. You can meet me back here in the rocks, bring me food, spend hours with me. And I shall tell you all about myself—the story of old Bill's death and the gold I found, of my mother and sister—about the false girl whose betrayal of me was a blessin' in disguise. I will tell you day by day all you should have known, about school an' play an' dances an' boys an' girls, an' children you should have known, all of the life you have missed."

"Oh, wonderful!" she cried, with eyes shining upon him, and she gripped him with strong brown hands. "To be with you day by day! A friend—a young man like my father was—who would be a companion, teach me, be all that my dreams have meant! ... You are no stranger, Kent Wingfield. I have known you always. ... But it must not, cannot be."

"It will be—unless, like that false thing who deluded me, you betray me."

"*I!*"

"You would not tell Jeff—your father—Slotte?"

"Never. But they would find you."

"Well, let them. I'd shoot Slotte on sight. An' I could square it with Bonesteel. I'd tell him I was on the dodge —a hunted man. That Elway sent me here to hide. That I met you an' was afraid to reveal myself. ... Then I'd join the Hole in the Wall outfit, an' I'd gamble an' drink an' rob an' fight like the rest of them—all to be near you, Lucy Bonesteel."

"All—to be—near me!"

"Yes. If I cannot save you I'll stay with you anyway!"

The shock she sustained then seemed as crushing as

the one that ruined her father's stature in her eyes. Mournfully, tragically she gazed up at him with eyes Elway had said were like the cornflowers of his youth. She accepted him then as something inevitable, like the fate that had made her a girl of the canyons.

"Kent Wingfield, you are determined to remain here to be with me," she affirmed, obsessed by the fact.

"Sure an' certain, Lucy."

"Your mother—your sister? Have you thought of them?"

"They are all right. They'd be proud of me. I left them well cared for. An' you mean more to me than they do."

"Then I'll hold myself sacred," she said, very low. "From Slotte—from the evil I didn't understand. I'll hide you safe. Oh, I can. Not even the eagles could find you. I am free here to roam as I want. All day—all hours of the night. I'll make up to you for this mad flinging away of your life."

"Well! —Reckon it's a—a grand prospect for—Kent Wingfield," he forced from his constricted throat, battling sternly to resist taking her in his arms. Then the need to be alone, to let himself go, so that he could regain control, thought, sanity, drove him to part with her. "Go now. Take Spades. Ride him—do anythin' to hide your grief from Jeff. . . . Lie, Lucy, lie for the man who came to save you an' who failed. Tell Jeff the horse came back of his own accord."

"I will."

"Don't stay away from me too long."

"Tonight when the moon comes over the wall, I'll meet you here. Jeff goes to bed early. I will come, Kent Wingfield. . . . Surely you are hungry?"

"Starved."

"I shall come right back."

"No. Make it tonight. You must be careful. You must think how best to be natural, to avoid hurry an' anxiety."

"At last I have a secret!" At a less portentous hour that would have been rapturously spoken. She gave Kent glimpses of an infinite variety of mood and charm.

"Go now," he said and kissed her hand, his first experience of that courtly act.

Her red lips parted in fascinated wonder as she glanced from her hand up at him.

"Good-by till the moon comes up," she whispered.

"Don't fail me!"

"I would not fail you if all the—the outlaws in Utah forded the river," she replied with a smile that was sweet and sad as she turned away, her hand on the black's mane.

Kent fled to his covert back under the wall. He was long in finding it, but time meant nothing to him. He bounded like a deer over the brook. He glided through the clumps of oak, under the spreading spruce, out in the sunny glades of sage, and in the gold-barred shadow of the wall. He was a man possessed.

When he found his camp he paced to and fro like a caged lion. A prodigious nervous energy attended the liberation of his emotion. He mounted the ledges, high above the trees, to find the wild beauty of rocky fastness too stingingly sweet to be endured. He must hide from the blue sky, the purple canyons, the red walls, the mosaic of the jumbled slope.

It was long before he could lie still in the deep shade, on the brown fragrant mat, close to the warm wall. The hours passed, the solemn noontide came and passed, the afternoon waned while he was realizing the profoundest meaning and glory of his life. It left him humble, reverent, passionate, fixed as the North Star, in hope and faith to save Lucy Bonesteel and make her happy. He had days and days, endless glorious days, and hours of night to love her, to have that love make him illusive as a savage, swift as an eagle, strong as the force of that terrible river and as unconquerable.

Sunset, twilight, dusk, and the mantle of night with a silver effulgence brightening behind the sentinel spires— he could not tell whether each and every one of them was exquisitely potential of loveliness and solitude, of the divinity of nature, voiced by the murmuring waterfall of golden fire and shading smoke and dark dim thread, or his mood had invested them with a glamour of the gods.

Long before the moon rose he awaited Lucy at the

appointed place with the silent patient Piute close beside him on the rock. A warm zephyr wafted across the valley, laden with the smell of new-mown hay and the low mournful thunder of the river. What a strange lost place, this hole washed out of solid rock by the contending tides of ages! The grand wall across the river crowned its black bulk with a rim of silver fire, momentarily brightening. The stars were blanched by a mightier light, rising from behind the spires and domes.

Piute lifted his sharp nose to scent the warm breeze. He growled low under Kent's strong hand. And on the moment the silver disk of the moon slipped up in sight between the spires, to lighten the dense gloom.

Kent heard Lucy's quick footsteps, the swish of her garments on rock and sage, moments before he saw her dark figure. She was coming to meet him, his fate, his love to be, this lonely canyon girl, whose salvation was his to achieve. And the greatness of it swelled to bursting his exultant heart. She was here, close, hesitating, peering under the moonbeams into the shadow where he sat.

"There—you are," she said, low-voiced and glad, and reaching his side she deposited a heavy pack upon the rock. "Meat and fried chicken—bread and butter—fruit, milk—eggs and pickles—jam and everything," she panted. "Oh, your dog! I didn't see him. . . . What strange green eyes! —Kent, he's a Piute shepherd, half-dog, half-wolf."

"Thanks for the grub. I'll eat after you are gone," he replied haltingly, sliding off the rock to stand before her.

"That won't be soon, I warn you," she added, archly looking up. "I've lots to tell you—to ask you. . . . I fooled Jeff—and somehow I kept the truth from breaking my heart."

The moon shone full in her face and she stood bareheaded. Kent had no speech to express his feelings, as he had no power to name her unutterable loveliness. She fitted this place. She had grown up there, somehow uncontaminated by the evil of her heritage, blooming like a canyon flower. He took her hands and drew her gently closer.

"Well?" she asked, with a little hurried catch in her breath.

"Nothin'. . . . I can't believe my eyes—my hands that hold you. If only God gives me strength—"

"My friend! We have days and days, nights on end before they come back. Let us forget until—"

Her whisper ended, muffled on his shoulder. Kent held her in awe, in unbelievable transport, as a precious treasure that was his only in trust, while he gazed up at the moonlit terraces and the silver crown of fire upon the walls. She leaned pliant in his arms, and it was not until he felt her breast swell warm upon his that he realized she was flesh and blood, a girl to whom such embrace must be a violation of her trust and gratitude. But she did not act like that. Kent lowered his gaze to find her head back upon his shoulder, her face upturned, white and rapt in the moonlight, her eyes closed under shadowy eyelids.

"Lucy, I quite forget myself," he said hurriedly, as he released her to a seat upon the rock. "You see I have thought of you so much these last long months. Oh, the awful nights in that furnace desert, with the moon red as fire! I lay awake and wondered if you were a real live girl —if I'd ever see you. An' then today I have been loco, as we say down in Arizona. So when you came—so like a ghost—girl from the moon—I just couldn't believe you were real. . . . An' I had to—to take you—hold you—"

"You may, if you want," she said, as he halted. "You felt good to me too. . . . It's all so sudden, so strange, Kent. We do not know each other at all. Yet you—I. . . . Oh, it's wonderful to have you. My heart is so full it hurts. I'm glad—glad. But, oh, it comes back often, my fear for your life!"

"Lucy, you said we had days an' days," he returned. "Now let us start all over. You do not know me. Well, I'll tell you my story, from as far back as I can remember, up until now. Then you will know me more than anyone ever did."

"Oh, tell me," she cried, with great starry eyes upheld to him.

98

9

SUMMER CAME early to the Hole in Wall.

Two thousand feet below the rim, sheltered from the upland winds, where the stone walls reflected the sun down upon the valley floor and retained the heat by night, it was hot. Not the torrid heat of the Sonoran Desert but the tempered heat of high altitudes.

Sun and water made a paradise of the Hole. Grapes and peaches, melons and corn, alfalfa and barley carpeted the rich soil with green and yellow and red. All around the gardens and fields patches of sunflowers ripened and blossomed, and waved in the hot breeze like golden wheat; the white sage grew as high as a house and scented the drowsy air with its fragrance; over the sandy levels the locoweed spread its crawling pale green vines and its lilac blossoms; the willow leaves took on a tinge of yellow.

At midday horses and cattle sought the shade of the western walls and switched at the flies; the sheep sought the grassy recesses of the breaks in the walls; the bees were at their harvest.

The Colorado boomed its thunder. Melting snow in the mountains where it had its source brought the July flood, and while that was running the Hole in the Wall was shut off even from the men who knew the secret of how to get there. It flowed darkly yellow instead of the green of winter and the red of spring. Driftwood sailed down in the current, and in the eddy behind the corner wall myraids of logs and sticks milled round and round, at length to lodge along the sandy beach. Day and night the menacing roar of turgid chafing currents filled the canyons.

Lucy's favorite hiding place had taken precedence in Kent's mind over all the marvelous prospects which he remembered he had looked for, dreamed and thought, waited then for he knew not what, but which now had come to him.

It was high up about the middle of the waterfall, near a deep crystal pool, where the brook paused from its several cascades, to eddy and swirl and rest before taking its long and final leap. The climb to the ledge was over steps of bare rock, in and out of the cracks in the wall, and along the level benches, under the cedars and spruces, at length to come out on a flat rock with a shallow cavern at its base where the sun never reached and the summer breeze blew the cool mist from the waterfall to temper the heat. Leaning spruce trees had for years shed their season's fall of pine needles, and the rock floor was a brown soft fragrant mat. The spear points of spruces from below swayed over the edge of the rock, hiding the nook from all but eagles. The open window in the foliage looked out over the golden precipice where the wide thin sheet of water glided over to fall and fall, like downward smoke.

The valley slept below in the afternoon sunlight, a colorful oval belted beyond the jumbled slope of rock and cedar by sage and sunflowers, and beyond that crossed by the vineyard first and then the green square gardens and fields of alfalfa, which emerged on the long grove of cottonwoods that sheltered Bonesteel's rambling log cabin. Through the widely scattered cottonwoods gleamed the yellow gliding river, sinister and terrible in its irresistible surging current and its thundering roar.

For more than a month of enchanted days Kent had spent hours there with Lucy, sometimes hours of the morning and always those of the afternoon, often the moonlight and starlight and the dark hours of night.

He dreamed with this strange girl of the canyons, idled and played with her, and in telling her all he had seen and known, listening to the story of her remarkable life he had learned to know her and to believe that if he could take her safely away he would be the most blessed of all men. From that first moonlit night Lucy Bonesteel had loved him, sweetly and wildly, without realizing that that was her state of mind toward him. And Kent had no restraint to battle in being for her just what she wanted him to be. When at numberless times her innocence and ignorance of the imperious desires and staggering consequences of love embarrassed or disturbed him he always found a way out or subdued the savage in him by the thought of what he owed her and how all satisfying and beautiful it would be when he could make her his wife.

Kent found both humorous and sad breaches in Lucy's meager education. Her father had left religion almost wholly out of her teaching. He had taught Lucy to read and write, the former of which she did very well and the latter laboriously and poorly, with many misspelled words. When Kent caught her up in this she grew most childishly grieved. He assured her it was only practice she needed, but that did not console her. Nor did Kent's earnest assurance that he could neither write nor spell much better himself. Her store of books had been pitifully meager and many pages had been torn out. She had never seen a history and of geography she had no knowledge. Utah was a vague land beyond the river; Arizona was a Navaho reservation; California was a gold field; and of other far off territories and states she knew but little. She thought most men bought and sold cattle, drank and gambled and fought. The rest of them took care of the planting and harvesting of the fields. Morally the worst man was a horse thief who should be hanged pronto. She quite mercilessly declared she would have helped hang Ben Bunge herself.

The few women who had at different periods come to the Hole in the Wall with her father's riders had been their wives according to Elway and Jeff, but Lucy had heard gossip among the men which was at variance with that. And of late years, since she reached fifteen, Bonesteel had grown testy and impatient with her curiosity until she had ceased to ask him. No child had ever been born in the Hole in the Wall. Lucy had seen several Indian babies, belonging to squaws who had followed their braves over the rocks into the canyon, and she had peculiar ideas of her own as to where these little papooses had come from.

Lucy talked as well as any of the other girls Kent had known; it was only when he got to know her intimately that her woeful lack of some fundamentals became manifest.

Idle, dreamy, glamorous days came and passed, but they were never quite the same again, as the summer waned and the river gradually fell.

They met as usual out in the shady breaks of the canyon, always in the afternoon and often at night. They spent hours on the waterfall ledge, with Piute and Jeff's dog Rover, now fast friends, talking, resting, loving, watching. Mostly they watched the river. As the thunder of its flow diminished, the terror of that red tide seemed to augment.

Lucy could not deceive anyone but herself. Kent saw she was such a child of nature that like a wild fawn she could be startled and then presently grow calm again. At times she grew contented, sweet, gay, teasing, pouting as of old, and but for Kent's awakening of her womanhood she might have returned wholly to her primitive unconsciousness. It seemed as if there was a step on her trail of which she was unconscious and that Kent heard. Her gaze followed his out to the red gliding terrible river; her ear turned to the low intermittent thunder; when Kent started at the rustle of the leaves or at Piute's soft padded step on the rocks Lucy sustained a shock.

The walls encompassed them, the solitude was as solemn, the loneliness as great as before. As the vivid greens took on different tinges of gold and browns the marvelous beauty of the Hole in the Wall reached its perfection. All their winged and four-footed friends, that had become almost tame, visited them with new mates and new young ones. The murmur of the waterfall lost some of its depth, but none of its melody. The bees hummed by, the eagles soared, the rock-squirrels chattered. The approaching Indian summer, that most gorgeous and beautiful of the wilderness seasons, with its first touches of color, its hints of purple haze in the canyons, its mystic silence, its waiting sense of something evermore to be, its poignant insect cry for the life that was dying—this poignant time only increased the love of Kent and Lucy, their torture of suspense, their generous affection for each other, their waiting for they knew not what.

When alone, Kent paced the glades like an Indian listening to the voices of the rocks. While with Lucy, despite his nervous strain, he was so wrapped up in worship of her, so enthralled by her charm, that he was not himself at all. Alone he became the range-rider again, with all his faculties, his sensibilities intensified.

Then one afternoon late at sunset, a little while after Lucy had left him, he was galvanized by sounds that split the serenity of the canyon—hoarse shouts of men, tramping of hoofs, booming of guns.

"My God—they have come!" he exclaimed, and his first sensation was one of relief.

It was too near dusk to climb up on the ledge to see down into the oval. He went on with his meal as usual and fed Piute, but he was preoccupied and sad. He left his chores unfinished and taking his rifle he hurried through the well-known aisles and lanes, under the shadow of the rocks. Piute led the way.

Darkness had fallen when Kent got out to the edge of the open by the brook where he always waited for Lucy. She would come. Surer this night than all the past nights! Across the dark flat he saw lights, several small ones, wide apart, and one large yellow glow, evidently a campfire. A trample and whistle of vicious horses came from the pasture over under the west wall. Kent strained his ears to hear voices, but in vain.

Piute stood up on the rock to sniff the air. He scented or heard something close. Then he rubbed his nose against Kent, who leaned against the rock.

Out of the darkness a dark form came swiftly and sure. It was Lucy, with a black cloak around her. She knew where to find him as well as in day, and she leaned into his arms panting for breath. The starlight magnified her great dark eyes.

"They—are here," she panted.

"I heard them, darlin'," he replied as he gathered her close and leaned against the rock. "It kind of relieved me."

"I am—burning up. I am—"

"Speak lower, Lucy," he interrupted with the coldness that had come to him with certainty.

"Are you—scared?" she asked.

"Not now. I have been for days. But real men can't scare me."

"Neither was I," she said with a daring low laugh, new to him. "I thought I'd sink in—my tracks. But I'm only mad."

"Well, that's not as bad as fright."

"We were at supper. Jeff thought he heard a shot. We were eating out on the porch. He jumped down to see under the trees up the river. And he whooped. After that I didn't need to hear the shots, the yells. Oh, I was sick. ... They had a boat, something Dad never allowed before. Thirty pack horses, heavily packed. They were wild, gay, some of them drunk. ... Dad, Forman, Rigney, Kitsap, Goins, Westfall, Harkaway, and half a dozen new men."

"Slotte?" queried Kent piercingly.

"Yes, damn him!" the girl replied, steadily and cold. "He came. In a new silk shirt and scarf! He rode across in the boat to keep them dry. He was drunk. ... In front of all—of Dad!—he grabbed me as if I were a sack—kissed me with his filthy rummy bristling lips! Oh! Wipe that off, Kent. Rub it out! Kiss that blistering stench away!"

"That'll be about all, Mister Slotte," said Kent, as if to himself. And he bent soberly to the task she had assigned him. Then his kiss brought the only unsteadiness she had shown.

"Ah! I'm clean—again," she burst out, with a fleeting smile. "Let me tell you, Kent. I slipped away and must not stay long. ... I had run down off the porch after Jeff. He met them out under the trees. I wanted Dad. I saw him

104

coming, black as a thundercloud. At first I thought he was drunk. But no. Slotte leaped off ahead of Dad and grabbed me—as I told you. ... I beat at him—tore loose—screamed: 'You dirty—horse thief!' They haw-hawed, all those men, except my Dad. I had a strange feeling he was about to kill Slotte. But he turned away—up the porch. Then that gang began to throw their saddles and packs under the trees, gabbing, laughing, cursing. Oh, they were in high spirits. All except Dad. I've seen him like that more than once. He stamped up on the porch with Jeff. 'Milk and fruit for me,' he said. 'Let that outfit cook their own grub. They've tons of it.' He slumped into a chair at the table. I went up to him, put my hand around his neck. 'Dad, I'm glad you're home.'—He crushed my hand against his face. 'By God, I wish I'd never come back to you, lass. Not with this outfit Slotte has forced upon me. They dragged lumber across the rocks—built a boat. It's the end of the Hole in the Wall'—I waited on him and then sat down to try to finish my supper. Pretty soon Silk Slotte let out a yell you must have heard clear out here. Dad cursed and I leaped up. Then I saw what had made Slotte bellow. Spades has the run of the ranch, you know. And he came whistling under the cottonwoods. After Slotte yelled he took a long, long look at my horse. Then he made for the porch, calling for Jeff. 'How'n hell did that black horse get back here?' Jeff stuck his head out. 'Wal, Silk, if it's any of yore damned business, Spades just sloped from you an' whoever stole him an' walked an' swum back home.'—'You're a — — liar! You're another Bill Elway! ... Bonesteel, this looks queer to me.'—Dad was slow and cool. He looked up. Something had changed him. 'Silk, I'm as surprised as you. If you don't believe Jeff ask Lucy. She doesn't know how to lie.' —Slotte snorted out, 'Aw, the hell she doesn't. Women are born liars.' And then he fixed me with those ash eyes of his, and asked me the same question he'd asked Jeff. I laughed in his face. 'Spades came back to me, Slotte. I knew he'd never stay with you.' —'Alone?' he hissed at me. 'Are you sure you couldn't lie?' —'Dad thinks too well of me,' I said. 'But I wouldn't lie to you to save my life.' Then Dad banged the table with his fist. 'All news to me, Silk Slotte. You'll answer to me later. Get off the porch.' —Then Dad turned to me and said: 'Lucy, believe me I knew nothing about it. You know I wouldn't let anyone ride your favorite horse. Slotte stole Spades. He ought to be swung for that. Lucy, old Bill's last words come back to me.' "Boss, Slotte is as slick as the silk he wears. You'll rue the day you drive me away for him." —'Lucy, that day has come. I have made a terrible blunder. Slotte threw in with enemies of mine. Swore he didn't know it. They're out there—Russ Harvey, Ney Roberts, Wess Simms, and three more men I didn't know. They met us at the crossing—had that boat already made—and the secret of my—my ranch betrayed.' "

"By heaven!" cried Kent, as Lucy paused to catch her breath. "How things work out! Old Bill was right. Lucy, this will ruin your father. It will split the Hole in the Wall gang."

"Oh, I pray it will. Split it—wipe it out, all except my father . . . Kent, he acted strange. He couldn't look at me. He spoke casually of cattle deals—that he had gotten rid of all his stock—that as his riders shared with him they were flushed with money. Oh, my poor father! Loving me yet hating himself. He fears nothing except that I will learn what he really is. Kent, let me not forget to warn you. If Dad ever finds out that *you* told me of his guilt he will kill you. We must keep that from him at any cost."

"Never fear. I'll not tell it. You must not let him know."

"He sent me to his room, which is the one beyond mine," went on Lucy. "I stayed there until dark. They were all down on the grass around a big fire, eating, drinking, making merry. I went into my room from the porch an got this coat. Before I could get out a bunch of them tramped into the living room. My door was open a little. I peeped in on them. Jeff lit the lamp and put wood on the fire. There were eight of them. I knew two—Slotte and Harkaway. The others, of course, were this outfit Slotte had brought. They looked about the same as all the men who've been here off and on. Only one—a tall slim man, the very opposite of Slotte—lean face like a fox's, eyes hidden, sandy mustache hanging down—he was a man like I've never seen before. Slotte told them the chief —that is Dad—would not come in. They talked for a long time. Another time I'll tell you all I heard—how they looked. I must hurry back now. Only Slotte is a snake. He means to drive Dad away or kill him. To take me! ... I gathered that Ney Roberts is as notoriously known in Utah as Dad is unknown—that as the head of a gang of rustlers he is a mortal enemy of the chief of the Hole in the Wall outfit. Slotte was sly. I guessed he is as deceitful with Roberts as he is with my Dad. They talked low. Sometimes I could not hear them. Slotte went often to the door to look out. . . . I'll tell you more tomorrow."

Kent walked with her in silence along the brook as far as the bridge.

"Be careful," he said, at length, holding her hands. "Keep in the shadow . . . We'll meet this somehow."

"You're forgetting," she whispered, holding up her face.

He kissed her mutely, and pressing her hands he tried to meet her dark eyes as she looked up bravely. The beauty, loyalty, the preciousness of her unarmed him at that parting moment. But out of his cold sick weakness leaped a passion that steeled him to flaunt fear and doubt. He watched the dark form glide across the bridge, turn once to look back, and then go on to vanish. He was alone again. The towering walls loomed black and forbidding; the stars burned down white and relentless; the river rolled out its rumbling menace.

Kent Wingfield had spent many sleepless nights in his life and some of them with friends on the verge of the grave. But primal fear and the hard creed of the range had nothing to do with the long hours of his struggle. From the moment Lucy had vanished in the darkness he had been confronted by the bitter choice of boldly facing Bonesteel and Slotte in their den or when Lucy came to him again, dragging her away with him into the recesses of the canyon and trying to find the way out over the rocks.

As he plodded to and fro under the black wall he

struggled vainly with this problem. For hours he leaned toward the idea of taking Lucy away forcibly if she would not go willingly. There were many cracks and crevices winding back into the rock fastness. He had not really made a thorough search. If Lucy knew where the trail began, she had thus far avoided telling him. If he lay low and hunted for it in the days to come, he might, very probably would, find it. But time was precious. What would happen to Lucy? What would become of the opportunity to put Slotte out of the way and befriend Bonesteel? It might be lost. And what of the new arrivals? Kent had heard of Ney Roberts, even in the far away Tonto. Bonesteel's regime was about over. This was, sooner or later, the fate of all outlaw chiefs. The very nature of their calling precipitated it. As they lived by the gun, so that way they fell.

There was one strong feeling in Kent which operated against his kidnaping Lucy: she was such a strange mixture of innocence and savagery. She might never forgive Kent for taking her away from her father in his extremity. Nothing was any surer than that if he could help Bonesteel she would love him always for that alone and cleave to him forever. The dark side of that choice had one chance in a thousand of success. Nevertheless, Kent found he could not shake the nameless insistent hold the slim chance had on his consciousness. He argued against it. His reason told him that way was folly. But it returned again and again during that vigil in the lonely canyon, while the Indian dog kept silent watch with him, and in the end it conquered.

The rest of that night he spent in evolving just what he would do and how he would do it, allowing for every possible contingency that might arise. He might be shot from a window of the cabin or from behind a tree. Such fatalities were common on the range, in the isolated rustler country and in the cattle settlements. But neither would happen to Kent Wingfield solely because there would be something about his action and manner that would preclude it.

Lucy was the only unknown quantity. How would she react? He could hardly gamble on meeting Bonesteel and confronting Slotte without Lucy finding out. Would she betray him by a woman's weakness in the hour of peril to her lover? Even if she did, it would not prevent his confronting Slotte, the outcome of which could not help but find favor with Bonesteel.

10

◨

DAYLIGHT BROKE with the cool night air slowly warming. Kent timed his approach to the stronghold of the outlaws at the hour when such men began to stir after long hard travel. He crossed the bridge where he had parted from Lucy the night before, and here he sent Piute back. This walk across the flat was his first in the light of day. Fields, vineyards, gardens, orchards, the encompassing walls were seen as mere approaches to the grove of cottonwoods and vague background to the Hole in the Wall. So it was with the bright sun, the drowsy morning, the horses in the pasture, all of which encroached upon the corners of his vision. But his eyes upon the grove and the sunlit patches under the trees might as well have been telescopes.

Kent strode straight through the cottonwoods toward the long irregular line of cabins connected by roofs across the porches between. Some portions of this habitation of logs were gray and moss-covered; the large end was new and square, a pretentious cabin built of peeled spruce poles. As Kent drew nearer he espied the lazy movement of men around a smoking campfire; canvas packs and saddles and bedrolls littered the greensward under the old cottonwoods. Some outlaw was singing a rollicking song of the cattle range. Beyond the camp, under the wide-spreading trees, gleamed the red river in the sunlight.

And as Kent saw it then he recalled Bill Elway's trenchant words.

His bold stalk took him clear through the grove into the glade before his roving eyes made sure that he had been seen.

A man coming out on the porch stopped short. He stooped to peer low. Then in a single leap he cleared the porch steps to land on the grass. His lofty stature, and the broad black sombrero, together with his eaglelike poise proclaimed him to be Bonesteel. At the very onset Kent's faith seemed to be working out.

The chief wore a white soiled shirt, a black belt with silver buckle, a low-hanging black gun, inconspicuous against his black pants, that were tucked into high-top boots. He looked precisely as Kent had expected to see him.

A shrill shout issued from some man round the campfire.

"Boss! Thet's the fellar who had Spades back at Logan's post."

These swift words, couched in harsh amaze, came from the outlaw Goins. Others of the gang stopped their tasks to stare. Two of those still in bed rolled on their elbows to blink sleepily. A man carrying water from the stream dropped his buckets. Four lean ragged men sitting apart under a tree rose in slow unison. Kent's encompassing eyes missed nothing.

"Who are you?" demanded Bonesteel. He had a deep, booming voice.

"My name's Wingfield," replied Kent, loud and clear.

"Where did you come from?"

"The Arizona Tonto. Maybe you've heard of it!"

"How did you get in here?"

"I rode the black horse Spades."

"Where did you get him?"

"Bought him from Bunge."

Bonesteel strode out into the open, shoving his sombrero back the better to see. He had long tawny silver hair and eyes like the points of daggers.

"Wal, my outspoken stranger, what do you want?" queried the chief, after a significant pause.

"Slotte!"

Bonesteel's start was something extraordinary to see.

"I'm head of this outfit. What's your business with Slotte?"

"You're Bonesteel?"

"Yes."

"All right, sir. I'll answer to you later. But first I want Slotte."

"Have you anything against him?"

"Ha! —I reckon."

"Then whatever it is, it's against me."

"No," rang out Kent. "I don't know you. I'm after Slotte. He an' his pard picked a fight with me at Logan's post. I've been on his trail since."

"Oho! Did you kill Neberyull?"

"They called him Neb."

"And it was you who beat Slotte to a gun?"

"Not satisfactory to me, Bonesteel," replied Kent curtly. "That's why I'm here."

"Haw! Haw!" laughed the chief mirthlessly. Something devilish in this outburst would have thrilled Kent but for his intensity.

"*Silk!*" shouted the chief piercingly.

The reply came from around the corner of the cabin in a rather impatient deep voice.

"Bad news, Silk," called Goins warningly from the campfire.

Then three figures came into sight, the most striking of which was not the brawny silk-shirted dandy with his bold handsome visage, but a man even more forceful to gaze upon than Bonesteel. His fox features, his drooping sandy mustache identified him as Ney Roberts, the notorious rival of Bonesteel in their nefarious trade, but these had little to do with his singular physical power. The third man was younger, upright as an Indian and as swarthy, his lithe figure belted from hips to waist. He wore two guns, sheathed low.

"What the hell!" ejaculated Slotte, taking in Bonesteel's stand, the lone stranger beyond, and the watching quartet under the nearest cottonwood.

Roberts showed his quickness of divination and his

111

subtlety by sheering aside to the campfire. But the younger man stayed by Slotte, sloe-eyed and intent.

"Silk, you're wanted," called out Bonesteel.

"So I savvy. Strikes me you're testy. What you want?"

"I don't want you," returned the chief sarcastically.

Then Slotte took a second glance at Wingfield. He crouched. He jerked up to stiffen in all his magnificent frame.

"Hell! . . . That rider!"

His shrill shout penetrated grove and cabin, echoed from the walls, rolled out over the river.

It fetched a pattering of swift soft feet—a sound Kent expected and dreaded. Lucy ran out of her room, up the porch, her golden hair flying. First she saw her father, then Slotte and at last Kent standing alone, motionless. She smothered a scream with swift shaking hand, and as suddenly her eyes became great staring black gulfs in a face blanched to snowwhite. Slotte saw all this as Kent saw it. But Bonesteel's back was turned to the girl.

Slotte's bull neck, suddenly black and corded, split his silk collar. The surge of dark blood puffed his face. His eyes were pale coals of fire.

"Bonesteel, look there—your bitch of a daughter!" he shouted stridently as he pointed at Lucy.

Bonesteel did not turn. "Slotte, I'll call you for that after your young visitor has his say," he said bitingly, and the sting of his words struck Slotte like a lash.

"Lucy, go in," ordered Bonesteel.

"But Dad—are they going to fight?" cried Lucy.

"I don't know. But this is no place for you. Get in the cabin."

Lucy fell back along the porch rail, suddenly to clutch a post and hang there. That was the last glimpse Kent had of her, and he caught that only in the corner of his eye. He concentrated on Slotte, on his swarthy companion, on the other men to one side.

"Hands off, men," shouted Bonesteel in harsh command. "This is Slotte's mix."

Kent was quick to follow that with his dry crisp speech —"Reckon you-all better stand pat. I'm playin' a lone hand. I'm callin' Slotte out."

That was a challenge, which struck at the roots of the instincts and feelings which were ineradicably ingrained in the hearts of desperate men. Kent knew how to appeal to the curiosity and the creed of Bonesteel's followers. What they might do afterward was another matter. If Kent had struck the right note they would be keen to see Slotte answer such a call.

"Bonesteel," burst out Slotte huskily, "I tell you that's the rider who stole Spades, shot Neberyull and marked me for life."

"Probably true, except the first," retorted the chief dryly. "I've a hunch this stranger who calls himself Wingfield isn't a horse thief so far as Spades is concerned. For he brought Spades back."

"But I tell you—"

"Talk to him!" flashed Bonesteel.

"What you want?" demanded Slotte thickly, when he and everyone present could see perfectly what the rider's lone stand meant. This worked powerfully on Slotte. And then his consciousness held the pregnant remembered fact that Wingfield had once before beat him to a gun and could do it again. Slotte might not have been a coward until then, but at that moment he betrayed as much. If he had been of the caliber of his assailant he would never have blurted out that husky query. In this crisis of his life he made the blunder to weaken his front and strengthen that of his adversary. He saw it. He knew Wingfield saw it —that they all saw it, and he suddenly burst into a sweat.

"Slotte, I knew I'd have to spur you into throwin' your gun," replied Kent scathingly. "An' I wouldn't be surprised if I had to shoot you in cold blood. Your greaser-skinned pard there shows more'n you got. But he'd better think whether you're worth it or not."

"Man, you've no show on earth to get away from here," raged Slotte.

"I'm not aimin' to get away. Now I'm here I'm goin' to stay. An' this Hole in the Wall won't be big enough for both of us."

"Aw, you — — fool! What you bracin' me for?"

"Do you forget you drew on me?" bantered Kent insolently. "An' you an' your low-down Neberyull drew on me because I had the horse you stole. I bought that black horse an' I can prove it. That was your excuse. You'd have murdered me if I'd given you a chance to shoot me in the back. I'm wonderin' if your chief here knows just what a yellow hombre you are. An' I'll gamble these men here don't know. You're doublecrossin' Bonesteel right now, as you have done for years, an' as you'll do for your new pard Roberts."

The rival outlaw leader responded to that with a glance of penetrating suspicion and an icy query: "Slotte, are you goin' to eat such talk as thet? This rider talks too much. He *knows* too much!"

"Say, you, keep out of this," broke in Kent, "an' you may learn somethin'."

"Go on, Wingfield, you're not talking too much for me," interposed Bonesteel.

"Slotte, I just happen to know what a lousy cheat an' two-face hombre you are," went on Kent tauntingly. "I was friend of an old prospector down on the desert. His name was Bill Elway."

Blank silence and consternation from all facing Kent greeted this statement. He let it sink in. He had the upper hand here, the best cards, and the longer he withheld his play the surer he was of his game, which was to kill Slotte and propitiate Bonesteel.

"Go on, Wingfield," ordered the chief.

"Elway was dyin' an' I stayed with him. Before he died he told me if I ever run across a man named Slotte to bore him. . . . I happened to run across your camp that night on the desert. I crawled up an' listened. I reckon Kitsap an' Goins will remember they heard somethin' rustlin' in the sage. That was me. I'd just met Bunge, who rode into my camp, swore he'd been robbed by Silk Slotte. He sold me the black horse. Well, I trailed you to Logan's post where you tried to kill me an' got that brand on your temple for your pains. I trailed you up the Segi, over the uplands, across the San Juan, down into the canyons. At the river ford I was stumped. But the black horse wasn't. . . . An' here I am, Silk Slotte. An' *this* time I'll mark your handsome mug nearer the middle."

When Kent ended that harangue Slotte was stamping

up and down, his head lowered like that of a bull about to charge, and his hands were spread, wide, low down, clawing in the air. He was a beast at bay. His back was against the wall and amazed passion had made a wretch out of him.

Bonesteel leaped upon the steps of the porch. "Look out, Crothers!" he called warningly, to Slotte's stiff-armed comrade. "Can't you see what you're up against?"

"Howdy," replied Crothers, his beady eyes on Kent, surely in recognition.

"Ha! I know you, Crothers, an' it's just as well," flashed Kent.

"Heah's to the Tonto!" shrieked the outlaw and lurched for the gun on his left side. His arm struck Slotte, who was also in a wrestling draw. Kent's gun had leaped with their intent. At its crash Crothers dropped like an upright log pushed over. His second shot destroyed Slotte's throw. He spun around with an inhuman scream, waving the booming gun, his face suddenly gory. Kent's third shot thudded on flesh, dusted his shirt, passed through him to spat on the log cabin. Slotte jerked spasmodically, his huge frame straining upward while his head swung back and his gun went spinning. On the front of his white silk shirt suddenly appeared a splotch of red. But such was his tremendous vitality that he did not fall. He staggered, swaying and reeling toward the porch, letting loose unearthly sounds—sucking intake of air through blood.

"Finish your job!" yelled Bonesteel in horror.

But the wary Kent did not choose to waste another shell on a man as good as dead. His eyes oscillated between Slotte and Roberts. This outlaw, too, was obsessed at the tragic end of the conspirator who would have betrayed Bonesteel.

"All—dark!" muttered Slotte, in guttural hoarse almost incoherent speech, as he groped for something, probably the life that was ebbing. "Can't—see. . . . Night already!" —Then he flung himself up in a last spasm of consciousness, a ghastly sight. "Aghh! —I'm killed! —That — — — —rider! . . . Lucy, damn your lying soul! . . . Bore him, men—bore him! ... Ney—Slim! ... It's—the—end. ... God!—"

He reeled up the porch steps and bounced from the wall to the rail, which broke with his excessive weight, and let him fall suddenly upon the ground.

Bonesteel gave one white look at the fallen man, then waved an imperious arm to Kent.

"Wingfield—come!" he shouted, and leaped upon the porch.

It was then he saw Lucy holding to the post, slowly sinking with her golden hair hanging over her face. Her father caught her and carried her under one arm into the cabin.

Kent backed toward the porch, his gun low, his menace holding the outlaws stiff. He backed up on the porch as Bonesteel stalked out again.

"Hey, Roberts—you and your outfit," he called trenchantly. "You understand that was a showdown for Slotte. I never saw this Wingfield before. I know only what he claimed. Slotte's front was yellow.... What's your stand on the deal?"

"Wal, Bonesteel, I reckon it's all a little sudden," drawled Ney Roberts, showing his teeth. "Suppose you come out with yore stand."

"I'm doing that. It turns out this stranger has done me a service. He doesn't appear to need any backing, but if you take up Slotte's side I'll stand by him."

"Wal, I ain't takin' sides with a dead man, whatever my relation to him might have been."

"Roberts, I never knew Slotte intended to fetch you here."

"He said you wanted me. I reckoned thet was kinda queer. But I came."

"Slotte was a liar," declared the chief bitterly. "He got what he deserved. I resent your presence here. I'm willing to make your visit worth while, on condition you leave and keep secret the way into my Hole in the Wall."

"Ahuh. So I savvy. You'll pay fer the inconvenience me an' my outfit have suffered?" drawled the wily outlaw.

"Yes, I will, in reason."

"Wal, I'll talk it over with Simms here, an' think about it."

"Roberts, that is equivalent to an admission you might not take my offer—or leave my ranch."

"Shore. It 'pears that way to me. Fer years I've heerd of this hole an' have always been curious about it. . . . Bonesteel, you ain't very hospitable."

"Agreed. But you'll admit the circumstances aren't favorable . . . . Goins, get somebody to help you drag these dead men out on the bank and bury them."

"Wal, Bonesteel, if you'll excuse me we'll do thet little job ourselves," rejoined Roberts. "Slotte had a tidy roll of greenbacks on him, an' as he owes me money I'd just as lief we searched him first."

"You're welcome to the money. But I'll remember the insult. . . . You'll find tools in the shed—and about fourteen graves of better men out there on the bank."

"So many! You must be a sociable outfit, livin' so like brothers all these years in this hole. Shore is a pretty sunny lonesome place. I'm gettin' kinda to like it."

"All right, if that's your say we'll let it rest there for the present."

"Thet's sense, considerin' it's been a thought-provokin' mawnin'."

During this curt colloquy Kent had stood in the door, listening and watching, with his gun still unsheathed. Only once, when he had first entered the door, had he swept a glance within, to be rewarded by sight of Lucy's white face and dark eyes peering from her room. She crossed her lips with a finger, an eloquent action which did not need to be translated into words.

Bonesteel strode up on the porch, fire in his eyes, and pushed Kent into the living room.

"Wingfield, can I offer you a drink?" he asked ironically, as if he doubted this young man had such things as nerves.

"No, thanks."

"Sit down there, where you can see out. . . . Well, I'm bound to admit it was as pretty a shooting fray as I ever saw. Slotte was an ox! . . . You must have met up with an old friend in Crothers?"

"Was he your man or Roberts'?"

"Not mine. And I've a hunch not Roberts'. Slotte knew him. Has been trying to get me to give him a job riding for me. What was Crothers down in the Tonto?"

"Just a mean two-bit rustler."

"Handy with guns?"

"Tolerable."

"Left-handed draw. Bumped into Slotte. But if Slotte had been there alone he'd have been too slow. . . . Wingfield, eh?—You've the cut of a range-rider."

"I used to be one. Rode with the Hash Knife outfiit."

"So? They've got a bad name."

"I reckon they deserved it. But I'm tellin' you there was two Hash Knife outfits."

"Ha! Ha! —Well, don't tell me you learneä a draw like yours ridin' for the good outfit. . . . What did Bill Elway tell you?"

"Not much. He was close-mouthed. An' practically nothin' until he was about to die."

"Ah! He did die, then?"

Kent briefly related the story of his wanderings with Elway, how they became lost and the death of the old man.

"Poor Bill! . . . Did he tell you anything about me?"

"You? —Oh, no," returned Kent in surprise, with gimlet eyes meeting that gray gaze.

"What did he say of Slotte?"

"Not much. An' I didn't pay strict attention. He was dyin'. . . . Slotte had ruined Elway. Said he frequented Indian tradin' posts an' Arizona towns. Gambled an' drank. Was hell on girls! . . . It was just my luck to have Bunge run across me, sell me that horse an' speak of Silk Slotte bein' camped close by. That's how I come to sneak up to spy on them."

"Where was that camp? Below the Segi?"

"Yes. Near Red Lake."

"Did you meet Logan?"

"Yes. I had supper there. That's whcre our row began. Neberyull was actin' up dirty toward Geysha, Logan's halfbreed daughter."

"I know Geysha. A decent girl. Logan is my friend. . . .

Wingfield, you don't expect me to believe you were way up there in northern Arizona looking to buy horses and befriend Indian girls?"

"I didn't say so."

"Well, what were you doing?"

"I was making for the rocks."

"What rocks?"

"The canyon country anywhere."

"Aha!—On the dodge?"

"That's right."

"Excuse my inquisitiveness. This is plain talk. What'd you do?"

"Bonesteel, that's none of your business. Believe me, I wouldn't have told you so much if I hadn't been caught here in a damn tight place."

"How long have you been here?"

"I didn't keep track. Weeks. But I've fared pretty well on fresh meat, vegetables an' fruit."

"Did you see my man, Jeff?"

"I saw a man workin' in the gardens."

"Did you see my daughter?"

"I saw a light-haired girl ridin' up an' down the sage."

"Why did you lay so low?"

"Well, I'd tracked Slotte here. I wanted to see him before I sprung myself on anybody. But I never savvied this place until this mornin'."

"Speak low," cautioned Bonesteel in a terse whisper, jerking a forceful thumb toward the adjoining room. "My daughter has lived here since she was a baby and she doesn't savvy. . . .Wingfield, how do you figure the situation you run into here?"

"Plain as print. I've heard of the Hole in the Wall for years. An' of the outfit that hid in here. You're the chief, Bonesteel. Slotte was plottin' to get your place, your stock, your money—an' your daughter. I just had the luck to stall him off the very mornin' after he got back with his gang. Don't overlook them, Bonesteel. This Roberts is a deal harder nut to crack than Silk Slotte. We know of Ney Roberts way down in Arizona—a gunman of the first water, hoss rustler an' bloody scourge of the Utah ranges."

"Right!" whispered Bonesteel heavily, wiping his pallid brow. "You heard me call him out there just now?"

"Yes. But it wasn't strong enough, comin' from you, Bonesteel."

"I'm not sure of my men," went on the chief haggardly, in a whisper. "Slotte has worked upon them, as he worked on me. I'd swear by Kitsap, Rigney. I hope Harkaway is loyal. But I'm not sure of him. Forman is on the fence and Goins has split."

"Thanks for your confidin' in me," rejoined Kent feelingly. "It looks bad, Bonesteel. I didn't drop in any too soon. My good luck!"

"You mean mine. Wingfield, is my hunch correct? You want to throw in with me?"

"I reckon."

"It's a bad move for a young man with a chance to go straight."

"Bonesteel, I'll back you till my hair blows out."

"What for? How much?"

"To hell with your money," retorted Kent. "Slotte an' his deal riled me. Sight of Roberts made me itch to try him out. . . . I saw your daughter. You just confided in me—that she didn't know the truth about you—your outfit an' this Hole you call a ranch. . . . I reckon if all else didn't make me keen I'd want to help her father for her sake."

"Here's my hand," rejoined Bonesteel, gripping Kent in a clasp of iron. "I like your straight talk, stranger from the Tonto. We'll more than match Ney Roberts."

"I reckon Roberts' play will be for time," said Kent shrewdly. "But if you have money—gold hidden here an' if Slotte knew it we've got that outfit to fight."

"Slotte only guessed I had. I see it all now. He waited, biding his time."

"Strikes me he waited too long, Bonesteel."

"Ha, he did that. But it was Lucy who stayed his hand. I guessed that last night when the drunken hound kissed her right before my eyes. I should have shot him. But he and the Roberts outfit had me worried, bluffed. To Lucy's credit she repulsed him like a fierce little wildcat—"

A rap on the door between the rooms interrupted the chief.

"Dad," called Lucy.

"What is it, lass?"

"Can I come in? —Those strange men are walking by my window."

Bonesteel cursed inaudibly, and hesitated a moment before replying: "Yes, come in."

The rude rough-hewn door opened creakingly on its leather hinges. Lucy appeared, pale and with parted lips. Kent dreaded the ordeal.

"Lucy, this is the young man who rode Spades home," said Bonesteel. "So you've something to thank him for as well as I. . . . Wingfield, this is my girl."

"Glad to meet you, miss," returned Kent, with a bow.

She acknowledged the introduction inaudibly, with wide dilated eyes upon Kent. Surely the cold forbidding side of him, still uppermost, made him a stranger to her.

"Lass, you disobeyed me," said Bonesteel reprovingly, with an arm round her. "I told you to go indoors."

"Dad, I couldn't."

"You saw it all?"

"Yes."

"I'm sorry. But it could have been worse. . . . Slotte double-crossed me, Lucy. He has involved me with this Roberts, a cattle rustler. I don't know how deep. But it looks bad."

"Roberts? I caught him watching me through my window. His eyes just burned."

"He has a nasty look, I'm bound to admit that. But you must not be seen by these men," replied her father vehemently.

"Dad, no good will come of it, if these strange riders stay here."

"They won't stay with my permission," returned Bonesteel, rising. "I'll go out and see what they're doing. . . . Lucy, you talk to Wingfield till I come back. Come to the kitchen presently. We haven't had breakfast."

He strode out, his steps firm and quick. Kent stood up uneasily, listening, and would have stepped to the door but for Lucy. She approached him with terrible eyes of reproach.

11

◘

THE NEARNESS of Lucy, the hand that went out to him, eloquent with appeal, released him from the stern icy clamp of his faculties. He was quick to respond.

"Why didn't you stay away?" she implored. "I was coming to you, the minute I could slip away."

"Lucy, I thought all night. There was only one way. I've taken it.... You're no fool, child as you are. With Slotte alive? My dear, be sensible. You are Bonesteel's daughter."

"Kent, you were terrible. I didn't know you.... I think you did right for Dad and me. But my fear for you! Oh! . . . I never had such feelings. I felt that I must die, but couldn't."

"You told me you'd seen fights before. That you'd seen men killed."

"I have—but I didn't love them. . . . Kent, I heard every word you and Dad said here. You lied to Dad. Oh, you were clever. You made him believe you were on the dodge—that you'd done some wicked thing. . . . You left him to guess and of course he made you out all that was bad—and a gunman to boot."

"Darlin', I never told you, but I guess I am—that last," he replied, dropping his head.

"Kent, a gunman isn't a thief, a rustler, a murderer."

"Not always. *I* wasn't Lucy. I swear to you."

"Oh, sweetheart! —You didn't have to tell me that.....

Listen. I don't care how wild you've been—how many fights you've had. I've sense enough to see that what you are may save Dad and me from God only knows what. But if Dad gets free of this mess he'd take you out with him, on those cattle trips I understand now. You've thrown in with him here. With my father—chief of a gang of robbers! Kent, I'll not let you do one dishonest deed. Not to save Dad's life—or—or that innocence of mine you've made me understand!"

"Lucy, how else could I make a stand with Bonesteel?" whispered Kent hoarsely.

"You couldn't. And so far it's all right."

"Lucy, if I played this game as I see it—if I went the limit with Bonesteel, always for one thing—to get you out in the end—would that kill your love for me?"

"Nothing could. I'm yours, Kent. But I'll keep Dad from making an outlaw of you."

"But, my heaven, girl! I'd rather be an outlaw than lose you. I'd—"

"Hush. There's Dad."

Bonesteel's heavy tread sounded without. His shadow blocked the sunny doorway.

"Come, let's eat," he said, and led them down the porch to where Jeff had a table outside of his kitchen. They sat down on wooden benches.

"Lucy, you're still pale around the gills. And Wingfield, you don't look so wound up tight as you were. What has my girl been saying?"

"I reckon she made me see this man-game a little from a girl's eyes. An' it's not so good."

"No indeed. I am selfish, self-centered. But if I live through this. . . . Wingfield, what did you say your first name was?"

"I didn't say. It's Kent."

"That's better. I hate long handles. . . . Well, the Roberts outfit stripped Slotte and Crothers down to their socks. They left the sad obsequies to my men. They're all eating together out there now, which seems well for the time being. I've a hunch there won't be any row unless I make it. This place is getting into Roberts. . . . Kent, what have you got out where you've been hiding?"

"Not much. A saddle and bridle, rifle, some shells, a blanket and a dog."

"Where'd you pick up a dog?"

"He came to me in the Segi. A Piute dog, half-wolf, I reckon."

"Suppose you go out there and fetch them back. You can bunk in the living room."

"Dad, I want my back window barred. Roberts stuck his head right in to leer at me."

"I'll have Jeff nail slats across it," replied Bonesteel ponderingly. "And Lucy, while we have these honored guests here you'll stay indoors or on the porch. We'll wait developments. . . . Kent, you keep your eyes and ears peeled, all day and half the night, at least while these hombres are up."

"There's where Piute will come in handy," said Kent. "He's an uncanny dog. Seems to know that I'm thinkin' about. A squirrel couldn't get near me when I'm asleep, with Piute around."

Piute was waiting for Kent beyond the bridge by the last stone that encroached upon the flat. Sight of the dog affected Kent keenly. Long since he had ceased to treat the Piute shepherd as he had other canine pets. Piute did not understand affection. He never leaped or cavorted; he never wagged his tail, or hung about Kent with glad eyes. The closest he ever got to such antics was when he sniffed with cold nose at Kent's hand. These morning hours were the first Kent and Piute had been separated since leaving the Segi. It had served to acquaint Kent with the knowledge that there was a very close and scarcely comprehensible relation between them.

"Howdy, old boy," was his greeting. "I don't know why I didn't take you with me. Afraid you'd hop a dog maybe. Come on."

Kent climbed for what he imagined a last time to the wonderful ledge under the waterfall. From there he gazed out over the colorful walled-in valley, to discover that in a few hours his feelings had changed. The appalling beauty and glamour of the paradise of the rocks had never struck him so forcibly. He realized then that the lonely weeks spent there with Lucy had taken him back almost to the nature of an Indian. He would have been content to live there always, alone with Lucy, until they grew old and died. But that would be going back in the scale of civilization. Besides, it was impossible. The crisis for Lucy and Bonesteel had come. Kent had to share it, in some way precipitate it to their benefit, to his own happiness, to Lucy's salvation. But he knew at that moment, as he felt the shuddering sweetness and wildness of the canyon wave over him, that all his life his heart would stop beating at the murmur of a waterfall, at the smell of cedar and sage, and at fields of gold and purple.

From there he went back along the ledge to his camp. He packed his tinned food supplies and stored them up in a hole in the rocks. His few belongings he rolled in his blanket, and taking up his rifle he retraced his steps down the trail to where he had left saddle and accessories. Burdened with these he emerged from the jungle of rocks and trees to cross the sage flat to the road, and he kept to that until he reached the grove of cottonwoods where he sheered off to put the cabin between him and the camp of the rustlers. He reached the cabin, and the room assigned him, without being seen by any of them, so far as he could tell. Lucy was not in sight, nor Jeff, nor Bonesteel.

Kent's first task, after he had laid down his belongings, and shut the door, was to see if he could not find the hole or crevice in the north wall of the cabin, through which he had spied upon Lucy and Jeff that first night. At last he found it, a tiny aperture on the inside where a bit of clay had cracked off from the chink between the logs.

His luck held and he could see everywhere on that side of the cabin. No change had been made in the newcomers' camp. The fire smoldered, with a skillet still on the coals. Pots and pans had been scoured, packs had been closed, firewood neatly stacked. Of the men lounging and sitting in the shade, at the end of the glade, Kent recognized Roberts and Goins. Kitsap was not present. He calculated that as there were only five in Roberts' outfit, and eight in all, that three of these men must belong to Bonesteel's outfit. But other than Goins and Roberts he could not tell which was which. Kent's self-imposed job was to watch these men, anytime and all the time, in their guarded and unguarded moments. He had done this sort of duty before. He was clever at it. He had served the Hash Knife outfit well in that regard. In this case Kent's task was to read the minds of these outlaws from their actions.

Noiselessly he drew one of the rude chairs in place, and sitting down found to his satisfaction that he could watch comfortably. He watched, resting from time to time, for what seemed hours. Occasionally he caught a word, as he had exceptionally sharp ears. In the stillness of night, he believed he could hear ordinary conversation out there.

About midday one of the men, a ruddy-faced stout individual, the least evil looking of the group, replenished the fire, carried his buckets to the stream and filled them, and was soon mixing dough in a huge pan. The others smoked and talked.

After hours of vigilant study of these outlaws Kent came to the conclusion that there was not enough intensity and furtiveness about them to warrant his suspicion that they had any plot that would call for immediate action. The cool Roberts might be able to fool Kent about the working of his mind, but they all could not do that. Men of unexceptional character reacted naturally to thoughts and plots, and to the careful spy, with time to watch, they would inevitably betray some clue to their intentions. This was an exhausted band of men, resting after a successful raid, lazily merry at some sally, or more often somber at some reference to the morning's tragedy. Such a state, of course, would not last long.

Therefore Kent concluded it was incumbent on him to show himself outside. The door to this cabin was large and wide; it swung easily, and when open let in a flood of light, which otherwise was excluded. Kent went out with the gray dog at his heels.

Jeff was repairing the rail where Slotte had crashed through and as it was evident he did not excel at carpenter work, he growled at Kent:

"Say, young feller, next time you feel destructive round

126

here, pick out some place that won't make a lot of work fer me."

"Gosh, Jeff, I hope I'll not feel that way again. Do you reckon I will?"

"Hell, yes. This Hole is the fightin'est place in Utah."

"Let me help you, I'm handy with tools," suggested Kent.

"Wal, thet's decent of you."

Whereupon Kent found himself engaged with Jeff in labor and casual talk. He made it a point to be agreeable and humorous, but not in the least curious. The approach to Jeff's friendship was not difficult of access. They repaired the rail and the section of porch floor that had ripped out with Slotte's heavy onslaught.

"Thar! Thet'll please the boss," concluded Jeff with satisfaction. "An' I'll bet you two bits he'll ask us if we don't want to do some more."

"I'll be glad to help, Jeff. Reckon it'd get on my nerves to loaf around all the time."

"Hev you got nerves?" queried the outlaw laconically.

"Sure I have. I'd go daffy here with nothin' to do."

"Aw, you'll have a hell of a lot to do."

"That so. I like your talk, Jeff, but your look makes me dubious."

"Lucy says I'm a deceivin' hombre."

"Where is she?" inquired Kent casually.

"In her room. She peeped out on us a couple of times. She didn't look happy, Wingfield."

"You could hardly expect that, man ... Has she been happy here?"

"Happy as a sunflower—when she's been alone here. It's a — — shame."

"What is?"

"Wingfield, our guard Roberts is amblin' over this way," said Jeff hurriedly.

"So I saw."

"Wal—He ain't packin' no gun," ejaculated Jeff. "Thet looks friendly. But, son, I'd take it with a grain of salt. Roberts is said to be as slick as he is bad."

"Thanks for the hunch, Jeff."

While the cook gathered up his tools and tin can of

nails, Kent gave attention to the approach of the outlaw leader. He was a man in the prime of life, tall, light but powerfully built, rather fair-skinned, blonde-haired, with a long narrow face.

"Wingfield, would you mind a few words with me?" he asked easily.

"Why, I reckon not. It's a free country," returned Kent slowly, trying not to appear overcurious.

Roberts leaned his tall frame against the end post of the porch, while he leisurely lighted a cigarette.

"I wanted to tell you that Slotte was no pard of mine."

"No? —He sure gave me that impression."

"Wal, things ain't always the way they look. Slotte fetched me here an' we had a deal, but he never fooled me none. An' I don't mind tellin' you I've no hard feelin's agin you fer borin' him."

Kent weighed this frank statement. At close range Ney Roberts had an insidious attraction, as remarkable as his appearance. Kent believed what he said, but did not trust that to be an example of the outlaw's honesty. He was deep. He had a motive.

"Naturally that relieves me, Roberts," rejoined Kent, just as frankly. "How about the other man—Crothers?"

"I didn't know him. Never saw him till Slotte fetched him to my camp. Wess had run into him somewheres. A two-bit cattle thief from the Arizona country an' we ain't missin' him."

"Ahuh. Then so far as those two hombres are concerned I'm not in bad with you?"

"Not at all. I told Bonesteel this mawnin'. He said pretty pert thet didn't change the fact of my bein' in bad with him."

"Roberts, can't you see his side?" queried Kent curtly. "After havin' this wonderful hidin' place to himself all these years to have strangers bust in here!"

"Shore. It's tough. But I come in good faith. Bonesteel an' me have been natural enemies without ever seein' each other or doin' each other dirt. Slotte swore we could get together. But I reckon now his deal was to get me to help him put Bonesteel out of the way."

128

"I guessed that. Bonesteel knew it, too. . . . Was that the deal Slotte had with you?"

"No. He made me believe Bonesteel would take me an' my outfit with him. It wasn't a bad idea. Things was gettin' hot fer me up where I held out on the Sevier."

"Did you tell Bonesteel that?"

"This mawnin'. But he didn't seem keen about it. What's your angle, Wingfield? We know what all Utah has been figerin' on fer years—who runs the Hole in the Wall outfit, an' where it hides."

"On the face of it," returned Kent ponderingly, "I don't know enough about either you or Bonesteel to say."

"Wal, you shore ought to have heerd about me," replied the outlaw, with a laugh.

"I have, an' it wasn't so flatterin'."

"Wal, no range gossip could do justice to me an' my outfit. But Bonesteel is a different proposition."

"I reckoned as much," said Kent, noncommittal.

"Wingfield, you're a young man in years," went on Roberts, feeling his way. "But you might be old in all the hard range deals."

"Sure, I might be," agreed Kent evasively.

"You needn't declare yourself to me. I never get curious about men of your stripe. All the same, Bonesteel said you was on the dodge an' had throwed in with him."

"That's what I told him, Roberts."

"Wal, thet'd be enough fer me, fer the present," went on the outlaw. "If we got together—Bonesteel an' me—then you'd shore be called upon to prove yourself, you can lay to thet. There's no gainsayin' your gall an' nerve, bracin' these two outfits singlehanded. I remember thet Crothers braggin' about some Tonto gunmen, how they all had Texas blood, an' was hell on the draw. You might be one of them, an' if you are, an' if you throw in with us thet'd jest be fine. On the other hand you jest might be a wild hombre from the Tonto—a gun slinger all right, for you shore showed thet—but neither a rustler or a robber. You jest might have heerd of this Hole in the Wall, an' say, about Bonesteel's purty lass. . . . Do I make myself clear, Wingfield?"

"You sure do," returned Kent coldly.

"Wal, no offense, an' thet's off my chest. An' now I'll give you a line on Bonesteel. You can use your own judgment whether or not to tell him what I say. Bonesteel is two men, really. An' I never heerd of him as Avil Bonesteel till Slotte told me. Thet, no doubt, is his right handle. The other I'll let you find out fer yourself. Under thet one he operates on the Utah range from Panguitch to the breaks of the canyon. He raises, buys, sells cattle in all kinds of little deals. He has a family across the river. Slotte did not tell me where, no more about it, except there was a woman Bonesteel set store on. Slotte said this gold-headed lass here didn't know who an' what Bonesteel was. Slotte reckoned she was a bastard—thet he was goin' to tell her. I figgered Slotte had thet up his sleeve in his deal to get the girl. Wal, if she's as innocent as it 'pears thet was shore a low-down deal.... Wal, Wingfield, I reckon you know thet Bonesteel doesn't spend as much as half his time here in this Hole in the Wall. His raids across the river are few an' far between, one a year, mebbe, an' its big. Then he holes up here till it blows over."

"Ahuh. So that's his game! What does he do with the cattle?"

"Wingfield, I'm comin' clean, 'cause thet's the way I am. Slotte wouldn't tell me. He said he didn't know Bonesteel's pardners. But he did say Bonesteel sold a slew of cattle to *himself,* an' then brand-blotted them, an' sold in northern markets. A great idea if it's true."

"But Slotte must have known."

"Shore. An' he wouldn't tell. You see he wasn't square with Bonesteel or me. I suspected thet, first off."

"Playin' both ends against the middle. . . . Roberts, you wouldn't be tellin' me all this just to hear yourself talk."

"Wal, if you're as smart as you look you can figger thet easy. Bonesteel an' me are goin' to get together—mebbe. If so, you'll have your test, my Tonto rider. If not—wal, I reckon you'll stand by him. An' thet ain't goin' to be cheerful fer Ney Roberts' outfit. Only my givin' you this hunch lays the cards on the table. You might help bring Bonesteel round. You might see it'd be more sense fer us to combine than to fight. . . . Thet's all, Wingfield. Take plenty of time an' think it over before you tell Bonesteel."

"Ahuh. I'd like to have about a year," returned Kent ponderingly.

"Wal, thet's onreasonable," concluded Roberts dryly. "If you're what you claimed you was to Bonesteel you'll show your hand pronto."

Roberts sauntered away, taking a last draw at his burned-out cigarette and flipping it away. Apparently his men had not paid any particular attention to his visit with Kent.

Kent went off for a stroll under the cottonwoods. Roberts might have been and probably was all that he had hinted he was, but it seemed equally probable that he exemplified what the frontier called honor among thieves. Kent believed what the outlaw had told him. Also he admitted Roberts' singular drawing power. He liked the man. If he had really been on the dodge, as he had made Bonesteel believe, he would have strongly considered joining Roberts' outfit. Could the outlaw have been keen enough to bring that very point out?

At length Kent walked across to the west end of the long succession of cabins. That portion was very old, and undoubtedly had been built perhaps even before Bonesteel's time. Beyond it were sheds and cribs, a wide-roofed structure without walls, where alfalfa was stored, coops and corrals. Kent reflected that he certainly would have liked to own such a ranch near Wagontongue.

On his return he walked down the porch, passing four of the cabins all joined by the same roof, but with the wide space between, before he came to the kitchen. From there it appeared to be all one cabin with partitions. Bonesteel's door was closed and so was Lucy's.

Kent shut himself in the room, feeling restless and uncertain. He knocked on the door that that led into Lucy's room.

"Lucy, are you there?" he asked, low-voiced.

He heard her light feet patter to the door. "Yes, I'm here, Kent," she replied eagerly.

"Are you all right?"

131

"No. I'm well, but how can I be all right if I can't be with you?"

"Will you let me in?"

"Dad told me to keep this door shut. Shall I do that?"

"I reckon you'd better. Where is he?"

"In his room. He slept for hours. But I hear him now —pacing to and fro. He's worried, Kent."

"So am I. —Lucy, let's take Spades an' another horse an' risk gettin' out over the rocks."

"Oh, darling," she whispered reproachfully. Don't bring that up again."

"I'm sorry. . . . Will your father object to our talkin' through the door?"

"I don't think so. If he does—or if we're afraid of being heard we can write and slip the paper through a crack between the logs."

"All same school days! —That'll be fine, Lucy. But I must see you or I'll go loco."

"I'll meet you outside tonight when there's a good chance. You be there after dark.

"When do we eat, Lucy?"

"Jeff has supper for Dad and me at four. The men eat afterward. What time is it now?"

Kent consulted Elway's watch to find the hour had passed four.

"It's after four."

"Jeff will call us soon. I hear Dad going out."

Kent went across to his peephole in the wall, and took a look at the outlaw camp. No one of them was in evidence. but he heard the ring of an ax. Kent remained there until Lucy called him. She was waiting outside, a little less strained of face and her smile was hopeful. Bonesteel was already at table.

"Howdy, Wingfield," said the chief. "Where have you been since morning?"

"I spent hours watchin' with my eye to a crack between the logs."

"Roberts?"

"All of them. After that I helped Jeff mend the porch rail. When we'd done with that Roberts came over an' talked to me for an hour."

"He did! —What's he up to?"

"Struck me he's disposed to be friendly to you an' me."

Bonesteel shook his head gravely. "You can tell me after supper. We mustn't worry Lucy with all this talk."

"I am worried, Dad," said the girl. "I know there's something wrong. I'm not blind and deaf."

Bonesteel stared at his daughter with gloomy, haunted eyes. He seemed to realize that she was no longer a little girl—that in her he might meet a bitter retribution. He did not answer, but soon finished his meal, told Kent to come to his room, and left.

Kent arose to comply. The girl looked up at him trustingly. He was aware that Jeff watched them with friendly speculative eyes. Kent did not fear this outlaw. He was too devoted to Lucy to be dangerous, no matter what he discovered. He might well be made an ally.

"Jeff, were you an' Bill Elway friends?" queried Kent, on intuitive impulse.

"Pards," replied Jeff gruffly.

"Then that little deal of mine this mornin' didn't step on your toes?"

"It shore didn't, young fellar."

"I'm playin' a lone hand here. An' sort of buffaloed."

"You can talk to me, Wingfield," replied the outlaw heartily. Then he leaned over the table, his big red hands spread, to look down at Lucy. "An' he can talk to you too, eh Lucy!"

"Yes," she whispered poignantly.

Kent strode back to Bonesteel's door which was open. The cabin was luxuriously furnished for a habitation so remote from settlements. Blankets, rugs, chairs, table, lamp, couch, a huge fireplace, shelves of books and racks of guns, contrasted markedly with the primitive bareness of the cabin outside. Bonesteel pushed a chair to Kent, and giving him a cigar bade him tell all Roberts had said.

Kent went into thoughtful detail and related the colloquy between Roberts and himself, withholding what Roberts had said about Bonesteel's double life. The outlaw paced the floor, his head bent, his hands locked behind his back.

"How did Roberts strike you?" he asked at length, halting before Kent to fix him with searching eyes.

"Well, I'd say tolerably favorable."

"Is he playing a deep two-face game?"

"I couldn't say, Bonesteel. If he is I didn't get any hunch of it."

"Would you trust him?"

"No. But doggone-me! That's my own suspicious nature."

"Roberts was damn curious about you," went on Bonesteel. "I heard him talking to Simms before I told him anything. And when I did, naturally I rubbed it on thick. Tonto gunman, hard as flint. Then I asked him if he needed any recommendation of your gun-throwing, 'Hell no!' he said. 'I *saw* him!' Not one of that outfit would provoke a fight with you. All the same what Roberts told you proves he wasn't sure you were on the dodge. And he wouldn't be sure until you threw in with him in some outlaw deal."

"Yes, I got that hunch."

"Wingfield, I took your word. Did you tell me straight?"

"Sure I did," returned Kent coolly, feeling he was on thin ice.

"You're an outlaw right now?"

"Yes, sir."

"You're a hunted outlaw?"

"I'd be afraid to tell some of your outfit the price on my head."

"Aha! —That settles that. By God, I'm sorry!"

Kent gasped his sincere astonishment. But the outlaw chief did not vouchsafe an explanation of his exclamation. He was in a passionate mood. Possibly the evil of his life rose up before him and at that moment he hated to see another young man go wrong as he had gone. He resumed his pacing up and down before the hearth. Kent sat there, forgetting his lighted cigar, trying to put himself in this man's place.

"Did Elway tell you I had gold hid away here?" suddenly queried Bonesteel.

"Elway told me to hunt for his enemy Slotte. That's all."

"That night you crept up to Slotte's camp to listen. Did you hear any talk then about the Hole in the Wall—and gold?"

"No. There was talk that they had not divvied money with Bunge."

"Elway thought I had gold hidden here. So did Slotte. And Roberts has the same hunch. But there is not." The chief's harsh statement did not convince Kent.

"That might account for Slotte's trick an' for Roberts wantin' to hang on here," ventured Kent.

"Yes. They've got it in their greedy minds. And there it'll stick."

"Ump-mmmm. Not in Slotte's case."

Bonesteel paced silently for a long while. When he spoke again he was haggard and fierce. "Wingfield, it's a bitter pill to swallow. But I'll have to take Roberts in my outfit."

Kent had half-expected the chief would be forced to such consideration. It would avoid a battle. And what Kent wanted so desperately was to play for time.

"That might be best," rejoined Kent slowly. "But I'd go slow. Let it grow on Roberts."

Bonesteel cursed. "Time no—ripe," he muttered, as if alone. Then, without further notice of his guest he strode out.

Kent stayed where he was for a few moments, deep in thought, trying to persuade himself that this plot was not growing darker when he knew differently. When he went out dusk had fallen. Shadows were deep under the cottonwoods. The outlaws sat around their campfire, waiting for their supper. No sooner had Kent gone into his room when Lucy rapped on his door. Hurrying close Kent whispered:

"Yes, Lucy, I'm here."

"Let's go now. Dad's gone. They're all outside," she returned excitedly.

"Wait a few minutes till it's darker. Where'll I meet you?"

"At the last cabin, on the river side."

"I'll be there in five minutes. Be careful."

12

◘

THAT FIVE minutes Kent spent at his peephole. The outlaws had two fires, one to cook on, and the other for light. In the blaze he saw an even dozen men sitting or standing in the circle, and prominent among them was Bonesteel. The moods of these two bands of outlaws seemed less dark and foreboding. They were taking stock of each other. Roberts sat in his shirt sleeves, still without his gunbelt.

All at once Kent Wingfield saw these bands of outlaws in their true perspective. So far as he could tell, except in case of Bonesteel, the girl did not enter into their calculations. Bonesteel was assuredly bent on his own selfish interest, as was Roberts. But for Kent the desperate fact was that Lucy was his cardinal and only objective, save his own self-preservation.

He stole out to meet her, once more divided between the icy sickening terror for her that waved over him and the passionate grim will to rise equal to any occasion. Crossing the porch he stepped on to the soft grass and glided west along the dark cabins. He had forgotten Piute until the silent dog brushed against him.

He had not been around that west end of the cabins. Once clearing it the sullen roar of the river came on the warm air. The colossal wall opposite appeared to lean over, a black and mystic bulk, along the base of which the current chafed. Kent stood there peering into blackness, listening for the light step he had heard so often. He heard a swish of moving foliage. Then he made out a line of willows and other brush which grew between him and the river. The lay of the cabins was such that they completely hid the campfire.

Cautiously he advanced until a slim pale form moved against the black line. Next instant Lucy enveloped him in a close embrace and kissed him as if such a thing as fear was not in her. And her whispered words were at once a passionate protest against the enforced hours of separation and an expression of fervid joy at being in his arms again. The feel of her warm tight arms, the fire of her sweet lips, the sense of his actual possession of this girl were all that Kent needed to make him again super-human.

"Come. I want to do something before we talk," she whispered, and taking his hand she led through darkness that was like pitch to him. Kent remembered she could see in the dark nearly as well as a little owl. She made no more noise than a slight swish of the grass or willows. She was so tense, so compelling that he had no impulse to halt or inquire, and he confined himself to stepping stealthily and listening with all his might. She was taking him east along the bank in the very direction he had gone that night Spades had carried him toward the wall. Presently she came to where the grass ended and the rocky ledge began. She had on moccasins, but Kent had to proceed very carefully not to make noise with his boots. At last she halted to bend down and peer intently.

They were close to the river, in fact almost over it, as Kent soon detected from the lapping of water at his feet. The pale starlight gleamed upon the sliding, muttering current.

"It's there—see it?" panted Lucy.

Then he made out the dark shape of a boat, square at each end.

"Yes. But heavens, child, we can't—"

"I'm going—to cut it loose," she whispered. "This morning—just after Dad went to his room—I heard him cursing about this boat. He hates it. —He never would have—a boat. So I'm going to get rid of it."

"Not a bad idea," agreed Kent, quick to see that a boat strengthened Roberts' stand there. "But wait a minute. We might be found out."

"How? We can't be tracked—not over grass and rock."

"All right. You sure are a brave kid," he said, thrilling at her. "You stay here. Keep your eyes an' ears peeled. I'll let it loose."

Kent peered back along the shore, by which they had come. A faint light flickered through the cottonwoods. It was quite far to the cabins. Then he turned to the task. In a few steps he had reached the boat, the bow of which rested on a rock. He felt for a rope, and finding it ran his hands along to where the end was noosed around a sharp corner of rock. Reaching it he stepped back and laid hold of the bow. He then became aware of a pack or sack about midship. Gently he pushed the boat free of the rock, then gathering his strength he expended it in a powerful shove.

Almost silently it shot out upon the river. He leaped up to Lucy's side. "There she goes," he whispered valiantly. She clung to him with tight hands. In the starlight her eyes were unnaturally large and dark. Gazing out he saw the boat slow down. Suddenly it seemed as if an invisible giant hand had laid hold of the craft. It swept down and turned round and round, to grow dim and vague, then vanish in the gloom. It was gone. And the low roar of the river swelled high, in the black distance below like underground thunder.

"Let us go back up by the wall. I know a place," whispered Lucy, and again she led him.

This time it was to a flat rock close to the wall, high up above, but not far from the river. Piute leaped upon it, as had been his wont on other occasions, while Kent vaulted to a seat. He put his hands out to lift Lucy up beside him, but she just sank into his arms.

"Do you love me?" she asked, with her face upturned.

"Lucy! —So terribly that I'm changed. All day I've been a shiverin' wretch. Tonight I'm aglow, fierce with the strength you give me."

"I am changed, too. It seems long since last night. What will tomorrow bring?"

"Let's don't think of that. Today has been hard enough."

"Kent, you are strange. I feel—"

"Don't think, darlin'," he whispered. "We must not stay out here long. But a little while, even a minute, would make me sure you are real—that you are mine in your heart. Only *they* could come between us."

"No one could. Not even Dad. Pretty soon I shall tell him."

"You mustn't."

"Jeff suspects us."

"Of what?"

"I don't know. He wouldn't tell. It's only if he can see I love you, Dad could, too, or anyone if they looked at me. I can't keep my eyes off you."

"Lucy, it's not likely at this stage of the game that your father or any of these men would be interested in us, unless they caught us like this. And that just can't happen. They're playin' for great stakes—Roberts to get this place—Bonesteel to hold it."

"If they don't fight they'll make some kind of bargain."

"That's what I think. And I don't believe they'll fight."

"Almost I'd rather see them fight. Dad will try to make an outlaw of you. But he can't. I won't let him."

"Lucy, I don't see how you could help it. I won't leave here without you. I'd do anythin' to get to stay."

"Oh, you must love me more than I do you," she cried piteously, clinging to him. "I'm torn between Dad and you. He's a part of me. And I'd die if I lost you."

Piute lifted his head and gave vent to a low growl. Kent silenced him with strong hand.

"He scents someone," whispered Kent, sliding down off the rock. "Listen."

After an interval Lucy said: "I hear men coming along the shore."

Kent did not hear them, but presently he saw a tiny red light that might have been the glow of a cigarette. He drew Lucy back from the rock, along the wall. The dog stayed close to them, his head up. Kent halted. Voices became distinct and the jingle of spurs and scrape of boots on stone.

"Wess, we can't go no further. The wall begins here."

"Yes, an' hyar's whar we tied thet boat. . . . It's gone."

"Drifted off."

"Drifted, hell. I tied thet rope. Did you ever know of a knot of mine come untied?"

"Wal, not of a rope. But how about thet Chandler woman—"

"Haw! Haw!"

"Harvey, I'll bust yore jaw."

"Wess, it shore ain't funny. Roberts will raise hell. He's afraid of this river, which ain't no damn wonder. He can't swim. An' crossin' up that on a hoss is no picnic."

"Who was last out of this boat?"

"I was. An' thet's why I know she's been untied an' shoved off. Who the hell could have done it?"

"Bonesteel, I reckon. His eyes shore blazed lightnin' when he seen thet boat. I thought he'd kill Slotte."

"Wal, it's a rummy deal. Let's go all the way down the shore an' see if it might have drifted in."

The three outlaws faded in the gloom, their voices gradually dying away.

"What did they want that boat for?" asked Wingfield, as much of himself as of Lucy.

"They didn't say. Perhaps for the pack."

"I think we'd better rustle back another way. . . . Lucy, your little trick will make trouble."

"We've got to make trouble between Dad and Roberts."

That spirited reply from Lucy gave Kent food for reflection. The girl was developing swiftly in this crisis. They kept to the wall for a goodly distance, then crossed the sage to the road, to follow that up to the cotton-woods, where Kent halted to reconnoiter. Under the trees it was thick with gloom. The campfire of the outlaws spread a yellow flare.

"Your eyes are better than mine," whispered Kent. "You lead. Keep to the left. An' go slow."

From tree to tree they glided. At last the campfire disappeared behind the blunt black bulk of the cabin. They had advanced toward the east end. Here under a cottonwood Kent whispered for Lucy to go back to her room. Silently she kissed him, strained him to her, and slipped away. Kent waited until a slight creak told him she had closed her door. Then he made his own way along the porch and gained his quarters. Once inside with the bar down he breathed easier. Slipping off his boots he hurriedly found the peephole between the logs.

A bright fire showed the group of outlaws about as Kent had seen them last. But on the moment a halloa brought their heads up alert.

"It's Simms. They're comin' back," spoke up an outlaw.

Then three forms slouched into the circle of light.

"Ney, yore boat's gone," announced the foremost.

"Wha-att?" sang out the leader, rising as a bent spring released.

Bonesteel's start was slight yet equally significant.

"Gone!"

"Wess, you missed it."

"Missed nothin'. I tied up thet boat an' I could have found it blindfold."

"I saw it myself, just before dark."

"Wal, a hell of a lot can happen jest after dark. Harvey reckoned it had drifted off. I knowed a damned sight better. But we went along the shore all the way down to where the rocks began again. No good."

"What's yore idee, Wess?"

"Thet boat was untied an' shoved off," declared Simms, with an oath.

"Wal, it's a —— good thing fer you fellars that I can't blame you," cut out Roberts shortly.

"What was in thet pack, boss?"

"Whisky. I left it in the boat cause I didn't want you men drinkin' just yet."

"All our whisky!"

"Shore all, except the flask I went after."

A chorus of curses went the rounds of that group. Bonesteel dropped his head a little and appeared to be studying the fire. Roberts finally resumed his seat.

"Bonesteel, what's yore idee about this?" he queried sarcastically.

"Good riddance, except loss of the whisky," returned the chief tersely, and looked up at his rival.

"Shore. But do you know anythin' about how thet boat got lost?"

"No. If I had shoved it off I'd certainly tell you."

"Wal, I reckon you would," said Roberts thoughtfully. "Now it just happens thet you an' all yore outfit have been around since I come back from thet boat. Hardly an hour ago."

"All 'cept young Wingfield," spoke up one of the other outlaws.

"Thet's so," said another.

"I was thinkin' the same." added Roberts dryly. "Wal, Bonesteel, mebbe you can give us a line on yore new gun-man?"

"Wingfield went into the cabin right after supper. I haven't seen him come out."

"Call him, Russ," ordered Roberts, and as the burly outlaw shuffled out of the group Roberts added with a caustic humor, "It might be a good idee to be polite—an' when you knock kinda stand aside from in front of his door."

Some of the outlaws laughed gruffly. Kent saw Harvey pass between him and the campfire, then heard his heavy boot thuds on the porch. Presently a loud rap sounded on the door, accompanied by a gruff voice: "Mister Wingfield."

Kent jumped into the air to thud down in his stocking feet, jarring the cabin.

"Hey! —Who's there? —That you, Bonesteel?"

"No, it ain't the chief," replied Harvey. "Just a committee callin' to see if you was in."

"I'm in, all right. An' you want to be damn careful how you wake me," growled Kent.

Harvey tramped off the porch again to cross Kent's vision. Roberts awaited him, sardonic and curious.

"Boss, he was in an' sleepin'," announced Harvey. "I heard his bare feet bounce on the floor. An' he was madder'n hell."

"Ahuh. Mebbe an' mebbe not," soliloquized Roberts.

"Boss, thet leaves Bonesteel's girl to take account of. She might have done it."

Bonesteel certainly voted death to that ruffian, if Kent was any judge of the look of a man. The chief rose to his lofty stature.

"Roberts, I don't think Lucy could have set your boat adrift. But suppose she did. What would you do about it?"

"Wal, thet's a stumper, shore. Let's find out first. Russ, see if she is in her cabin?"

"I'll go with you, Harvey," said Bonesteel coldly.

Kent tiptoed across his cabin to call low at the crack of Lucy's door. She had her lamp lit. She heard him. In a moment: "Kent! —What is it?"

"Turn out your light—pretend to be in bed," he answered low.

Then he watched the faint light that shone through the crevice. It went out just as the footsteps of her father and Harvey sounded without. They passed by Kent's room, on to Lucy's. Then came a knock and Bonesteel's voice:

"Lucy, are you there?"

No answer. Bonesteel knocked and called louder, with a hint of alarm in his hurry.

"Dad! —Is that you?" cried Lucy, as if awakened in fright.

"Yes."

"I'm in bed. What do you want?"

"Have you been in your room since supper?"

"Yes. Why?"

"Never mind, lass. I'm sorry I disturbed you. The boat Roberts brought here has disappeared. He thought you might have sent it adrift."

"The lousy rustler!" cried Lucy in a feigned fury.

"Eh! —What?" ejaculated her father, no doubt as thunderstruck as was Kent. Then he stalked off the porch, followed by Harvey.

Kent stole back to his peephole, elated with his sweetheart, and most curious to see how Roberts would take this sequel.

"Roberts, your suspicions were unfounded. And I'll hold them against you," announced Bonesteel in scorn.

"Boss, the girl was in bed, sound asleep," added Harvey, with a heartiness that augured some satisfaction. "Bonesteel woke her up an' told her you thought she'd stole yore boat."

"Hell! I didn't say thet or think it," protested the outlaw vigorously.

"Wal, Bonesteel told her so an' she called you a lousy rustler."

Roberts gaped and his lean visage turned a dark red in the firelight. He sat down abruptly amid the loud guffaws of his men. Suddenly with a gesture of violence Roberts silenced his mirthful outfit and then flashed at his rival:

"Bonesteel, this girl of yore's doesn't know what an' who you are!"

"My God! —No!" exclaimed Bonesteel, transfixed with alarm. His face changed as markedly as had Roberts', only it turned white.

A long silence ensued, during which these rivals and foes glared at each other, and their men, grasping the passion and tragedy of the moment, watched and listened mutely. Then the tension broke unexpectedly.

"Boss!" burst out Simms, leaning forward. "I heerd somethin'."

"What?" In a twinkling, the mood of these outlaws changed. Whatever their hearts held of primal instincts the greatest one was fear.

"Either I'm dotty or I heerd thet boat," proclaimed Simms hoarsely.

"Man, you're drunk. You got hold of thet liquor yourself."

"No! —Listen, I tell you. If I didn't hear them oars creak I'm wuss off than drunk."

The outlaw subordinated all faculties to that of hearing. Kent did likewise, turning his ear to the little hole.

"There!" hissed Simms.

"Yes. I hear somethin'."

"Boss, it's the boat."

"Like a dry wagon axle."

"What the hell!"

Kent finally caught a faint high-pitched squeak that might have come from labored oars in a boat. He

144

wheeled to peer out again and was in time to see Roberts wheel and actually count his men.

Bonesteel had heard and he too had fallen under the spell of the moment. From dark face to dark face his glance swept. "Jeff—Goins—Kitsap—Rigney—Forman —all here!"

"So help me Gawd!" muttered Roberts, leaping up, gun flashing.

"It's our boat, Ney. I remember that squeak."

"Boss, if it's a movin' boat somebody is rowin' it."

"Bonesteel, could thet boat have fallen into the hands of Piutes?"

"No. They couldn't row it if it had."

"Then it's another boat."

"Comin' down the river?"

"Sounds thet way."

"Fellars, it's comin' up river. Close to shore now. . . . Rowin' easier."

"Bonesteel, one thing is shore. Somebody else—besides us—knows yore secret Hole in the Wall."

The chief leaped across the campfire and drew his gun to face the dim road leading down to the river.

No more was said. In the breathless silence Bonesteel's and Roberts' men alike, in a common cause, awaited the intruders with drawn weapons. Kent pasted his eye to that peephole. Whoever was in this boat, whatever brought them, would be more likely to further his cause, one way or another, than make it more hazardous. Nevertheless he felt tight and cold with suspense.

The squeak of oarlocks ceased. Faint splashes followed and then a scrape of something hard drawn up on sand. Whoever they were these invaders were bold or ignorant of the nature of this break in the solid walls of the canyon. Moments passed and for someone, Kent thought, death drew closer. Kent thought also that never would he forget that picture of wild men in a wild place, standing or kneeling in the firelight, like panthers about to leap.

"Who comes there?" shouted Bonesteel, his eagle head bending low.

"Better shoot first," advised Roberts caustically.

"It's me, boss," came a shrill reply.

"Bunge!" rang out Bonesteel.

"Do you know him, chief?" queried Roberts sharply.

"One of my men. He's alone or he wouldn't come."

"Kit, if it ain't Ben I'll eat my boots," shouted Goins in bewilderment.

Kent Wingfield had the surprise of his life and one not unaccompanied by increased alarm. But when he saw that red-faced Bunge enter the lighted circle, to stand aghast, he sustained a shock that made him shake.

"Bonesteel! . . . It's me. Bunge. Wait before you—use thet gun," panted the newcomer, his eyes rolling to and fro.

"Sure it's you, Ben?" queried the chief, lowering his arm.

"All thet's left of me. . . . Who'n hell air these strangers?"

"A visiting outfit, Ben."

"Oho! Thet accounts fer the boat. . . . Air they friends, boss?"

"Hardly—yet. . . . Where'd you get that boat?"

"Boss, it came driftin' to me—when I was about to drown. . . . I tried comin' in over the rocks. Lost my hoss. Had one orful time gettin' down—to the river. Found I'd missed the Hole. I came out below—jest round thet fust point. Reckoned I could make it climbin', wadin', swimmin'. Wal, I been all day. I shot all my shells tryin' to make somebody hear. An' I got stuck round the corner. Thought I could swim around. But I shore was drownin' when thet boat bumped into me."

"Wal, Bunge, I reckon I owe you somethin'," spoke up Roberts. "Thet is my boat. An' loss of it shore riled me."

"Who air you?"

"My name is Ney Roberts."

Bunge's consternation and silence attested to his recognition of that name.

Bonesteel intercepted with an angry gesture. "You fool! Why'd you come over the rocks? I'm the only white man ever got in or out of here that way."

"Huh! . . . Aw, I knowed thet," replied Bunge, quick to get his cue from the chief. "But I had to. . . . Boss, I shore got one hell of a story to tell. But I'm starved. An' thet drink I found in the boat ain't enough."

"Why did you take to the rocks?" demanded the chief.

"Cause I was chased to hell an' gone by the Piutes, thet's why."

"Piutes! —They are our friends."

"Like hell they air. They was!"

"What changed them?"

"No less than a gun-totin' hombre from the Tonto Basin. He was ridin' Spades, boss. *Spades!* What you think of thet? . . . Wal, he run plumb into Matokie an' some of his braves. The Piute knowed thet black hoss an' he reckoned he'd been stole—which was shore correct. They got to arguin' about Spades. Matokie wanted to get the hoss, meanin' to fetch him to you. But thet rider bored him an' another Injun."

"Bunge, if the Piutes chased you to hell an' gone how'd you learn all this about Matokie."

"Logan told me. It's all over the country. I run into a Navaho in the Segi. He told me. An' when I got up on top the Piutes didn't look to see who I was, but took after me hell-bent fer election. They chased me across the San Juan, where I give them the slip over the rocks."

"What'd you do with the money you were carrying down at Red Lake and the horse you were riding?"

"Didn't Slotte tell you?" asked Bunge, swallowing hard.

"No. Slotte hadn't been here long enough when he became afflicted with a peculiar disease that's likely to get contagious."

"Where is he?"

"Buried this morning."

"Wha—att! . . . Goins an' Kit? . . . Aw, there they air," ejaculated the outlaw, floundering in the predicament he had built upon falsehood. "Pards, shore you tole the chief how sore I got about the money Slotte wouldn't divvy?. . . How I rode off takin' Spades? . . . How I meant to fetch both the money an' the hoss back to Bonesteel?"

"Correct, Ben, except we didn't say nothin' about your comin' back 'cause we didn't know thet," drawled Kitsap, concluding with a grin.

"Bunge, where's the money—and the horse?"

"Boss, thet Tonto hombre held me up—robbed me!"

"Where?"

"On the trail south of Red Lake. Then I run into a posse who was trailin' thet very same galoot. Did they ask me if I'd meet him and' did they tell me who he was? . . . Wal, I should snicker they did. . . . Only Gawd Almighty knows why thet hombre didn't murder me! —He's got Billy the Kid skinned to a frazzle!"

13

◫

KENT WINGFIELD, standing there at the cabin wall, with his eye glued to the peephole, felt shot through and through with swift sensations, prominent among which was red-blooded anger at this monumental liar.

For some reason impossible to guess, Bunge had been shunted back upon his comrades of the Hole in the Wall. He was clever enough to know that his mere return would look well to the chief. Slotte's death had been sheer good luck for the outlaw. Both Kitsap and Goins were his friends, which fact strengthened his case. For the rest he could resort to crafty and brilliant lies.

"So this bandit who held you up has Billy the Kid skinned to a frazzle, eh?" queried Bonesteel, tremendously impressed, probably as much by the fact that he had been harboring this Tonto rider as by the notorious reputation Bunge was giving him. Roberts and his outfit looked and listened in profound interest. Bunge's fellow outlaws gaped at him, gripped by the fascinating fact that this bandit was already in their midst.

"Wal, I guess he has," replied Bunge, beginning to breathe like a man who had slipped his neck out of a noose. He wiped his sweaty face. He made a motion as if to squeeze the water out of his bulky coat, but suddenly desisted. "The posse wanted him fer killin' a sheriff down at Payson. He's done a heap of shootin', thet hombre. He damn near killed Slinger Dunn in the Drift Fence War down there. An' up to then Slinger had the edge on all the gun throwers. At Wagontongue, where the posse took me after losin' the trail, I heerd a lot more. They called him Wing Field, 'cause he had a gun arm swift as a bird's wing. He rode fer the Hash Knife outfit for three years when thet outfit was tough. He was in thet Yellow Jacket feud. An' before he was twenty he was jest plain cold death on the draw. There's good said of him as wal as bad. Fer he croaked some mean greasers, redskins an' bad hombres thet the range was glad to get rid of. His rep hangs most on a job he did in the Verdi. He was out with some riders who was trailin' a bunch of rustlers. Ole Jim Stevens' outfit. You knowed Stevens, boss. Wal, this young feller Field got separated from his outfit an' run plumb into Stevens with three of his outfit. It was jest too bad fer them. While they was pullin' their guns young Wing popped them out of their saddles like so many turkeys from a roost. An' he was shootin' from a jumpy hoss. Aw, he musta been hell with a gun. I looked into his without bein' scared, but if I'd of knowed him I'd shore sweat blood. . . . Thet Stevens fight is true, boss. I can't swear to the rest. You know what range talk is. The latest story about him is thet he went off to Sonora with an old prospector, an' came back to Wagontongue alone, an' packin' a heap of gold. They say he murdered the old prospector. . . . An' thet's the hombre who robbed me of Spades an' the cash belongin' to you."

"Bunge, you can be excused for not going for your gun," replied Bonesteel. "Sure you didn't know him, but you had a hunch. It's not safe to crook your finger when there's a killer like him around. . . . One more thing. Did you tell the posse or anyone down there what he robbed you of?"

"Boss, I discreetly kept that to myself," returned Bunge modestly.

Bonesteel shifted his sardonic face toward Roberts. "What'd you do about it?"

"Wal, I'll tell you if you'll do what I say," replied Roberts.

"Certainly, if it's reasonable."

"Make this tall, storytellin' Bunge step round the corner of yore cabin there, pound on the fust door an' yell."

"What?"

"Wal, considerin', thet bandits don't hold people up an' introduce themselves I'd have him yell, 'Hey, Wingfield, you fetched the hoss back. But I want my money.'"

"Ben, you heard?" roared the chief.

"Shore I heerd."

"Go then and yell that."

"What the hell, boss . . . What's the idee. . . . Who's in there? I—I might get bored," ejaculated the bewildered outlaw.

"You *will* get bored if you don't," thundered Bonesteel, and he lifted the gun that all the while he had kept in his hand.

Bunge knew his chief. Without another word he stalked out of the circle and stamped up the porch steps.

Kent heard him puffing, feeling his way along the log wall, to halt at the edge of the door. Kent drew his gun, grimly humorous at the thought of giving that outlaw a scare.

"Damn poor joke, I'm thinkin'," muttered Bunge. Then he pounded on the door. "Hey—"

"Who's there?" yelled Kent, at the top of his lungs.

"Owi!" Bunge sounded as if he had exploded in that outcry. Then he blustered: "Who's in thar?"

"Say, I know your voice."

A ringing order from the chief reminded Bunge that certainty in his rear was more perilous than uncertainty in front.

"Hey—Wing," he bawled, as if strangling. "You fetched the hoss back, but I want my money!"

"Who're you?" yelled Kent, louder, if possible, than before.

"Ben Bunge."

Kent worked the action of his Colt so swiftly that the reports merged almost in one continuous deafening crash.

150

The big bullets were like hammer blows upon the door. Then Lucy's shriek pealed out.

Cursing, Kent ran to call at the crevice. "It's all right, Lucy. That was Ben Bunge."

Kent reloaded his gun, grimly listening to Bunge's thudding boots on the grass and the hoarse glee of the outlaws. By the time they had recovered from their mirth Kent was watching them again.

"Roberts, it might be wise not to rile Wingfield any more tonight," said Bonesteel, curtly to his outlaw guest.

"I savvy thet. I'm sold," replied Roberts coolly.

"You all better turn in," concluded Bonesteel, and left them. He went up the porch, to halt boldly at Kent's door.

"You awake, Wingfield?"

"Awake! —Bonesteel, are you all drunk out there?" answered Kent testily. "If I get wakened up again I'll be sore."

"Just a little fun. My man Ben Bunge came back. He mentioned having met you. I wanted to convince him you were here. . . . By the way, Wingfield, did you fetch the money?"

"Oh, that? Ha! Ha! Ha! . . . Good night, chief."

Bonesteel bade Kent good night and passed on to Lucy's door, where he called. "Lucy, did you hear the racket?"

"I am—scared stiff," replied Lucy, which, judged by her shaky voice, was no doubt true.

"We played a joke on Wing Field."

"Wing . . . Field?" echoed Lucy.

"Yes. The gentleman who has been trying to repose in the cabin next to you. Just a little innocent fun. But the joke is most on Roberts. Good night, lass."

The hour was growing late and Kent was tired standing with his eye glued to the cabin wall. His peephole required the pressing of his face between the chinks, which position was most uncomfortable and finally became painful. He took a last look at the outlaws around the campfire. Their number had diminished. Some had rolled in their blankets. Bunge went off with Goins and Kitsap

151

toward the west cabins. Roberts and Simms sat beside the dying fire, their heads together, conversing low.

Kent had noted a couch covered with an Indian blanket. Here he sought rest he needed exceedingly. The night before had been sleepless, and this day endless and full of nerve-racking moments. Bunge's return had been the climax. The addlebrained liar had completely persuaded Bonesteel that he was harboring in his midst the wildest and most dangerous young desperado in the West. Bonesteel had betrayed a mocking gratification, the reason of which was obvious. Roberts had reacted as subtly, but differently. He was a rustler, not a rival gunman. With the revelation of Wingfield's real status, as promulgated by Bunge, the whole situation took on a different color. Roberts would exercise more pains to conciliate Bonesteel, and the latter would be less amenable.

These thoughts ran through Kent's whirling mind as sleep began to weigh down upon him; and his last conscious effort failed with the problem of how to meet this extraordinary situation.

The ringing stroke of an ax roused Kent out of deep slumber. Sunlight filtered through cracks in the rough shakes that served as shingles. Some one of the outlaws was astir. Kent listened for sounds in the next cabin, but none were forthcoming. The hour could not have been very early, for the sun surely must rise high to peep over those walls. Refreshed in body and clear in mind again Kent lay there considering how best to meet the issues of the day.

Bonesteel would accept and welcome him as a wild youth deadly on the draw. For want of a better part, that suited Kent and he would play it to the last card. Roberts would hate him, fear him, and not be above having one of his men shoot him from ambush. Not one of them would meet him openly. This probability had its bad and its good sides.

Lucy would be the stumbling block. If she had heard the loud talk of last night—which was likely—she would very soon grasp that her father and all these outlaws took him for a bloody ruffian, with a price on his head, and she would rebel with all the surprising temper which had developed within her.

Bunge would have to be met. Kent could kill him easily enough, but could not convince himself that would do any good. In the event of a battle between Roberts and Bonesteel the thieving, lying Bunge might be needed. They would all want to get hold of some of the ten thousand dollars Kent was believed to have stolen from Bunge, if not by gambling fairly for it, by foul means. This was a ticklish side to the predicament. For the rest Kent decided he should live up to the reputation accorded him. If there were any chance at all for him it would lie in that.

Kent got up and took a peep at the outlaw camp. The cook, a red-faced individual, was whistling at his tasks. No one else appeared to be awake, or at least no one was stirring. Kent strapped on his gun belt and pulled on his boots. Then he bethought himself of a much needed shave.

Throwing open his door he stalked boldly out on the porch. Passing Lucy's room he was surprised to find it open, and to catch a glimpse of an even more vivid, colorful interior than her father's room. But he did not see Lucy. Jeff was banging pots and pans around in the kitchen. Kent loomed in the doorway.

"Hand it out, Jeff," he yelped.

"Wha-what you want?" asked Jeff haltingly, after a violent start.

"A pan of hot water, you locoed flapjack slinger," replied Kent, in cheerful ferocity.

He got it in double-quick time. Then he repaired to his open doorway, and spreading his little pack on the bench he proceeded to begin the great luxury of a shave. When about half-finished he heard Lucy's step.

"Mornin', big eyes," he called gaily. "Have you such a thing in this camp as a clean towel? Mine is dirty and—bloody."

She did not come quickly, but she came; and when he saw her his breast felt like it had caved in. For Lucy to be pale, grave-eyed and trembling was only to enhance her allurement. She murmured something as she handed him a towel.

153

"What's wrong with you—darlin'?" he asked, whispering the last.

"What do you think?"

"Your rest was distrubed, I reckon."

"I lay awake all night—shivering."

"No? Why didn't you call me?"

She gasped a little, as if the actuality and audacity of his presence were profoundly different from the incredible thoughts she had been entertaining.

"Kent—if that's your name. . . . I—I heard every word Ben Bunge said last night."

"You did? What a darn shame! I'm sorry, particularly about the shootin'. Fact is I forgot you."

"Oh, Kent!—Have you lied—to me?"

"What? . . . Gosh! See there. You made me cut myself. Made me spill blood, Lucy Bonesteel!"

"I'm sorry. I—I didn't think."

"You stand right there, Lucy, till I get this job over," ordered Kent, and with swift strokes he completed his shaving, after which he washed and wiped his face. Then he deliberately looked out into the grove, up and down the porch.

"Where's your father?"

"He went out early."

"Jeff?"

"Still in the kitchen."

"Come around behind the cabin." Kent led the way to the end of the building away from the kitchen and out of sight of Roberts' camp. Then he transfixed her with all the terrible sternness of eye of which he was capable, prompted both by grief and alarm at her apparent distrust. In his heart he could not blame her. What did she know of such a man as he claimed to be? At his look she turned white as a flower. Her sweetness and loveliness were such that Kent grew beside himself with love. He shot out a hand to clutch her waist and in one pull he jerked her off her feet, almost into his arms. He shook her hard, until her hair danced all over her head.

"Lucy Bonesteel, you think I lied to you?" he demanded.

"I—I . . . No, Kent, you couldn't be so—so—"

154

"Listen, you poor frightened child," he interposed, abruptly changing to earnest tenderness. "Doubt your father, or anyone, but never me. I am Kent Wingfield. All I told you about myself is true. I swear it. That Ben Bunge is the damndest liar in the world. He made up most of that stuff. He was tryin' to hide his tracks. . . . Lucy, once an' for all. I love you madly. I am honest, an' worthy of your trust, if no more. I would die for you—an' very probably will."

"Forgive me," she begged, trying to get into his arms. "I've been loco. All last night. . . . It was only—I thought how horrible—if you had lied. . . . And just now you looked so strange, so devilish of eye. . . . For God's sake don't—don't say you're going to fight—"

"Hush, honey," he whispered, bending to kiss her wet cheeks. "I was to blame. I must have scared you out of your wits last night. Brace up now. Our case is hopefuller this mornin'. Sure your dad, an' all of them, reckon me to be the bloodiest killer unhung. It's funny, Lucy, but it'll serve our turn. Run now, an' don't—lose—your—nerve —again!"

At breakfast Jeff was respectful where formerly he had been friendly and loquacious. Bonesteel did not show up at this meal. Lucy showed signs of a sleepless night, but she was cheerful, and if she dared not speak in front of Jeff what her eyes expressed when opportunity afforded, she did not hesitate to press her little moccasined feet all over Kent's boots. There seemed to Kent to be something incredible and cruel about these moments with her, when their love spoke so poignantly, while all the time it was as if they were sitting on a powder magazine.

"Jeff wants some help today," ventured Lucy, at the conclusion of the meal.

"What with?"

"Out in the garden. There's a lot of work."

"Work in that hot sun? Not much."

"It's really not hard to pick peaches and beans," protested the girl in surprise. It was the easiest of things for Kent to deceive her.

"I couldn't think of it," drawled Kent, mostly for Jeff's benefit.

"What are you going to do?"

"Reckon I'll hobnob with the men."

"Drink, gamble and fight?"

"Not the first you can bet on that."

"Wouldn't you rather help me help Jeff?"

"Oh, that's different. But your Dad. Won't he kick at a bad hombre like me bein' with you?"

"I've never been with a bad hombre before. Let's see what Dad does."

"Fine. Have Jeff call me when you're ready."

Kent got his second gun out of his pack, a huge bone-handled Colt of older model, and stuck it conspicuously in his right hip pocket. Then he sauntered out to the camp. He did not swagger, but pretended the insolent nonchalance of a young desperado, to whom fear, life and death were nothing. Most of the outlaws were sitting on the ground around a tarpaulin. Bonesteel was there, eating with them.

"I'm tired of beef. Can't we have some venison?" Roberts was saying.

"Howdy, men," Kent said. "I never met you-all, but I reckon Bonesteel will introduce me."

"Not necessary at all," replied Roberts, in dry cordiality. "Least ways not with them hardware cards you have on you."

If there was any tension on the moment it eased at that.

"Sit down an' eat," added Roberts as an afterthought.

"Thanks. I just had mine. But I'll take a smoke, if you have one of them two-bit cigars."

"Mebbe I'll dig up one later, if you set in with us."

"Poker?" asked Kent indifferently.

"After we have a little powwow," replied Roberts significantly.

"I reckon you-all got me well heeled," said Kent, with a grin.

"Wal, accordin' to Bunge, you are, tolerable."

"Bunge? That —— ——!" ejaculated Kent. "Bonesteel, why'd you send him to wake me up? I'm mean when I get jarred that way."

156

"Suppose we let Bunge speak for himself," rejoined the chief.

"Where are you, Bunge?"

Finally Kent located the outlaw at the far end of the tarpaulin, and it needed no second look to see that worthy was between the devil and the deep sea. "Say, you — — redhead. What were you bellerin' about last night?"

"Wing, I figgered you could hev heerd Bunge if you was dead," put in Roberts. "He was bellerin' about money."

"What money was thet, Bunge?" launched Kent.

"Wal, my money," returned the outlaw.

"Oh, I see. Yours? . . . Bunge, are you sure you'll need that money where you're goin'?"

"Whar I—I'm goin'?" stuttered the perplexed and desperate outlaw.

"Yes."

"An' whar's thet?"

"Well, you won't need your heavy coat where you're goin'," returned Kent deliberately. The significance he had attached to that bulky garment the night before added to his suspicion this morning. It was more than an inspiration. Kent flipped a hand at his gun. As it whirled brightly up he caught it with the barrel aligned with Bunge. "Peel out of that coat."

"Coat!— What you . . . don't shoot."

"Throw your coat over here or I'll put a round hole in it."

Livid of visage the redheaded outlaw divested himself of the coat and tossed it over the heads of the men where Kent stood up to catch it.

"Feels kinda heavy, Bonesteel," said Kent, weighing the garment. He gave it a savage shake which brought out a jingle of gold coins. "Rip it open!" he ordered, and threw the garment at Bonesteel's feet.

As if hypnotized the chief spread the padded coat out on the grass. Roberts stretched his neck like a buzzard. They all resembled birds of prey. They scented gold. But Bonesteel found little of consequence in the pockets. He breathed hard as he seized the knife offered him and slashed the lining open. Packs of greenbacks, tied thin

157

and tight, greeted the greedy eyes of the outlaws. And the other side of the coat spilled forth the same, and also a small buckskin bag obviously full of gold coins.

"Boss, thet gold is mine," gulped Bunge, ghastly and leering of face. "I was fetchin' the rest back . . . jest jokin' about thet holdup."

"Kill him, Wing!" replied Bonesteel, black of brow.

"Aw, hell, I haven't any hard feelin's. Bunge was just loco."

"You won't kill him?"

"Ump-umm. Leastways not in cold blood. If Bunge feels bad about it an' wants to draw on me he's welcome."

"I'll kill him," shouted Bonesteel in bitter wrath. The disloyalty to himself more than the lie to Wingfield brought his gun out glittering. But Roberts knocked it up.

"Hold on. . . . What's the use? If Wing here won't bore him there's no sense in yore doin' it. Bunge was only goin' Slotte one better. I don't say I'd've done it myself, but most fellars would. Let him off, Bonesteel."

"Get out of my sight," fumed Bonesteel, reluctantly sheathing his gun.

"An' see here, Bunge," added Kent, his voice high-pitched, as the outlaw scrambled up with alacrity. "You — — — —redhead! If you ever lie about me again I'm gonna get mad!"

"Haw! Haw! Haw!" roared Roberts, and others of the gangs joined him in coarse mirth.

"Gentlemen, I fail to see the fun in it," observed Bonesteel, once more composed. "I've shot more than one man for less. . . . Kitsap, count and divide this money. Keep your share and give Goins his. . . . Wing, will you take Slotte's share?"

"I don't care if I do," said Kent coolly. "Shore I'd hate to hang around poker games an' not set in. It's only fair, though, to tell you fellars that all the coin gravitates to me."

Roberts rose erect, with dynamic vigor that suggested instant decision.

"Bonesteel, an' all of you, I'm declarin' myself," he began, speaking as one who knew his power over men.

158

"This here Wing Field has hit me plumb center. If he hadn't throwed in with Bonesteel I'd hev got him in my outfit one way or another. Fer the job I've been plannin' —the biggest ever undertook in Utah—we need a young devil like Wing. So I say to you, Bonesteel, an' to yore men—let's get together. I busted in here where I didn't belong. Thet was Slotte's fault, not mine. But I'm here now. It'd never do fer two outfits to know the secret of the Hole in the Wall. Only one outfit should hide in here, an' work out of here. Because if we worked separate we'd step on each other's toes. No! We might as wal face the facts. Say Bonesteel wouldn't throw in with me. An' say I wouldn't throw in with him. An' say I wouldn't give up this Hole in the Wall. Thet'd mean a clash. There wouldn't be many of us left. . . . Thet's all. We don't need a vote. Is it yes or no, Bonesteel?"

"Roberts, have you sounded my men on this deal?" queried the chief.

"Shore. All except Wing."

"No outfit can serve two masters."

"I'd be satisfied to work under you as chief."

"All right. I accept. My one condition is that we do not use a boat."

"Chief, I knuckle. But use the boat this once—when we cross. We can turn it adrift then."

"I agree to that."

"An' now one thing more before we shake an' call it a draw," concluded Roberts in sonorous elation. "It concerns our new hand, Wing Field, of the Tonto. . . . Wing, what's yore stand?"

"I stand by Bonesteel."

"You're new out here. Thet's why our first job depends on you. It's the biggest I ever planned. An' tough for you!"

"Aw, I'm game for anythin'."

14

□

BONESTEEL HAD subtly changed during the day. With the die cast he had lost his somber pondering. It struck Kent that he avoided Lucy, an occurrence to which she was blind. Her mind was full of her meeting with Kent. But Kent read the meaning of Bonesteel's quick step, his intent eye, his thoughtful brow, his closed lips. If Roberts had not revealed the plan for the great job he had acclaimed he had at least fired the chief with his keen daring enthusiasm. In that dark rustler's brain there had evolved a project too great for him alone, hence his eagerness to propitiate Bonesteel and win him over.

Kent's one glimpse at the outlaw camp, just before dusk, recorded the unusual spectacle of Bonesteel and Roberts walking off together, their heads close.

"Hell! The fire's out!" muttered Kent. "I'll be roped into some dirty deal pronto. . . . By heaven I'll try Lucy once more!"

This time he meant to be unmerciful and relentless.

The nighthawks were whistling overhead; the canyon owls to-whit-to-whooed; the river voiced its low sullen roar at the confining walls. Somewhere far away real thunder rumbled. The dusk was thick, warm, sweet-scented and full of the lonely haunting glamour that seemed peculiarly to belong to this deep secret canyon. How many dusks had fallen under those walls! It was a place where the sculpturing of time manifested itself grandly, where towering monuments had been left to the ages.

Shadows of specters of the past attended Kent Wingfield as he stole out to keep tryst with the daughter of the outlaw. There might have been a romance of lovers in that canyon before Lucy's and his, but he doubted it had had the anguish of theirs. Indian brave and maiden might have sung their songs of love and told the legends of their clans under the ancient walls. Cliff-dwellers and cavemen surely had fought and died there. And the primitives who had first peopled these caverns of the canyons had felt the mystic mantle of the melancholy dusk, had seen the bold and mighty walls sheer up into the star-vaulted sky.

It all made Kent sad. These things were eternal so far as the age of man was concerned. They were indifferent, though by their very nature they made his life crueler and shorter. The actual situation presented to Kent that hour was almost insupportable.

He found the fence of peeled poles and heard Lucy's low whistle before he saw her dark form perched upon the topmost bar of a gate. She had seen him first. He hurried a little.

"Why, Kent!" she whispered, as he, in excess of emotion wrapped his arms round her, and dropped his head in her lap. It was almost too much—to meet her there in the dusk, to know beyond any doubt that she was one girl in a million, that she loved him—and he had no idea how he could save himself, let alone her.

"You were troubled today," she whispered anxiously. "Forget it—and love me."

"Let's do the love-makin' last, if we have heart enough for it;" he said, almost bitterly, raising his head. "Lucy, how do you keep your hopes up?"

"Kent Wingfield, I have grown ten years older since Father came home. I have begun to realize what life is— life for us as lovers—and life for these outlaws. It has been like heaven to be with you—when we were alone here. It is hell now. . . . I have been trying to hide it from you, because I did not want to make your burden heavier."

161

"You know then I'm in danger?"

"Indeed I do. Jeff told me. He said: 'Lass, thet boy is likeable. But don't let yoreself like him too much.' He wouldn't tell me why, but I know."

"Jeff is a decent fellow. Your father is hard as flint. Roberts is callous. . . . Lucy, they have joined forces."

"Kent! —Oh, you don't mean Dad has taken Roberts into his outfit?"

"He has. I saw them shake hands on it. Couldn't you tell tonight from the way your father looked and acted?"

"It meant little to me. Dad is always like that just before he leaves on one of his trips."

"No wonder. To leave you an' this beautiful refuge—to ride out to steal an' kill."

"Oh, Kent, don't say that. To run off cattle, perhaps. They all do that. But not—to kill."

"I said steal an' kill," repeated Kent. "Your father knows dead men tell no tales. He must hide his tracks. When a man leads a double life, plays honest rancher while he's the greatest cattle thief in Utah, he has to have a bad outfit an' to shoot."

"I—can't believe—you," she cried, almost sobbing. "If I—knew that—to be true—"

"What would you do?"

"I'd hate him. I'd almost kill him!"

"Why don't you find out, if you won't believe me?"

"How can I?"

"Spy on him. Stay up at night, instead of goin' to bed. You're like a cat in the dark. Slip up on them an' listen. You'll find out pronto. They're hatchin' some bad eggs, Lucy. They've got somethin' big on. Roberts has a thunderin' hand up his sleeve. An' he's goin' to play it. . . . They've elected me for the tough part, which I'll bet is to ride to some great Mormon ranch, get a job as a rider, an' at the right time, say on a night watch, to kill the other riders so Roberts an' Bonesteel an' their men can swoop down an' run off a thousand head of cattle or more. Those Utah ranges are big. The steal might not be found out for weeks. An' that's always too late. . . . Yep, I'm elected, Lucy."

"How do you know?" she gasped.

162

"Roberts asked me my stand. I told him I stood by your father. An' I had to say I was game for anythin'."

"But you didn't mean it."

"I reckon I had to. Lucy, these outlaws actually believe I'm a notorious desperado from the Tonto. Both leaders welcomed me into their outfits. If they knew I was honest —they'd shoot me in the back. What has saved me here is my quickness with a gun, an' then a reputation a lot of which I invented an' that liar Bunge exaggerated to save his own hide. . . . I've got to live up to it!"

"Kent, you intend to go out on this raid?"

"I had to promise."

"You'll never go. I won't let you."

Kent laughed in sorrowful bitterness. "Poor kid! It's the thought of you that makes me miserable. Are you any better off for my comin'?"

"You ask that? Oh, Kent! You have given me love."

"Yes. An' sufferin', too."

"I used to love Dad, and Bill and Jeff—my horses— pets, all without suffering. That came with you. All the rest was childish. . . . Kent, I'll save you—if—if I have to kill—"

"Hush, child! —For God's sake, you couldn't kill your own father."

"How could I? —Yet—" she replied strangely, her great eyes like the caverns of the canyon. She was learning the rage and passion of a woman's heart. Kent realized that he had been slow to realize the inherent strength in this girl. "What's the use of being a woman—if you can't stop men," she concluded as if to herself.

"Women never stop men. They make them go on— lovin', hatin', sufferin', fightin', dyin'."

"Then they're no good. . . . Kent, you'd steal for me?"

"Yes."

"You'd kill for me?"

"I'd do anythin'," he said helplessly.

"Then I ought to do the same for you. . . . I would steal from Dad. I could murder Roberts in his sleep. I could—"

"Run off with me!" he whispered passionately. "That'd save us both."

163

She slipped off the fence into his arms and hung there until she found the lowest bar with her feet. Then she clung to him, yet appeared to be fighting him at the same time.

"I—can't. . . . I daren't."

"You love your father better than you do me."

"Yes. . . . No! It's tearing me apart . . . but this is—*home*. Could any other place be home to me? . . . And the people—the world I've never seen—thought of it terrifies me."

"People would never know you as Bonesteel's daughter —as a rustler's child. An' the world outside is beautiful— some places as beautiful as this, an' more so. Only different. Lucy, my darlin'—I beg you."

"No!"

"Not to save me from bein' a low-down thief—a murderer of honest men whom I have no call, no right, to meet with guns?"

"*No!*—I'd hate that more than I could hate anything else, except my father. . . . I'd fight to keep you from it. But if I couldn't—I'd still have you—here for long weeks and months—to love me!"

"You will not, Lucy Bonesteel," he flashed passionately, thrusting his face close to hers, white and convulsed in the starlight. "So after all, you *are* your father's daughter. You'd have me be an outlaw rather than lose me? You think the love of a degraded man here would be preferable to that of an honest man out there in the world?—All right, Lucy Bonesteel, you won't get either."

"*Kent!*"

"I'll get out of here tomorrow if I have to walk over the rocks."

"*No! No!—No!*"

"Yes—by God! . . ."

"Kent! —You'd—leave me?" she wailed as if crucified.

"I am leavin' you."

"But how could you—after teaching me love?" she implored. "I was happy. I didn't know my father's infamy. *What*—I—am!".

"I don't care. I'm goin'."

"It will kill me!"

"I hope to God it does. That'd save you from becomin' a slut for Roberts or one of his kind."

"A slut! . . . You could let me? After all you have said —you could abandon me here—to be fought over by these beasts of outlaws?"

Kent broke under that. His pretense of fury could not hold up. He snatched her off the fence to his breast and leaned his face against her hair. If then she had already become what she prophesied he could not have left her. The preciousness of her was heart-rending.

"No, Lucy!—No darlin', I couldn't abandon you," he cried brokenly. "I will stay. . . . Let them do their cursed worst!—I can always kill you—an' myself."

She lifted her arms round his neck. "My love!" she sobbed. "You almost—broke my heart. . . . You must not kill me—or yourself."

Kent Wingfield, with his life depending on the turn of a card for time, and for any break which might come his way—a fight between the two outlaw factions which might eliminate some of the dangerous men with whom he would sooner or later have to cope; or an opportunity to tell Bonesteel the truth and convince him of the hazard to Lucy as long as Roberts and the others remained in the Hole, or even alive for that matter. Neither seemed a likely prospect along with the outlaw chief's present mood.

In the event he had to leave with them, he planned to turn back the first night out, swim his horse back across the river and take Lucy by force if necessary. They could get such a lead on Bonesteel and Roberts they would be hard to catch. This would have to be a calculated risk, as would the problem of outwitting Jeff or, failing that, crippling or killing him which he wanted to avoid. And Lucy herself would be a problem with time being such a factor.

Late the morning of the third day Bonesteel led the chosen of his confidence back away from the cabins for a final colloquy.

He chose the structure where the alfalfa was kept dry —a large open-sided, wide-roofed shelter where danger-

165

ous interruption or discovery seemed apparently impossible. They might be seen by the other outlaws, but not heard.

Kent knew that Bonesteel had of late developed an extremely nervous apprehension in regard to Lucy. She had disobeyed him twice to approach him while he was with Roberts. These brief moments, nevertheless, afforded ample opportunity for the rustler to see Lucy in all her alluring charm. Kent had more than once caught a leaping look in that outlaw's eyes which he would have given years out of his life to extinguish.

Bonesteel led round on the far side of the big mound of alfalfa, which stood in the center of the roofed space. It was a shady, dry, odorous place, well suited for rest and talk.

"Reckon you better not smoke," said Bonesteel. "Some of this hay is old and would burn like tinder. . . . Sit down."

Roberts' right-hand man, Simms, was present, and the thin-lipped hard-eyed Westfall. Of Bonesteel's outfit there were Rigney and Kent. It occurred to Kent that both leaders had chosen their respective followers not alone for confidential reasons.

"Roberts," began Bonesteel, darkly forceful, "your plan to wait here alone without me won't do."

"Wal, an' why not?" asked the outlaw.

"Because it might take long for Wingfield to build up his part of it and for me to arrange for immediate disposal of so many cattle—both very important details to this raid."

"Suppose it does take long?" protested Roberts, just as forcefully as his rival. "The longer the better, up to late fall, jest before the snow flies on the Sevier range."

"I wouldn't leave you here alone."

"Alone? I'd have my outfit an' some of yore's, all ready to go off at half-cock. I agree to see there's no drinkin', no quarrelin'."

"You didn't strike me as thick-headed," returned Bonesteel impatiently. "I wouldn't choose to allow you to stay here—with my daughter."

"Aw!—So thet's it?"

"I've seen your interest in Lucy. Do you deny it?"

"Hell, no! I'd like to marry her," replied the outlaw frankly.

"No doubt. That has happened before. It doesn't reflect upon you, but is simply impossible."

"Thet girl will have to marry somebody, an' it ain't likely he'll be what you might have been once, Avil Bonesteel. If she doesn't marry— Wal, somebody will take her anyway. An' seein' she's such a nice, modest lass —thet ain't so good."

"I'll take care of my daughter," returned Bonesteel. "Now let's get back on the main issue."

"Jest a minute or I might get my back up," said Roberts in slow, cool deliberation. "How long do you reckon it'll be till somebody tells this kid of yore's thet you've got another woman an' another name over there in Utah?"

Kent saw two things then—the leap of murder in Bonesteel's steel-gray eyes and in his rival's gaze the knowledge and the will to prevent it.

"What do you know about that?" demanded Bonesteel hoarsely, his face the hue of ashes.

"Wal, I've heerd range talk thet didn't mean much till I got here an' put two an' two together. Then I guessed the facts. An' I reckon, Bonesteel, thet the last thing you want is to hev yore girl find thet out about yore double-crossin' her. I don't know yet exactly *who* you are, but fer a thief, a robber, a secret bloody chief of a killin' outfit, you can't be beat in all Utah."

"Yes, it is—the last thing I'd want Lucy to find out," replied Bonesteel, the shaking of his iron nerve betrayed in his voice.

"Wal, I wouldn't hold thet over yore head. I'm not low-down enough fer thet. I'm jest pointin' out thet somebody will tell her. It's the way things happen."

Bonesteel's haggard visage attested to a long, long fear of that very thing happening.

"What is more—in the nature of events this Hole in the Wall will be found out. They come to the end of their ropes, Bonesteel, sometimes in nooses."

"That's enough, Roberts. Do we go on with our plans?"

"Why shore. We might as wal, seein' thet I hev to go on till I get bored, an' so do you."

"Very well, then. Since you respect me as chief, go on with details of your plan, such as you outlined to me. I've told Rigney the general idea. He likes it. But Wing here, upon whom so much depends, knows nothing yet."

"Wal, here goes," rejoined Roberts. "As I said, it's in the Sevier valley. Thar's a cattle baron who's runnin' I'd guess twenty thousand head over a wide range. His name is Casell. He's such a skinflint thet he has never more'n half a dozen riders to his name. He keeps them till they holler fer their wages an' then he lets them go. He'd hire any rider thet come along. Wal, we'll mosey up there an' locate in some wild hidin' place while Wing here goes an' gets on with Casell. He'll learn the lay of the range. I know enough already, but some more won't hurt. Casell's stock ranges low along in the fall an' before the snow flies it'll be fifty miles an' more from his ranch, an' farther'n thet from any settlement. Now, believe it or not, half of Casell's cattle heven't any brand at all. We can cut out as many head as you think you can market an' we can take our time about thet. Wing's job is to do away with the riders, or if there happens to be more'n two or three he'll signal to us when the time's ripe, an' we'll ride over an' help along. It's no job fer inexperienced hands an' it'll have all Utah by the ears. It's a cold proposition an' pretty dirty—or I should say bloody. But thet's the easy an' the safe way. The weakness of my outfit was lack of market fer so many cattle. . . . All right, we'll drive thet herd out of the valley without bein' seen. We can gamble on thet. It'll be weeks an' mebbe months before any of Casell's riders would be expected in. An' meanwhile we'll hev the herd travelin' ten miles an' more a day. Once down out of thet high valley we'll be workin' toward the breaks of the canyon country, where we can head to the south or west, accordin' to what range Bonesteel has his market."

"West. To the sage flats under Trumbull Mountain," added the chief.

"West? Trumbull?—Thet's not so lonesome as some other parts of Utah. We've rode some of thet country. Big outfits—the Utah Cattle Company—the Double XX Bar outfit—an' Cheney. You've heard of Cheney. Hell on rustlers. He drives big herds to St. George an' Nevada. Mormons against him. Reckon he's Gentile. But he undersells them."

"*I* am Cheney," said Bonesteel.

"*Wha—att!* —So that's it! You Luce Cheney? ... An' Bonesteel, too?"

"Yes, Roberts. And that must be your secret now. I'll bind you all with blood oaths."

"Gawd! ... Fellars, don't hit me with a feather. — Chief, which name is yore right one?"

"That's no matter. Let's—"

"But yore girl's name is Lucy Bonesteel—not Cheney."

The chief waved his rival's curiosity aside as irrelevant and annoying.

"Roberts, the plan is tremendous," went on Bonesteel. "Simms, you an' Harvey declare yourselves."

"Wal, I put the idee in Ney's head," replied Simms nonchalantly.

"Great. Only one weak spot. Thet's killin' Casell's riders," said Harvey.

Bonesteel turned last to Kent.

"Wing, he's put his finger on the spot. What do you say?"

"That's no weak spot," returned Kent, meeting the chief's scintillating glance, and veering from that to the hard eager eyes of the others. "Leastways it doesn't faze me."

"Thar's yore Tonto rider!" ejaculated Roberts in elated admiration.

"Done! Settled!" flashed Bonesteel, his dark face lighting. "We leave tomorrow. ... All right, Roberts, Wing, all of you—it's a deal."

The outlaws stood up to face each other, each in his own way expressing the dark potency of what that fateful deal meant to him.

At this juncture a quick rustle of hay sounded from the

top of the alfalfa mound. Kent smelled dry dust in his nostrils. An awful fear contracted his heart.

"Dad," came Lucy's voice in clear treble, like ice on metal. "If you're through now, I'll have my say!"

Kent saw the girl rising on hands and knees from the top of the mound where she had been hidden. Her face was pearl in its pallor and her eyes magnificent fires. She whirled to slide down, her skirt above bare shapely legs, and she landed upon her feet, upright against the mound.

"Oh God!" Bonesteel staggered back mortally stricken, his dark mask of avarice and passion fallen. Kent did not recognize that quivering visage. If he had never pitied Bonesteel he did then.

"Wal, chief, as you 'pear to be in fer a family ruckus we'll take ourselves off," said Roberts with a derisive grin, and he stalked away followed by the three outlaws. Kent, too, would have left but for Lucy's detaining hand.

"I heard it—all," cried Lucy, her breast heaving as if to burst.

Bonesteel fell upon the seat from which he had just arisen, and he covered his face with the action of a man who attempted to hide something hideous. In that bowed head, its silver tawny hair disheveled, Kent read the appalling despair of guilt, of unforgivable truth before the daughter he loved and whom he had tried so desperately to keep innocent and ignorant, all to no avail.

"Your secret!—The mystery of your Hole in the Wall!" went on the bitingly terrible voice, youthful, relentless, inexorable. "Your secret!—All told. . . . My father—a liar—a cheat—a thief—a murderer—a plotter with outlaws as vile as you! My father—Luce Cheney! . . . *Who and what am I?* . . . You hid me here. You kept me here. You had me taught, guarded, brought up like a decent girl whose father—mother were good. You kept me from the unclean hands of men. For mercy's sake why? . . . All for this. This hateful hour when I *see*, I *hear* the truth of your crookedness. . . . Oh, my *father*!—I worshiped you. I had no one else. I was born to love. . . . And now? I hate you! I loathe you!"

Bonesteel arose as one flayed upon his raw flesh, to

170

whom inaction had grown unendurable. He looked his debasement.

"Enough. . . . Lucy, I was what I am—before you were born. I loved your mother. I married her—brought her here to keep her from finding me out. When she did find out—it killed her. I kept on. . . . And before I knew life passed so swiftly—you were a girl—as you are now a woman. There's no—more to say."

"There is. This plot I overheard. This terrible thing you would set Kent Wingfield to do. . . . He is no thief, no rustler, no outlaw. He is an honest man whose gun had to be ready. . . . He has fooled you. Old Bill Elway sent him here. . . . To rescue me!"

"Hell's fire!" raged Bonesteel, whipping out his gun with the nature of his curse in his lightning eyes. "Wingfield, is she crazy?"

"It's true, chief. An' God knows I'm glad to confess," replied Kent.

"I'll kill you," hissed Bonesteel, but quick as he was Lucy was quicker to leap in front of Kent.

"Kill me! Let your murdering bullet go through my heart first. . . . I love this man. I met him the very first day he got here. I took him food—back into the canyon where he hid. And we were together there—day after day. . . . Father, a proof of Kent Wingfield's honesty and honor is here—for any man to believe. I was a child in mind—a woman in body. And he said beautiful!—I loved him as if my heart had been damned to love. But I knew nothing of love and life. I wanted him to marry me himself. But he would not take me that way. When you came it changed all. He had to pretend to be on the dodge, a hunted man. Always he begged me to go away —to run off with him. And I never would. I wouldn't leave you. I never, never deep in my heart could have believed what you are—until I heard you prove it."

Bonesteel sheathed his gun with palsied hand, which then plucked at Lucy, to drag her from Kent. But she only whirled to encircle him with protecting arms.

"Kent—is she mad?" he demanded huskily.

"Bonesteel, she's mad indeed with grief. . . . With grief an' love an' fear," burst out Kent tragically. "But what

171

she says about me is true—as true as what you must have felt for Lucy's mother. . . . Bonesteel, I'm on the square. Old Elway told me of Lucy. The story inflamed me—called to good I didn't know I had in me.—You must believe! I can't prove it here. If you'd go with us to Arizona—"

"So help me!" Bonesteel struck his forehead as if a light had illumined his murky brain. "Girl, you've saved my soul—if not my life!"

"Oh—father!" she faltered, weakening when her woman's steel and fire had wrought this miracle.

"Lucy, run to your cabin and bar yourself in," ordered Bonesteel. "Leave Kent with me."

She wavered, lost between hope and dread.

"Go!" he commanded, with nameless emotion piercing his stern authority. "Stay in your cabin until Kent comes for you. . . . Go! It's the last time you will ever obey me . . . the last—time. . . ."

Lucy fled with an anguished cry of divination.

15

◘

"SOONER THE better! I'll gamble on surprise," Bonesteel breathed hard through his teeth, and cracked his fist into the mound. The greatest decision of his life ended in that gesture.

"Come, Kent," he called, stalking forth. "Walk slow while I think."

Kent felt a tremendous intensity in the man. They walked by the corrals, the sheds, along the pasture fence until they reached the cottonwoods. With the cabins in plain sight Bonesteel walked slower, halting at length by the woodpile adjacent to the porch that connected Jeff's cabin with the first empty one.

"Kent," he said suddenly, "you planned taking Lucy away the first chance that offered!" It was not a question, but a statement of fact.

"Y-yes!" stuttered Kent in his eagerness.

"You know where the waterfall leaps off the flat cliff into a pool!"

"Yes. Lucy and I spent many a day there." ·

"You ride under the fall—not through it," went on Bonesteel, his brow corded, his eyes like gold balls. "Once you are under it you see light. There's a hole through there, cut by an underground stream ages ago. It leads to a side canyon blocked off from the Hole by slides. My secret begins there. It leads over the rocks in and out, up and down. It never touches the old Piute trail that comes down above here to the ford of the Colorado, until you reach the San Juan. It comes out below—a bad place to get down. But Spades can make it. And my horse, Clubfoot, will lead you. Follow him no matter where he goes. For that will be the way out. You couldn't find it. There really is no trail . . . Are you marking all this down not to forget?"

"I am, Bonesteel. Go on."

"Spades and Clubfoot will be there tonight, early or late. That doesn't matter because you have to wait till dawn. But you must not leave the cabin until after dark. Some of these outlaws might be left to see you. . . . You will find the horses there. Clubfoot will have a pack of food, a blanket, a slicker. Spades will have a heavy pack, long, tied down to the saddle. This pack will contain gold and a wide belt full of paper money."

"Gold!—Money!" gasped Kent, revolting.

"A fortune. Some of it blood money—the fruit of a rustler's work—but most of it is money that I earned and saved long ago and hide here for safety. There will be no time, no way for me to tell you which is honest money and which is dishonest. Give half of it away if you'll feel better. No matter! There's enough. . . . You are to start rich—to make Lucy happy—to give her everything she has missed. . . . Are you marking that down?"

"In words of flame, Bonesteel."

"You accept it—with her?"

"Yes."

"You love her. I see that, thank God whom I failed."

"Love her!—Bonesteel, I was ready to give my life for Lucy, or live it as you have lived yours."

"No need now. She is young. She will outgrow the—the . . . She will be such a woman as the sun shines on but seldom."

"Bonesteel, she is your blood. She may not go willingly. For weeks I tried to persuade her. She might—"

"You must make her go. But don't fear that. I will be dead in reality, or failing that—dead to her. Because you are to tell her that I was killed in the fight I'll start soon."

"Ahuh. I see," replied Kent somberly. The man was great in his extremity.

"Let's find Jeff. He's one man I can rely on. He will be glad to help Lucy."

"Wait—Bonesteel. . . . You mean to fight it out with Roberts! Alone against that bunch! You'd never make it. You could put him off if you couldn't drive him away. Tell him you crawfished on the big Casell job. Then go with Lucy and me."

"I'll kill him," returned Bonesteel implacably. "I have one single chance. . . . None if he or Simms or Harvey are alive."

The outlaw's mind was revolving round his dual nature, the other self, the respectable Cheney and another woman that had come into his life to make it worth a battle to the finish.

"What am I supposed to do?" queried Kent.

"Watch your chance to sneak out the things you need. In a coat. Or a bundle of clothing to wash. Take these to Jeff. For the rest stick in your room—keep Lucy in hers till dark. That's all."

"Funny deal you're givin' me. You hand me a fortune —an' more a million times than that—Lucy—sure a treasure beyond all the gold that was ever mined. An' you expect me to see you face that outfit alone!"

"Not alone. Rigney, Kitsap, Forman, Harkaway, possibly Goins, all will fight for me."

"Not Goins. An' maybe not Harkaway."

"We shall see. . . . Kent, your duty is not to stand by me. But Lucy! All depends on you."

"Sure. I get that. Nevertheless it's the damndest deal. I don't like it. I can take care of Lucy an' still help you. I would know what Roberts an' his outfit couldn't guess in time. All the difference in the world, Bonesteel!"

"Right. But you might be killed—and probably would be wounded. Not to be thought of! . . . The answer is NO!" Bonesteel's edict, as far as he was concerned, was final. "Come. Let's brace Jeff." They found the cook in the kitchen, idle for once, his wrinkled face wearing a grim cast.

"Talk low," whispered Bonesteel, bending over the table. "Jeff, I've got a bag of gold hid in there for you."

"Boss, I'll do it fer nothin'," he said. "Save yore breath aboot what's gone on hyar. I know. . . . What do you want me to do?"

"Pack some bread, cooked meat, dried fruit, a canteen of milk, some salt—you know what. A blanket and a slicker. Watch your chance to sneak this pack out to the barn. Meanwhile I will make a pack myself—a heavy one —all you can carry. This you will put in a bag. If it looks like a bag of corn well and good. But don't be seen. When the row starts out here you rustle to saddle Spades and Clubfoot. Put the heavy pack on Spades—the light one on Clubfoot. Lead them out behind the corrals into the brush, and around and up to the waterfall. Slip saddles and packs there. Tie the horses. Then you might get back here in time to be of further use to me."

"Go slow, boss, an' I shore will be hyar. I'm sayin' this is the happiest job you ever give me. As fer you, young fellar, if I hadn't savvied you long ago—you'd hev been deader'n a doornail."

"Enough. Rustle now."

Kent, with his creed learned on the range and inviolable even for love, tried again to protest, but the rustler chief, obsessed with his desperate idea, shoved Kent back and entered his cabin, to close and bar the door. Kent had no recourse but to do likewise with his.

Then his next move was to spy upon the outlaws. They were all out there, sprawled on the grass or lounging on their beds, smoking and talking. Several were squatting like Indians, playing cards. The absence in most of them of that tenseness which Kent easily read in Roberts and his two lieutenants proclaimed that they had not yet disclosed the plot. There was something else on Roberts' mind. And Kent's intuition grasped that to be Lucy Bonesteel.

Spreading his coat on the couch Kent packed in the capacious pockets all that he could pack of his personal belongings. He chose and discarded, replaced one with another until he was satisfied that he had all of the indispensable things and a few he might have done without.

That was the extent of his preparation for the flight. He faced the door, listened for Bonesteel's footsteps, peeped again upon the outlaw group. The moments seemed interminable, but he knew they were passing. Bonesteel would hurry, consistent with caution. It would not be long now. He swallowed to relieve a constriction in his throat, which returned again and again. Dared he whisper to Lucy—prepare her for the uproar soon to split the morning calm? No! He needed his nerve—his wits— to think more—to decide. What? He thought all decisions had been made for him. He paced to and fro until he sweat. Bonesteel should hurry, he was losing precious time. At last Kent lifted the bar and shoved his door out a very little. He was just in time to see Jeff, shouldering a burden that made him sag, pass out of sight beyond the last cabin. And at the same moment Bonesteel backed out of his door, showing the butt of a gun protruding from his hip pocket. An extra gun!

Kent swept his door open, and taking up his rifle, which leaned against the wall, he stepped outside to meet Bonesteel's piercing eyes. Only the chief's glance betrayed his passion. He looked careless and at ease; he had a cigar in his mouth.

"—— —— you! Go back!" he cursed in an undertone.

"Ump-umm. I'm goin' out to hunt skunks," replied Kent.

The chief recognized the futility of changing his young ally, and time was precious.

"When I open up jump for cover," he hissed with a concentration of mingled passions that was hypnotic. Then he walked to the porch steps and leisurely turned to look back, while he puffed at his cigar. Kent joined him there, lifting the rifle to his left shoulder, after the manner of hunters.

"By the way, boy, Lucy's real name is Bonesteel. That name ends when she takes yours."

What a magnificent actor he was in that vital moment! Kent's spirit leaped to match him, if that were possible. Bonesteel seemed relaxed, almost gay, as they walked toward the outlaws. He talked, but Kent never caught the sense of his words. It was no accident that Kent stopped beside the great cottonwood.

"I raise you two bits," Bunge was saying.

"Call," replied Goins.

"Whar you goin' with the long gun?" asked Roberts genially. In the last minute of his life of acumen he was deceived.

"Reckon I gotta brush up on distance shootin'," replied Kent.

Fate had jockeyed that line-up, in favor of the chief. His men, excepting Goins, sat somewhat to the right. Roberts sat at the left, with Simms and Harvey a little back and close together. Westfall was on his knees, digging into a pack, and the other two outlaws were beyond, one asleep and the other smoking.

"Roberts, have you sprung our little deal on the gang?" inquired Bonesteel with the faintest of icy edges on his voice.

"Nope. I left thet fer you. Reckon'd you'll celebrate it with a party."

"You read my mind.... But I'll ask a question first.... *Goins!*"

The outlaw named almost jumped out of his skin, and all the others suddenly went stiff.

"What you want—boss?" stupidly queried Goins, batting his eyes, as he slowly got up, the cards falling from his hand.

"If Roberts and I split whose side are you on?"

"*If* you split?" returned the outlaw gropingly. His instinct sensed catastrophe, but his wit seemed checked.

"Goins, I know, but I wanted to see if you had the guts to come clean with it."

"Wal, if you know so damn shore let it go at thet," replied Goins sullenly.

Bonesteel's gun leaped and cracked. He shot the outlaw through the heart. Goins expelled a whistling breath and fell soddenly, to quiver on the grass. Surprise succeeded to paralyzed shock. The thing Bonesteel had gambled all on manifested itself.

"Aw! You—killed him!" rasped out Roberts haltingly.

"Yes."

"Fer Gawd's sake, man! . . . What fer—when we hevn't split?"

"But we have split, Roberts!" yelled Bonesteel, releasing a passion that rang hate throughout the grove.

Roberts' reaction was instantaneous. Up he sprang with a deadly shout and his hand clapped low for his gun. It was not there. In the heat of the warm day he had left off his belt, transferring his gun to his hip pocket. As he corrected the error and jerked at the gun, Bonesteel ended his action, his flashing malignance. Roberts fell sheer back upon Simms who was heaving up with strident yell, his gun out.

Kent killed Simms on his feet and in a flash swerved his gun upon Harvey who was shooting from his hip. He ducked behind the cottonwood, and as he turned Bonesteel fell flat, knocked down by a bullet. Then a crash of guns and a chorus of curses filled the grove. Bunge fell face down upon the cards on the tarpaulin. Bonesteel jumped up, a gun in each hand, to bound behind another cottonwood. Smoke obscured Kent's gaze. Through it he aimed at Westfall, who on the instant threw up his gun and fell.

The concerted crash of guns ceased as suddenly as it had begun. The hoarse yells thinned out.

"Thar they go, Kit—over the bank!" bawled a man to Kent's right.

"Head 'em off!"

"They're makin' fer the boat."

"Look out!—Harvey is up!"

Crash! Bonesteel's guns boomed again. Kent looked up from the other side of the tree to see Harvey, shot, wobble and sink in his tracks.

"Hold chief!" warned Kent piercingly.

"Give me—that rifle," panted Bonesteel, as he rushed over to Kent, bloody in his lust to kill.

"Sure. But wait, man," cried Kent, getting an iron grip on the chief.

"Some of them—run for boat."

"I saw. They might plug you from cover. No rush, Bonesteel."

"They must—never get away."

"They can't. . . . There goes Kitsap."

Shots from the river shore spanged out and bullets pattered through the willows.

"Hey, boss," bawled Kitsap. "They're after the boat. Fetch that rifle."

Bonesteel snatched it from Kent and plunged away under the trees, keeping from the bank of willows. Then Kent surveyed the ground in front. Roberts lay still. Harvey's body had the grotesque hideousness of a terrible muscular frenzy stiffened in death. Westfall had come in, instead of retreating, and lay stretched face down, a gun in each hand. Kent's estimate of that outlaw had been correct. Bunge lay ghastly beside the limp Goins. Forman, too, was dead. The last man was Rigney, alive, trying to sit up. Kent ran to his side.

"Are you bad hurt, old man?" asked Kent, lifting him.

"Bad enough, Wing, but not—too bad," choked Rigney.

"Where?"

"It's my groin."

"Anywhere else?"

"Not thet I feel. But it hurts so —— —— bad I can't —feel nothin' else. . . . Did the boss cash?"

"No. He ran with Kitsap to stop some of them."

"Say, it was short an' sweet! You gotta pat the chief— on the back. Wasn't he mad? . . . Thet Westfall killed Forman an' Bunge, an' damn near did fer me. If Simms had got to shootin' we'd all been done fer, 'cept mebbe you. . . . Wing, you bored him an' Harvey. Thet's what saved the boss. Reckon he was gamblin' on thet—or he wouldn't hev braced Roberts' outfit. . . . What's thet?"

"More shootin'. . . . I hear the squeakin' of oars. They're in the boat."

"Run out there, Wing. But keep behind somethin'.".

Kent hurried to the right, from tree to tree, across the road, and then down the bank, to keep behind the willows until hoarse yells on the shore told him where to cut in. He came out upon the sandy beach below where it ended in the rocky ledge. Kitsap was kneeling on the sand loading his gun with a bloody hand. Bonesteel stood high on the rocks with rifle leveled. On the moment a gun spanged and a heavy bullet struck the water close to shore and went plock! into the bank.

Then out on the river Kent saw the boat. Two outlaws were in it, one of whom knelt low in the stern with his gun extended. The other was frantically rowing. They had gotten several hundred feet away. Again the rifle cracked. And the man in the stern lurched half up, to fall out of sight into the boat.

"Thet was Harkaway, boss," called Kitsap. "Bore the other one. . . . Take yore time an' shoot high."

Bonesteel scarcely heeded the advice. He shot and worked the lever of the Winchester—again and yet again. The third bullet brought a shriek from the outlaw, whose right arm flopped, losing the oar. It floated away on the swift current. The doomed man hauled on the other oar, only to turn the boat downstream. Then he ceased to struggle and yelled for help. There was none, even if mercy had awakened in the rustler chief. The boat he had hated sped on into the middle of the river, on into the swifter current.

"No use in him yellin'," said Kitsap. "The old river's got him."

They watched the craft speed on the current, the outlaw's appalling cry soon drowned in the sullen greedy thunder of the rapids below, until its bobbing hulk, its single upflinging arm, vanished round a bold corner of wall.

180

Bonesteel turned away, remorseless, and grand in his triumph. The whole front of his shirt on the right side flapped wet and darkly red.

"Bonesteel! You're shot!—Let me see," cried Kent.

"Hell. I'm not—shot," panted the chief, swaying, yet keeping his feet. "It's nothing—a scratch.... Not from Roberts' gun!—Son, did they hit you?"

"No. I ducked in time."

"How about Simms—Harvey—Westfall?"

"Dead."

"And my—men?"

"Rigney's bad hurt, but will recover.... The rest are dead, Bonesteel ... gone!"

"Jeff?"

"He hadn't time to come back. It all happened too fast."

"Ah!—It's over—better than I'd dared to hope.... Kent, go back. Do what you can for Rigney— till Jeff comes. I'll stay here with Kit.... Tell Lucy I'm dead.... Drag her away! ... May you—always be—as happy—as I am—this moment!"

16

◘

KENT WAS impelled to rush immediately to Lucy but the lie he had promised to tell held him back. How long she would remain in her cabin he could only guess. When he called Jeff to help him bury the dead outlaws it was in a voice loud enough to be heard across the river. Lucy certainly knew he was alive. Surely she must wonder about her father. While he labored, Kent kept watch on her doorway; but Lucy made no appearance. Had her love for the outlaw chief turned entirely to hate?

The afternoon waned with a thickening of the atmosphere, the ominous darkening of the sky, the muttering rumble of thunder presaging a late storm.

Once finished with the grim task, Kent made haste to remove the blood and red earth stains from his grimy hands. His rifle leaned against the cabin door where Jeff had brought it. Kitsap was with Rigney. Bonesteel had hidden himself well until Kent and Lucy should leave. The magic hour of deliverance had struck.

Kent reloaded the Winchester and put on his coat which would have to carry the few items he was taking. He had decided on the trail over the rocks even though it might now be safe to go around the wall through the river. He remembered the Piutes. Perhaps that part of Bunge's story had been true. Interception on the rougher trail would be less likely.

Then, gritting his teeth he went to Lucy's door and called.

"Lucy, I must come in."

"Oh, come—come!" she pleaded.

With a powerful shove he swept back the heavy door leading into her room. In the dim light he made out objects of furniture, at last a couch where Lucy lay.

"All—in the—dark," he said unsteadily, and strode to throw open her outside door. The sun had set gold and red and purple. A marvelous veil of color enveloped the canyon. Lucy's room lightened to disclose her lying spent and white, with haunting terrible eyes he dared not yet to meet. Kneeling beside her, with strong hands seeking hers, he said huskily:

"Lucy—it's over!"

"Oh, Kent! . . . You are safe—unhurt?"

"Yes. My luck held. . . . It seemed like a short fight. But bloody!"

"I heard—all the shooting. I thought it would never end. I grew old—waiting for your step. . . . My—dad?"

"Aw Lucy! —I'm . . . It's bad news. Brace yourself. He's gone, child—gone!" whispered Kent, lowering his head.

"It didn't seem like that. . . . I didn't feel it. . . . Poor wicked distraught man! . . . Are all the others dead?"

"No. Not all. That—that's why we must leave pronto,"

said Kent, hating the falsehood. He kissed her pale tear-wet cheek. "Bonesteel told me where to find the trail. We'll go that way. Come Lucy. Take a few things you'll need, but quickly. Take your jeans, boots, gloves, sombrero—a coat. Oh! You'll need them pronto. It'll storm. I'll carry them. We must rustle, Lucy."

Kent's fears for her strength eased. With swift hands he took her bundle and the clothes she gave him and rolled them in a blanket. He tucked that under his arm and took up his rifle. With the fading of the afterglow dusk stole into the room. He went out calling low: "Come!" Silently she glided out, slim in the black coat, pulling her sombrero over her head. He had a glimpse of her face. Shifting his rifle into his left hand he took hers and led her down off the porch, out under the dark cottonwoods. She almost ran, so that he had to stride to keep up with her. The grove was gloomy, silent, brooding. Soon they were out in the open, crossing the gardens, into the sage. Darkness was coming on apace. Night had trooped out from under the walls. But overhead day still fought the gathering shades. Pale rifts of blue showed through the murky sinister clouds. From over the towers and domes pealed a menacing thunder, as if it was gathering the mighty forces of deluge. A strange rose-tinged glow, emanated from somewhere, lighting the sage and the scrawled rocks beyond. The great sentinel spires pierced the dusky canopy overhead.

Suddenly at the bridge over the brook a wild wolf form appeared. "Piute!" exclaimed Kent gladly, realizing he had not seen nor thought of the dog for days. Or was it just that hours had seemed as long as days?

"You old doggone Piute!" The dog whined and turned up the trail.

The dusky light lingered while Kent strode on behind Lucy and Piute, under the spruces and the isolated rocks, back into the aisles, and up the cedared steps to the grassy ledge under the waterfall.

Kent dropped his burdens and removed his heavy coat. Hot and wet he labored to get his breath.

"Spades!" cried the girl, breaking her silence in a note

of surprise and gladness. The horses were haltered in a glade back from the ledge.

"Sure—Spades," panted Kent. "Did you think—we could walk? . . . Sit down, Lucy. . . . This will be our last time in the old place."

Under the shelf of the cliff Kent found the saddles, from one of which the pack had been removed. He felt it with a hand not steady. Removing the other pack he untied the slicker and blanket to find a number of canvas bags. These contained food, carefully packed by one who knew bad trails.

"Lucy, we stay here until dawn. Will you eat somethin'?" asked Kent hopefully.

"I couldn't."

He did not insist, thinking it best to let her alone. He spread the saddle blankets beside her and then the other blankets upon them. After this task he gazed out upon the weird and darkening canyon with fixed eyes focused to limn forever on his memory the wonder and the grandeur of that Hole in the Wall.

The waterfall was so thin that he heard only the slightest of water sounds, a silken soft splashing, and a falling as of gentle rain. Sheet lightning glowed, creating the most spectacular and magnificent of canyon scenes. Now a wide flare would blaze along the ramparts of the walls, silhouetting them bold and black against the lightning; then another in another direction would illumine the inky sky behind the great towers and domes, crowned for an instant in silver fire. Thunder boomed, to roll down the river, under the walls, to bang and clap, and die away in almost endless echo.

Lucy crept to Kent presently and close in his arms, as if seeking protection, or something she had never had in her life; she wept away the bitter tension of her ordeal until, worn out, she fell asleep. He laid her upon the blankets, with Piute close by and paced the hours away in a sorrowful vigil that yet held thoughts of gratitude and joy. Gazing out upon that void of spectral shadows, listening to the thunder of the river rivaling the thunder of the storm, thinking of the hardened outlaws, dead, in their graves, and the strange man who had meted death to them, Kent could not credit his senses with authenticity. Yet when he passed close to Lucy, and gazed down upon that white face, he knew she was alive, that he had saved her, that through her he had worked out his destiny, had changed and grown incredibly. And in his heart he blessed old Bill Elway. There was good in these outlaws, in Bill, in Jeff, in Kitsap, and strangely true, in the dark and secret soul of Avil Bonesteel.

Toward dawn Kent wearied and dozed at intervals, until the east turned gray and lightened. Coyotes made the welkin ring with their piercing staccato cries. They heralded the day, and with that to Kent came the stern realities of a perilous unknown trail, of a desert river to cross, surely in flood from the rains at its headwaters, of a band of Piutes, a chief of whom he had evidently slain.

He built a fire, heated some meat, toasted some biscuits, and poured milk into one of the two cups. Then he stooped over Lucy to call her. Asleep, with worn stained face, and great dark shadows under her heavy lids, her golden-hair spread over his dark coat, her slender graceful form relaxed in all its alluring curves, she was beautiful in a way new to him, with a helplessness that curbed his yearning.

"Lucy." And as she stirred: "Lucy—the horses are here. Spades is ararin' to go!"

Her eyes opened wide. Kent had a fleeting glimpse into a realm he reverenced if he could not comprehend, and then the day, the time, the place leaped into her consciousness.

"Spades!—Oh, Kent, was I dreaming?—We are leaving—"

"You bet. Roll out, lazy, an' wash your dirty pretty face an' brush your rumpled hair. I'll saddle an' pack the horses. Then we'll eat an' hit that trail pronto. We've a long way to go."

Spades and Clubfoot were fat. Days of grazing on the rich grass below, with no exercise to work them out, had left their flanks thick.

"Well, hosses, you'll sure need all that fat when we hit the uplands an' the desert."

Kent had never seen Lucy's saddle and bridle until

then. They were of Mexican make, rich and black, with silver mountings, the finest trappings for a horse he had ever seen. If Lucy could ride what a picture she would make on that black horse—for the girls and boys of Wagontongue to marvel at. Ride! He wagered she could ride like a Piute.

"Hold your hosses, Wingfield," he soliloquized. "It's a long hard trail to Wagontongue."

He saddled the black, carefully. Then he turned to the pack, a nondescript sack, thin in the middle, thick at each end, with long leather thongs hanging from it. Kent lay hold of the sack. The effort scarcely budged it. "Heavens!" he muttered, aghast and thrilling. "Is it full of rocks?" Then he drew a deep breath, took strong hold, and heaved powerfully. He had all he could do to lift it upon Spades. Was it altogether the weight that made Kent sweat? Ponderingly and thrillingly he tied it securely, thinking the while that with Lucy's light weight added it would not be too much for a horse as big and strong as Spades.

He found Lucy gazing out upon the valley. Her posture was enough for Kent; he dared not look at her face.

"Come an' get it, Lucy," he called.

He ate like a rider who had far to go, and pressed the victuals upon Lucy without glancing up at her. Obediently she ate and drank in silence. Presently Kent turned to the bundle, to haul forth her jeans, boots, gloves.

"Climb out of that dress, honey, an' into these. We got a trail to ride—an' a river to cross. . . ."

Then he went to saddle Clubfoot. Upon his return Lucy was in her riding outfit, ready to start.

"We must be rustlin'. See, Piute thinks we ought to be on the go."

"Kent, don't ever say 'rustling' again," she asked softly, her head down.

"Eh?—Oh, sure. I won't ever, Lucy. . . . There, your little pack will go inside the big one, keepin' the slicker out."

Before Kent mounted he went around to the waterfall to take a look. The volume had so thinned out that he could see the mouth of a cavern on the far side. He had noticed this depression in the wall long ago, but had never felt curious enough to investigate. Here, practically under his nose all the time, had been the way out. He went in to find a tunnel, with dripping roof, leading back over rugged rocks to a distant hole where daylight entered.

"By gum, it would take an Indian to find this," muttered Kent, marveling. Then he hurried back, eager to get out of the canyon, as eager as he was sad.

Lucy was again gazing back into the valley. And it chanced, or Kent's emotion made it appear so that the transfiguration of sunrise greeted them with its loveliest effects. The river slid on as red as flame down into the black shades; the tips of the walls shone brightly; in the valley sunshine had not yet touched the soft mellow greens and browns, the grays of sage and gold of cottonwood; all lay wrapped in slumber down there, except the cavorting colts in the pasture. The great break in the walls resembled a jumbled avalanche, which it really was, a flowing down from the heights of splintered cliffs and weathered rock and ruined mountain, all greened and purpled over with cedar and spruce and manzanita, to tumble in a mosaic of cascades down to the sage.

"Oh! Oh! . . . *Oh!*" Lucy's cry would haunt Kent for many a year, perhaps forever. He looked no more, but called. And the crack of Spades' iron-shod hoofs told Kent she was coming. Clubfoot entered the tunnel as a horse turning into a lane he knew. In the gloom there was no trail visible to Kent's peering eyes, but Clubfoot followed a trail. The gloom deepened, then soon lightened. Kent rode out of a hole the roof of which he reached with his hand. Piute was waiting. Spades pounded the rock, to thud into a dry streambed. The stream that had run here had gone underground.

"Did you know about this?" queried Kent, gazing up the slanting yellow walls, at the distant V-shaped notch above.

"Yes. Jeff told me. I never rode through. I would have shown you long ago if you had ever agreed to leave. Later I was selfish and couldn't."

"Where are the round places? The mounds an' ridges an' arches, with the holes between?"

"Up on top, Jeff said."

"Ride, Lucy!"

Clubfoot did not live up to his name. If he had a limp it was barely discernible, and affected neither his walk or trot. The floor of this split in the rocks ascended gradually only because the streambed meandered. In a straight line it climbed steeply. Steps of gravel and sand and rock gave place to solid rock; and high up, where the gorge branched to the right, Kent came upon the ancient streambed again. Looking back often Kent always saw Lucy riding with head bowed, seeing nothing, lost in her loss, still too close to that to realize freedom and gain. But she was riding Spades there close behind Kent, and his heart sang. Bare walls converged until Kent could spread his arms and touch them on each side. They sheered up at a slant so far and high that no sunlight got into that rift in the rocks. Here there were pools of water, green and deep, sometimes up to the flanks of the horses.

They reached a divide, from which Kent looked back. The hole that had been his refuge and Lucy's home might have been any one of a number of purple clefts. It was gone and he would never see it again. Lucy looked only down.

The divide was a pass that led in broken fields of red rock and cedar thickets to the ascent of the scalloped surfaces, the denuded slopes. Kent was curious to see what Clubfoot would do when he came to that climb up a bare mountain of rock where any one of a dozen courses might have been chosen. The bay kept swinging to the right, to take the farther slope, a steep smooth incline where faint scratches on the brown sandstone showed Kent that padded hoofs had climbed. Clubfoot's iron spikes cut into the stone. And likewise Spades' left fresh cuts. Kent wondered if Bonesteel and Jeff had forgotten the pads, or if the day had come when they cared no more to hide tracks. And it was Kent's conclusion that they did not care.

Then came a steep face of rock, where Kent dismounted to lead his horse. Lucy stayed on Spades; she did not appear to see the ascent until Kent called her attention to it. She looked. "I've ridden Spades up steeper slopes than this," she said indifferently.

"You have? All right. But ride him," returned Kent sharply. He climbed the long hill of curved rock on foot, resting often, getting behind Spades often. The black new where to go, though not so certain as the bay.

From the summit, long winding ridges wound above and between hollow swales in solid rock, and clefts choked with cedar, and oval pits with floors of sand, on toward higher mounds. Kent got in the saddle to stay there. Clubfoot deserved the trust imposed upon him by Bonesteel. He never faltered, he never failed. Sometimes he slowed on slanting narrow ledges, to edge one hoof before the other. Spades was as sure-footed as a mountain goat. And as for Lucy, the invisible trail over the waved rocks at last became something to make her handle the mettlesome black like a range-rider.

So the hours passed while up over the rolling red horizon white clouds peeped and bulged on all sides, to spread toward the zenith. The sun shone down hot, the horses sweat and smoked.

By noonday the riders had scaled the undulating plateau of stone to the heights. Here the unparalleled sublimity of the scene compelled Kent to halt and exclaim: "Look, Lucy!—So you will never forget!"

The dark sad eyes brightened with awe and wonder. "Beautiful! But so wide—so far! It frightens me."

"You have been shut in between walls all your life. You are up on top of them now, free, in the open. There are the purple uplands—the black mountain. An' there to your left the red escarpments runnin' out over the canyons."

"Go on, keep going," she said, almost with entreaty, as briefly she looked back down the league-long descent they had been hours in mounting.

The white clouds reached the dome of the blue vault overhead, and on all sides they changed and darkened. Alternately the sun shone with blistering heat and disappeared behind the white, dark-ribbed sails.

In another hour, when Kent began to fear they would

be caught in a storm before they forded the San Juan, the clouds on three sides had darkened to let down flowing veils and sheets of rain. And rainbows appeared to brighten and blaze in the heavens until the spectacle appeared gloriously unreal. Kent counted nine rainbows, some of which were near and others far, some dim and others brilliant. One curved across the heavens; another sank into the lilac haze of the yawning abyss under the great mountain; yet another retreated as the riders descended, its wondrous hues trailing just before them, like a transparent curtain to reach out and touch.

To the west the slopes and waves began to glisten and glance with rain that thickened to white palls and sent misty waterfalls down into the depths.

But the glory of rainbow storm and sloping rock never drove from Kent's mind the dread, the worry, the vigilance that beset him. He caught Lucy's increasing awareness of her new surroundings. Storms and rainbows and rocks were a part of her life, but she had never been out from under the confining walls. The miles, the boundless vistas, the ever-present opening distance with its beckoning buttes had begun to pierce her grief, to lengthen hours into days. With so much Kent was deeply grateful.

He recognized not one slant or curve, over which they traveled, but it grew on him that they had cut across to the south whereas his ride into the canyon country had been to the north and west over the Indian trail to the Colorado, a much longer route. Therefore he was not surprised, though tremendously glad and thrilled, when Clubfoot led out of a rounded defile to a deep square-cut canyon—the San Juan. They quickly came out upon the rim, showing the muddy boiling river below, high, but not in flood.

Clubfoot halted at a niche, as if to wait for Kent to relieve him. Sliding off, Kent looked over with a shiver, then looped his bridle on the pommel and bade the faithful horse to lead. Kent turned it to see Lucy off leading Spades, and close behind. His fears for her seemed unfounded so far as horses, rocks, trails and rivers were concerned.

190

"The San Juan, Lucy. Once across that ford an' the worst of our trail will be passed," he said tensely.

"It's bad here. But Clubfoot is not afraid. And Spades knows he can go where any other horse can go."

That five-hundred-foot descent was a nightmare to Kent. Yet they made it with only a few slips and no mishaps. The trail ended under the base of the wall, invisibly joining the main one where Kent's tracks, made months before, still showed in the sand, still untrampled by other horses.

"Spades and I used to have fun in our brook when it ran high," said Lucy. "He could wade upstream in water clear to his neck, but when he lost his footing—then we got a ducking."

"Here I am worryin' about you!" ejaculated Kent, ridiculing himself. "The river is a little higher, a little faster than when I crossed. Lead off there, Lucy, an' head a little up river, for that trail on the bank opposite. I'll fall below you, sure, but if Clubfoot is as good a mudhen as Spades—"

Lucy did not need to urge the black. With a snort he plunged in to breast the current, running most heavily near that shore. Clubfoot followed. For a few moments both horses labored to keep their footing. The muddy torrent tore at them. Current and horse matched even for a third of the distance, then in the shallowing water the battle went against the river. Clubfoot fell back and below Spades, while Piute was carried swiftly down stream. Lucy looked back over her shoulder, excited with the action, to call encouragement to Kent. She had no fear of physical things. Both horses waded out, heaving and snorting, fifty feet below the trail, and Piute trotted up the shore to meet them.

"Aw! Aw! My good luck!" exclaimed Kent, beside himself. The San Juan was crossed. "Lucy, since my first thought of you some angel has watched over me!"

She gave him a wistful smile, but no word. Kent remembered his cache of tinned foods, and rode up the ridge to find it intact. Hooking the sack over his pommel he led Lucy on to the red rocks bearing the Indian inscriptions. This crude art of the desert dwellers, so raw and expressive of primitive animals and men in action, was the first thing in which Lucy had shown more than passing interest. She had never seen the like.

"But what do these drawings mean?" she asked.

There Kent found a split in the trail which in his haste he had overlooked before, one branch that he had traveled coming down out of Noki Canyon, and the other, new to him, swinging up to the plateau, and leading off to the southeast through a narrow break in the red wall, evidently a tributary of Noki. Kent felt relieved that this outlet appeared to lead away from the Piute uplands. Over an easy trail the horses proceeded at a trot and the miles grew apace. They passed wet belts where the storms had flooded cliff and wash. Piute led the way and Kent kept sharp watch. But that copper-hued canyon gave no sign of man or beast. It widened. Sagebrush and greasewood began to green the benches; waterholes showed at intervals in the rocky streambed; a first scant cottonwood tree heralded others to follow.

A sudden action by Piute halted Kent. The dog had his sharp nose pointed up at the nearest wall, a copper-hued bluff that formed the western rampart of the desert area.

"Look," said the girl calmly.

Kent's swift gaze located Indians on the rim. At first sight the striking effect of pinto mustangs, with lean dark riders motionless and wild held Kent to the mere physical beauty of the picture they made, how it gave the lonely desert the lift it needed. But presently he noted, even at that considerable distance, the high-peaked sombreros some of the Indians were wearing.

"Piutes!" he flashed.

"They are watching us, Kent."

"I reckon they are," replied Kent grimly, as he swept a range-rider's keen gaze along the rim to see if there was a break anywhere near. It was sheer and unbroken as far as he could see in either direction. And he remembered he had noted this right barrier of the copper-hued canyon was unscalable as far as they had ridden.

"I'd like that pinto with the red mane," observed Lucy, squinting up at the wall.

"Aren't you even scared?"

"Not with you along."

"Lucy, I'll bet the Segi cuts through that upland somewhere over there to the west an' south. Some Piutes wouldn't be friendly to me. This bunch can't get down short of hours. If we hadn't seen them . . . Whew! —Piute old dog, reckon you saved us."

"If they are hostile he probably has," returned Lucy soberly.

"Ride on Lucy. If they chase us it'll be the real old Injun thing. But they can't catch you on Spades. If it gets hot I'll throw the packs and hide them. If Clubfoot can't keep up an' they get close I'll throw a few rifle bullets back at them. I don't think they'd bother you anyway."

They set out at a brisk trot which soon slipped into a lope. Clubfoot went along well.

Kent was surprised to see the Piutes gallop their shiny mustangs toward the north, soon disappearing from sight. This was a direction that gave Kent less apprehension. But out of sight they could circle and this way Kent could not be certain how soon the Indians could find a descent.

Lucy abruptly reined in.

"Piute is not coming," she said. "He looks and acts queer."

Kent yelled to the dog. The result was that Piute again took to the trail and followed. Kent made sure he would come. Presently Kent looked back again. Piute had halted. Soon, however, he trotted on again, and Kent lost sight of him behind an intervening rise of ground. The trail was open, straight and still easy to travel.

"Look back," called Lucy, again stopping.

Piute stood on a rise of ground, white against the sky, like a wolf in its wildness.

"He'll never come," averred the girl. "We've had wolf dogs. They always go back."

On the moment, Piute, after a long look, raised his lean wild head high, no doubt to wail his lonesome plaint, then he turned away to vanish.

"Gone! . . . I'll be darned," ejaculated Kent. "He was always queer. Aw, I'm sorry. I liked Piute."

"Kent, don't ever keep anything that does not want to stay with you."

"Four-legged or two-legged?" queried Kent.

"Even a centipede," retorted Lucy.

"Ride ahead. An' let's make the best of good trail."

Clubfoot kept up with Spades. He had long won Kent's admiration for everything a horse could have to make him great, except good looks and great speed.

The valley opened out, the walls behind the riders began to lift, which proved their height. In the middle distance a single copper-colored sentinel rock towered from a slanting base. It had fluted sides, a strange formation. In an hour they passed it. Kent kept looking back, searching the desert with experienced eyes for signs of riders. But as mile after mile passed under the steady clip-clop of hoofs, and no dust clouds puffed yellow above the sage, he began to lose his fears of the Piutes. The lay of the walls made it impossible for him to be headed off. In a few more hours uncertainty would cease. Soon they would be in Navaho country.

The sun still shone bright and warm. But the desert here was not hot like the bare-rocked canyon country where no breeze blew. Here on this wasteland there was room for violent storms. Clouds began to creep up all around, to sail white and beautiful up into the blue, to thicken and change color as the day advanced. And the time came when the curved rainbows and the down-dropping rain veils gorgeously canopied the desert.

In the foreground, ten miles or more, a black spur peeped up over the red wall toward which the trail ascended. It had a familiar look to Kent. Once a range-rider ever saw a landmark he never forgot it. This tip he had first seen from somewhere south of the Segi.

Rain fell upon the riders during the afternoon. When it rained no dust clouds would arise. Another gradual league-long climb, however, afforded opportunity to see back down the trail for miles. Kent halted to look. No moving dots! No black specks!

Again they were off over the fragrant plateau, and it was not long until the gray expanse appeared to end in the sky. This Kent knew was another jumping-off place, but it did not worry him because the trail led straight on. Sight of the black spur thrilled him anew. They were getting somewhere. Still he was wholly unprepared to come out round a corner of crag upon a magnificent panorama.

Lucy gazed down spellbound and mute. The tremendous void and space, rather than the beauty and grandeur, accounted for her shock.

The void yawned—a gulf streaked red and floored with green—an immense valley of widely separated monuments. Kent gasped and came back from the far distances to try to grasp this place, as marvelous as the canyon country from the uplands, as different as if it had been on another planet.

The depth was great, the distance deceiving. In the foreground of the vast valley rose a mountain shaft of rock, a black wedge-based monument, rising, sharpening to an incredible crown on which tiny specks, eagles, were circling. To the right of it, thirty miles or more, the valley headed into rugged rocks of red. But to the east its scope widened and the boundless green bowl lifted from its dark floor on terraced elevations, so far apart as to make them isolated, monuments of red rock. A world of earth and stone had washed, worn, weathered away here in the ages past, to leave these harder shafts and pillars of rock rising to the sky. To the eye used to enclosing walls the scene must have been incredible. Lucy might have been gazing off the rim of the earth upon a silent barren valley of the moon. It had greatest of all a sublimity that deadened the grasp of mortal eye. When Kent had mastered that he listened to its dead silence, a silence no sound could break; he saw the sculpturing of the gods, monuments in massive buttes, shafts like spears, columns like smoke, castles with turrets and minarets, all red, red as blood, in the sunset light. He felt the awful solemnity of the eons that had produced this phenomenon, the august reign of a spirit to which time, life, death were nothing, the invisible proof of eternity.

At last when he called Lucy she murmured: "I want to stay here."

"Land of the Navahos, dear. It's grand. I'm just happy over the way you feel. But we must ride down an' on!"

"I could live down there forever. Could we have a

ranch here, so that I could ride and ride—to see it always?"

"That valley would not support cattle nor white men. It's tough enough for Indians."

They descended a winding trail that turned to the glorious monuments and as well turned away from them, until down on the floor only the great black tower loomed over them. The trail led away toward where the valley notched. Sensations of time had been dwarfed. The fugitives rode on and on. And all at once it seemed the sun sank and the trail led into rocky, hummocky land, where scrub cedar and pinon grew, down to a shallow wash of running water.

On a bench several hundred yards off the trail with a cluster of high rocks to hide them, Kent halted for the night.

"How far?" asked Lucy, leaning to him as he stood to help her off.

"Close to fifty miles, I'd guess. With heavy packs an' Clubfoot part lame! Some ride!" he cried heartily. "You are the best girl rider who ever forked a horse."

Tireless and swift, with eyes flashing here and there, with the insistent voice of triumph at the door of his heart, he made short work of camp tasks. Dusk had not yet stolen down out of the canyons. Thunder rumbled lower and lower, far off. A few bright stars glittered white out of the blue lakes in the purple cloud. Over the escarpment in the west blazed a clear golden lightning of sky which brought out the bold black horizon line with startling vividness.

Lucy had been at his heels every moment until at length, when the meager supper was ready, he placed a blanket seat for her and forced her into it. She was hungry for this meal and thirsty. They ate, sitting close together. Kent missed the feeding of morsels to Piute. The desert night stole upon them Kent was first to break the silence.

"Tomorrow we'll circle to Logan's. I know where we are now. Then four or five days, an' Wagontongue."

"Oh Kent! Oh!" cried Lucy, suddenly breaking the

196

silence, "It'd be so wonderful—so—I don't know what—if—if only—"

Her voice ended in a sob and her head fell against him. That outburst crystallized a vague and gathering thought, which had tormented Kent at intervals all during the day, and now reached its culmination. He put his arm around her.

"Lucy, I have lied to you," he said.

"Lied to me!"

"Yes. But it was Bonesteel's fault," went on Kent swiftly, realizing now the truth and good of his inspiration. "Your father was not killed. He's alive—wounded in the fight, but alive, not even bad hurt."

"Alive? . . . Oh, my father! You tricked me into leaving him."

"Don't leap like that. Come back—an' listen. . . . You remember, Lucy, when Bonesteel struck his forehead an' said so strangelike, 'Lucy, you have saved my soul if not my life?' That was when the idea came to him. Oh, I see it all so clearly now, my dear. His mind is an open page to me. Since I was honest an' true, an' you loved me—he could send you away with me. He would kill Roberts an' his men, partly in hate—for Roberts meant to have you —not as I first thought, to keep the secret of the Hole in the Wall, but the secret of Luce Cheney. In that hour of your denunciation—he ended his thievin' career. . . . That mornin' he sent you to your cabin an' kept me back. Jeff would take horses, food, money to the waterfall, where the trail began. When night came I was to go to you, tell you he had been killed, an' drag you, if need be, out of the cabin an' to the horses at the end of the trail. I agreed. I offered to help him in the fight with Roberts. But he refused. When the time came, however, I went out an' met him. Too late to drive me back! He had to accept. He was as cool, as calm as I ever saw him. Only I felt his deadly intensity. While we walked toward the outlaw camp he said: 'By the way, Lucy's name is Bonesteel. An' when her name becomes yours thet will be the last of the Bonesteels.' We went on, an' he provoked the fight—as easily as throwin' a spark into powder. . . . I'm glad to say, Lucy, that I did help some. Simms, Harvey, an'

197

especially Westfall were bad hombres, fortunately which I didn't underrate. . . . They were snuffed out. Goins, Bunge, Forman also. Rigney badly hurt, but would recover. Kitsap untouched, except a crease on his hand. They were loyal to your dad. Bonesteel shot high up in the shoulder—a wound of no consequence. Jeff was not in it. . . . That's the story, Lucy. I could never have had peace if I had not broken my promise to your father."

"How strange! How terrible! —But, oh, it changes everything!"

"You will not run off from me—to go back?" queried Kent jealously.

"No. I could not go. He does not want me. You do. I have no one else in all the world to love me. But you are all I need to make me happy. Oh, that weight off my heart! . . . Kent, *why* did Father want me to think him dead?"

"The bitterness of his degradation before his daughter. Oh, he loved you, Lucy. But after you denounced him so unmercifully an' justly, he did not want to look upon your face again . . . or you upon his. That reason came first with him. An' secondly, it was indeed the end of Bonesteel. If he were killed, well an' good. If not he'd bury the name in his Hole in the Wall, an' take up that other identity—that of the respectable Cheney, rancher over in Utah. Sometimes it's not too late for a man if he sees right."

"Then there is another woman?" whispered Lucy.

"Yes, an' that is well. . . . Lucy, I'll say Bonesteel was great in his wicked career. God only knows what drove him to it. An' he will be greater in this newer, better life. Forgive him for his cruelty to you, as I forgive him for the torture he gave me. An' believe that the spirit old Bill Elway saw—the love he bore you—guided me to save you an' give your father his last an' only chance."

The night was black with star-filled sky; the coyotes wailed; the horses cropped the sage; Kent watched over Lucy as she slept with her cold pure face upturned. The man took only snatches at sleep, loathe to lose even for a few moments the reality of his blessed fortune.